P9-DMZ-043

what comes after

what comes

STEVE WATKINS

First edition 2011

Library of Congress Cataloging-in-Publication Data

Watkins, Steve, date.
What comes after / Steve Watkins. — 1st U.S. ed.
p. cm.
Summary: When her veterinarian father dies, sixteen-year-old Iris Wight must move from Maine to North Carolina where her Aunt Sue spends Iris's small inheritance while abusing her physically and emotionally, but the hardest to take is her mistreatment of the farm animals.
ISBN 978-0-7636-4250-1
[1. Child abuse — Fiction. 2. Grief — Fiction. 3. Moving, Household — Fiction. 4. Domestic animals — Fiction. 5. Farm life — North Carolina — Fiction. 6. North Carolina — Fiction.] I. Title.
PZ7.W
[Fic] — dc22 2010038711

11 12 13 14 15 16 BVG 10 9 8 7 6 5 4 3 2 1

Printed in Berryville, VA, U.S.A.

This book was typeset in Fairfield Light.

Candlewick Press
99 Dover Street
Somerville, Massachusetts 02144

visit us at www.candlewick.com

For Janet

Life is a battle in which you are to show your pluck,
and woe be to the coward.

— Henry David Thoreau

Mother, Son Accused in Beating

A Craven County, North Carolina, woman is accused of ordering the beating of her 16-year-old niece as punishment for letting loose a family goat.

Susan A. Allen, 43, of 9 Cocytus Rd., has been charged with malicious wounding, conspiracy and child cruelty.

Allen's son, Book Allen, 18, is charged with the same offenses. Both are being held in the Craven Regional Jail.

Prosecutor F. Lee Trenis said Susan Allen had custody of the victim, who moved to Craven County from Maine two months ago after the death of her father.

On October 3, Trenis said, the girl, upset at the Allens' plans to slaughter two young male goats, let the animals out of a pen behind the Allens' semirural home. The Allens caught one of the goats, but the other got away.

The missing goat showed up at Craven County High School later that day—two miles through the woods from the Allens' home. School officials called Susan Allen to retrieve it.

When Allen arrived at the school, she told school officials she needed her niece at home to help with the goat.

Trenis, the prosecutor, said Allen told the girl she would be punished. Allen ordered the girl to do chores until that afternoon, when Book Allen, a senior at Craven High, came home from football practice.

The Allens took the victim to nearby Craven Lake, where, according to Trenis, Susan Allen ordered Book Allen to drag the girl out of the car and "punish" her.

The girl suffered numerous contusions as a result of the subsequent beating.

Trenis said Susan Allen ordered the victim to explain her injuries by saying she had been feeding the goats when one "got spooked" and butted her into a fence.

According to Trenis, the girl told school officials that story the next day, but they didn't believe it. She eventually told a school counselor about the assault.

The girl was hospitalized for two days, then released. She has been placed in a foster home.

If I'd stayed in Maine, I would have done all that, and would have gone by my old house sometimes, and the barn and Dad's vet clinic, and maybe I would have gotten a job with the new vet who took over from Dad back in the spring when his cough got so bad that he couldn't work. I would have visited the cemetery where Grandma and Grandpa were buried, and now Dad, too. I would have weeded all their plots and planted flowers.

But life doesn't turn out the way you expect. Ever. I didn't expect Dad to die, not even at his sickest, not even when he didn't know who I was anymore. Not even in those last hours at the hospital, when the *click* and *hush* of the oxygen were the only sounds in that dark, awful room, and Reverend Harding hugged me and prayed with me, and said the Twenty-third Psalm—"Yea though I walk through the valley of the shadow of death, I will fear no evil."

When he finished, he whispered, "Iris, I'm so, so sorry. It's time we let him go."

I hadn't expected that, either. I'd thought we were praying for God to let Dad live.

Beatrice had been my best friend since elementary school, and her parents promised Dad that they would take care of me. It was the thing he worried about most in his last weeks.

But things changed not long after he died. Beatrice's parents started arguing, usually late at night. And they kept arguing—in their bedroom, with the door shut and the sound muffled.

one

I was never supposed to end up in North Carolina.

I was supposed to stay in Maine instead. I was supposed to live with my best friend, Beatrice, and her family. Go back to my old high school for junior year. Play on the softball team where Beatrice pitched and I played center field with standing orders from Coach to go after every ball hit to the outfield.

If I'd stayed in Maine, we would have gone riding on Beatrice's horse down pine trails to the bluffs overlooking the Atlantic. We would have gone sea kayaking and shared her bedroom and made fun of her little brother, Sean, who had his hair in a rat tail—a style nobody had worn since the 1980s.

We would have made fun of Coach, too, who told us he used to play for a Red Sox farm team, which we doubted. We looked him up one time on the Internet and couldn't find him on any farm team rosters.

We could hear their voices, even if we couldn't make out what they were saying. Beatrice put on her iPod and turned up the music. I didn't have an iPod. Sometimes I left the house and rode my bike down to the batting cages. Sometimes, after Beatrice fell asleep, I sat up in my bed until the arguing stopped, as terrified then by the silence as I had been earlier by her parents' harsh voices.

Mr. Stone spoke to me first. It was a month after the funeral. "We're very sorry, Iris," he said. "Things have gotten difficult for Mrs. Stone and me. I know we promised your father, but that was before—"

He didn't finish, but he didn't have to. I knew what it meant, and it hit me like a line drive to my stomach. He tried to smile. "This doesn't mean we won't have you back for a visit," he added. "Would you like that? Would you like to come back for a visit sometime?"

He didn't look at me. He didn't look at Beatrice. Or at Mrs. Stone. My heart sank.

Mrs. Stone said she was sorry, too. "I wish we could keep you with us, Iris," she said. "There are just these things in the way. . . ."

Her voice trailed off, too. She brushed some hair out of her face and tucked it behind her ears. They were red. Her whole face was red—either from crying or because she was about to. Then she wandered off, the way she often did in the middle of conversations.

"That's OK, Mrs. Stone," I said, knowing Dad would want

me to be polite no matter what. But it wasn't OK. I should have screamed at her instead. I should have screamed at all of them.

Aunt Sue was the next of kin.

She was my mom's older sister. I had only seen her once before, but I didn't remember because it was when I was a baby. She drove up from North Carolina right after I was born. Dad told me about it. She had a son named Book, who was two then. I never heard about Book having a father. Aunt Sue didn't want to stay in our house, so the night they arrived, she and Book slept under the camper shell in the back of their truck, even though it was February. They only stayed part of the next day. Aunt Sue looked at me but wouldn't hold me, got in a fight with my mom about some things that had happened a long time ago, then climbed back in the truck with Book and drove home.

I didn't know what to expect from her now, all these years later. When I called her from Beatrice's, she was smoking the whole time. I heard her light a cigarette, and every time she spoke, I heard her exhale first. She said she was sorry about Dad but didn't sound as if she meant it. She said Book was looking forward to having me live with them, but that didn't sound sincere, either. She didn't say much else.

I asked if she ever heard from my mom, and there was a long silence.

Then she said, "No."

Then she said, "And I don't ever expect to, either."

I handed the phone off to Beatrice's dad. I hadn't really expected my mom to be an option. She left when I was five, and no one knew where she was—not even Aunt Sue, apparently. No one had heard from her in years.

I went back to the batting cages after getting off the phone, my face burning from anger and frustration, and I swung at high, hard fastballs for an hour until I was too tired to lift the bat.

Beatrice and I stayed up late the night before I left, packing and repacking my stuff. She kept wanting to add more, trying to make me take clothes that were hers: socks and T-shirts, sweaters and mittens and scarves—as if that would make up for her family abandoning me. I didn't want any of it.

"You're going to come back for Christmas, right?" she asked at one point. It was well after midnight.

"Yeah," I said, though I really wasn't sure of that, or of anything. "If I have the money."

"I'll get you the money," Beatrice said. "I bet my parents will pay for the whole thing. It's the least they can do."

"Yeah," I said again, suddenly doubting there would be any Christmas visit. "Maybe."

Beatrice's boyfriend called—his name was Collie—and they spent half an hour whispering, which gave me time to finally finish packing. I had an old hat that Dad used to wear, a green fishing cap. I ran my fingers over the frayed edges and traced the curve of the bill. I pressed it to my face and imagined it smelled like Dad, but probably it didn't. Probably it had been too long since he'd worn it.

I put it on, thinking it would be too big, but it fit me just right.

At three in the morning, Beatrice and I climbed out her window and wandered around town one last time. Nobody was awake but us. We didn't talk; we didn't do anything. We just walked down the middle of the street, east toward the harbor. The wind had picked up, blowing in off the Atlantic; it was threatening to storm.

Our reflections, distorted in the darkened storefront windows as we walked past a row of shops, magnified what a funny-looking pair we were — Beatrice tall, with her black hair and high cheekbones and perfect smile and model's legs; me short and skinny, with a sharp face and freckles and chopped hair and middle-school boobs; both of us in practice Ts, gym shorts, floppy socks, dirty New Balances. It was about all either of us wore in the summer.

Beatrice started crying.

"I'm so sorry about my mom and dad," she said. "I wish I knew what was going on."

I waited for her to say more, to at least try to explain what had happened. Something. But she just cried. I started to comfort her, to act polite and tell her it was OK, like I had with her mom. But then it hit me again how messed up the whole thing was. Maybe her parents were splitting up, but so what? My dad had *died,* and my best friend's parents had broken their one promise to him. And all Beatrice could do was cry about it. What about fighting for me? What about insisting that I stay with them no matter what?

But as much as I wanted to shout all that at Beatrice, I just couldn't. She and her family were still all I had, even if it was for just this one last night in Maine. So I took off running instead.

Beatrice yelled "Wait!" but I wouldn't, so she raced after me down the street, past shops, through people's yards, down alleys, down to the bay. I let her catch up with me where the land sloped down to the black water—usually calm in the harbor, but churning tonight as the wind kept blowing harder and the rough ocean waves skirted the seawall.

The storm broke over us as we stood there—a summer squall, as sudden and fierce as a nor'easter.

"Come on!" I yelled over the roar of the wind and the rain. "Let's go out on the seawall."

Beyond the dark harbor we could see whitecaps rising, smashing hard onto the rocks. The seawall jutted out a quarter of a mile, no longer so high above the tide line. A blue beacon light shone faintly above a small stone cabin at the point.

"You're crazy," Beatrice yelled back. "It's too dangerous!"

I ignored her and slid down the muddy embankment to the water's edge. The rain kept pouring as I climbed over wet rocks and finally onto the wall.

"Iris!" Beatrice yelled after me, but when I didn't stop, she followed me.

Soon we were running, stumbling, leaning into the wind and the hard, slanting rain that pelted us, sharp as needles on our arms and legs and faces—anywhere we were exposed. We struggled on, with the wind howling, the waves rising higher, crashing harder, the spray blinding us.

It took ten minutes to make it to the end, battling through the wind and that spray, until we fell inside the shack, exhausted. There was no door. Everything was slick and wet. Wood shutters strained but held in the one window on the ocean side. We huddled together at first, crouching low on the floor.

Beatrice wanted us to stay like that until the storm passed, but I had a different idea. I got up to open the shutters—they slammed against the outside wall—and then I stood there for the next half hour, facing the Atlantic. I gripped the frame tight until I couldn't feel my hands, just the blasting wind and the needles of rain and the incessant spray. The waves rose dangerously high, threatening to break over the seawall.

My face burned. I was sure I would have welts from the slicing rain. For a minute it even seemed to be raining backward, the water falling up and into my face from the ocean.

Then the wind shifted, and slowly, gradually, died. The waves receded. The storm passed.

There were stars out. I shivered violently from the cold, then turned and helped Beatrice off the floor. We stood there for a couple of minutes more, leaning on each other, then staggered together back home—back to *her* home. We didn't speak. I used to always know what Beatrice was thinking, but now, and for most of the past month, I didn't have a clue. Maybe she kept quiet because she was mad at me for dragging her out onto the seawall, or maybe she just didn't know what to say anymore.

I didn't know what was left to say, either, and didn't have the words to explain to Beatrice—or to anyone else—how good it had felt to be out there on the seawall in the middle of the storm. How it was so much better than lying awake at night, worrying about moving to North Carolina, thinking about my dad, thinking about all the things I forgot to tell him, all the ways I hadn't been a good enough daughter, how much I missed him and how awful and deep this black hole of grief was that threatened to pull me all the way in and turn me into something the opposite of myself.

two

I stepped outside the next morning to a world lashed clean by the storm. The sun was blinding, the sky blue and cloudless. Beatrice and I struggled to fit my suitcases into the trunk of her dad's car but kept getting in each other's way. Everything seemed off—the house, the yard, the street, *us*—as if it had all been erased, then redrawn: close to the original, but not quite the same. Angles a little different, sight lines no longer clear. I put on sunglasses, but it was still too bright out. I couldn't see the ocean.

Once we were done, Beatrice and I both climbed into the backseat. Mr. Stone got in behind the steering wheel and looked blankly at the empty passenger seat for a minute.

Finally he shrugged. "Off we go, then." Mrs. Stone waved from the front door, sagging against the frame as if she needed the support to help her stand.

We'd only gotten a few hours of sleep, but I was still surprised that Beatrice passed out ten minutes later, not long after we pulled onto the Portland highway. Mr. Stone and I didn't talk. He fiddled with the radio until he found the oldies station that my dad and I always used to listen to, but the ones playing today seemed to have been selected just to make me feel awful: "So Far Away," "Operator," "Wish You Were Here."

I pulled my hoodie up over my ears to try to block out the sound, and spent the rest of the trip looking out the window at the blur of pine stands and strip malls and little towns and glimpses of the coast, trying to memorize everything as if seeing it for the last time, which maybe I was.

Once we got on the interstate, the real Maine vanished, though, and it seemed as if we could have been almost anywhere in America—not that I'd been very many places before: Portland a dozen times, Boston twice for softball tournaments, Nova Scotia once on the ferry. I'd never been on an airplane, but I couldn't get excited about it, knowing what I was leaving and where I was going.

There was a lobster-roll stand where we got off the interstate, and I asked Mr. Stone if he would stop.

"You're hungry?" he asked, looking at the clock on the dashboard. It was ten in the morning.

I shook my head. "I just wanted to get some Whoopie Pies for my aunt and my cousin. I don't think they have them in North Carolina. I thought I should probably bring them something."

Beatrice stayed asleep when I got out of the car and didn't wake up two minutes later when I climbed back in. I had to elbow her awake when we finally reached the airport. She was slumped against my shoulder and left a string of drool when she sat up.

"Sorry," she croaked.

"For what?" I asked. "Falling asleep or getting drool on my hoodie?"

She blinked and wiped her chin. "What?"

I shook my head. "Never mind."

Mr. Stone looked over the backseat. "Almost there," he said. "All ready for your big adventure, Iris?"

Beatrice sniffed. "God, Dad. She's not going to Disneyland."

"I'm aware of that, Beatrice," Mr. Stone said, his voice sharp. He reached back without looking and gestured at me with an envelope. "This is some spending money for your trip, Iris, and any expenses that might come up when you get to your aunt's."

Beatrice grabbed the envelope and counted the money: two hundred dollars in a stack of crisp twenties. Her face was red when she handed it back over, and I shoved the money into my jeans pocket and mumbled thanks.

Beatrice's cell phone rang as we pulled up to the terminal, and I knew from the ringtone that it was Collie. They barely had time to launch into one of their whispery conversations, though, when Mr. Stone stopped at the Departures curb.

"Gotta go," Beatrice said into her phone. "Love you, too."

Mr. Stone said he would wait in the cell-phone lot for Beatrice to go in with me, and she started chattering the minute he drove off, I guess trying to make up for all the things she hadn't been awake long enough to say in the car. "Call me when you get there, OK? And e-mail me as soon as you get to a computer. Tell me everything. See if you can take pictures and send them to me. And find out when you can come back to visit."

Her phone rang again. "It's Collie," she said. "He must have forgotten to tell me something."

She scooted off to talk while I got my ticket and checked my bags.

I wanted to reach over and snap her cell phone closed, but instead I just stood there seething. Beatrice had changed in the past month. The worse things were between her parents, and the closer I got to leaving, the more obsessed she'd become with boys.

She finally got off her phone, came back over, and threw her arms around me. It seemed to finally be hitting her that I was really leaving. I hugged her tight and started to speak, but before I could figure out what I was going to say, her cell phone went off again.

The ringtone wasn't Collie's, but she pulled away quickly. "Oh, hey," she chirped. By the time she finished the new conversation, I was in the security line, and all she could do was call my name and wave.

• • •

I kept my eyes tightly shut during takeoff—not because I was afraid of flying but from the effort of holding it together. The minute they turned off the FASTEN YOUR SEAT BELT sign, I squeezed past two passengers in my row and made my unsteady way to the lavatory, where I finally crumbled into tears. I'd been holding them in for weeks, since Mr. Stone first told me I couldn't stay with them, that I would have to live with Aunt Sue in North Carolina. But now it was actually happening. I was leaving Maine, leaving everything I'd ever known, leaving my whole life behind. I sat trembling on the toilet seat in that tiny airplane bathroom, knees drawn up to my chin, face buried in my hands. I might have stayed there sobbing for the entire flight, but people kept knocking on the door and I finally had to force myself to stop. I washed my face, pressed my hands over my puffy eyes, took a deep breath, and went back to my seat.

As we cruised over Massachusetts, I sipped a ginger ale and stared out the window. My thoughts kept circling back to Beatrice, to the bribe money Mr. Stone had given me, to the last glimpse of Maine coast through the salt-streaked car window. Finally I dug through my bag and pulled out a pen and my notebook.

Dear Dad,

You won't believe where I am right now. I've got my face pressed against an airplane window and I'm looking down on

Boston. I think I can see Fenway Park, but it might just be one of those Super Walmarts. . . .

I kept writing. I told Dad I loved flying, which might have actually been true if I hadn't been so distracted. I told him about sneaking out of Beatrice's house the night before, and about the storm, but not about the seawall. I knew he would have thought it was a foolish thing to do, even if he'd have understood why I did it. I didn't tell him about how angry I was at Beatrice and her parents, or about how much I dreaded moving to North Carolina. I kept my letter upbeat and positive; I didn't want to upset him.

I'd written Dad other letters like this since he died. They weren't journal entries, or diary entries, or anything where I poured out my heart and soul. Just letters. Just the Iris news. I wrote them at times like this, when I got hit by one of these tsunamis of grief and needed something, anything, to keep me from drowning.

It had started with one of the last conversations we had. Dad had gotten confused. He thought I was going on a trip. He kept talking about my trip, and he wanted me to promise to write to him.

I tried to make him understand. "I'm not going anywhere, Dad," I said. "I'm staying right here with you. There's no trip. I'm staying right here."

"It's OK," he said, his eyes squeezed shut, his hand locked

tight around mine. "Just promise you'll write me a letter when you get there."

So I wrote him these letters, not that there was any place to send them. Usually I tore the letters into strips once I finished, and then tore the strips into scraps, and then threw the scraps away. I kept this one, though. I didn't have much left of Dad, and I didn't want to leave it on the plane.

Aunt Sue was waiting for me at the Raleigh airport, and she looked just like her voice: raspy and hard, though she was kind of pretty, too, in a fading, crow's-feet, farmer's-tan way. I could see my mom in her a little, though my mom had been younger and thinner than Aunt Sue the last time I saw her. Aunt Sue had on an orange baseball cap with a sweat stain in the front, jammed tight over her short gray-brown hair. Her charcoal Harley-Davidson T-shirt was tight, too, and showed off her figure. She wore old jeans, and socks and sandals, the same as me—I wasn't sure what to make of that—and she held a sign with my name on it in all capital letters, spelled wrong: IRIS WHITE.

Book wasn't with her.

I walked all the way up to her before she actually looked at me. "Aunt Sue?" I said.

Our faces were about level, though when she shrugged and straightened up I could see she was a couple of inches taller.

"You Iris?" she said.

"Yes. It's Wight, though. *W-I-G-H-T.*"

She shrugged again. "That all you got?" She nodded at my shoulder bag. I also had the sack of Whoopie Pies.

I held them out to her. "These are from Maine. They make them up there. I just got them this morning."

She nodded again and nearly smiled. "Yeah, I had one of them once. They're right tasty. Thanks."

"You're welcome," I said, happy about that. Aunt Sue turned to leave, expecting me to follow, but I had to stop her.

"There is some more stuff," I said. "I have two suitcases I need to pick up at the baggage claim."

That erased any trace of a smile.

"I got a truck parked in the parking deck, and we're gonna have to pay for having it there," Aunt Sue said. "They give you any money for your trip here?"

Her question caught me off guard, and it took me a minute to understand that she expected me to pay for the parking. I pulled out one of Mr. Stone's twenty-dollar bills and handed it to her.

"All right, then," she said, and headed for the escalator with the sack of Whoopie Pies dangling at her side.

She ate one while we waited for my bags to show up on the carousel, then said, "What I wouldn't give for a cup of coffee right about now."

"There's a Starbucks back upstairs at the Arrivals," I said.

Aunt Sue snorted. "I'll wait for a 7-Eleven."

I didn't say anything else. Neither of us did. Despite our one strained phone conversation, I'd thought Aunt Sue would be warmer, happier to see me. At least curious about this niece she'd never known. At least sympathetic.

The bags were slow, so after ten minutes, she went outside to smoke. I went up to the Starbucks. Dad never liked me drinking coffee but knew I was going to anyway, so we always compromised and drank half-decaf and half-regular when we made it at home. This time I got all regular.

I still had my cup when Aunt Sue came back inside, reeking of cigarettes. She sniffed when she saw it and said, "I guess you must be made of money."

My face flushed, but I didn't say anything. I couldn't tell if I'd done something wrong or if she was just this way with everybody. I crumpled the cup and tossed it in the trash just as the carousel jerked into motion and suitcases tumbled out of the chute—mine first of all, which seemed like a miracle. Aunt Sue watched as I dragged them off the conveyor belt; she didn't offer to help as I struggled behind her with them on the long walk to the parking garage. Once we got there, she had me throw everything in the back of her truck, an old Ford with a rusted-out bed, and when I said it looked like rain, she dragged a moldy tarp out from behind the driver's seat and told me to tuck that around my stuff if I was worried.

We stopped once on the two-hour drive to Craven County—at a 7-Eleven. Aunt Sue finally got her coffee; I paid for the gas. It was mostly flat and mostly country there in eastern

North Carolina—peanut fields, tobacco fields, pine forests—and I fell asleep an hour in. I hadn't expected to doze off, but I guess I was exhausted from not sleeping at all the night before.

Rain whipping through my open window woke me. I rolled it up, but the truck didn't have air conditioning and soon it got too hot, so I ended up cracking the window even though the spray came through. Aunt Sue lit a cigarette, and I cracked it open some more. I imagined everything in the back, which was everything I owned in the world, getting soaked under the leaky tarp.

It was dark when we finally reached the farm. A dog started barking when Aunt Sue stopped the truck, and that made me happy. I'd have at least one friend in North Carolina, anyway. Aunt Sue yelled at him to shut up, and he did. Right away.

"His name's Gnarly," Aunt Sue said. "And he isn't worth a damn."

Gnarly's leash was clipped to a long, drooping clothesline in the yard. He ran back and forth a couple of times but then settled down. I knelt in the dry grass—the rain hadn't reached Craven County—and let him lick my hand, which calmed us both down a little. He was some sort of mongrel hound with a lot of slobber, and I liked him right away.

I smelled pine trees and something funky and familiar: manure and damp straw. There was a field, a fence, and a barn, so they must have had other animals, not that Aunt Sue had mentioned any.

My bags were soaked, just as I had feared. I grabbed a dripping suitcase and followed Aunt Sue up the steps and onto the back porch, and then into the kitchen. Book was there, a hulking guy with a shaved head and a gray, grass-stained T-shirt that said *Property of Craven County H.S. Athletics.* He sat hunched over a giant sandwich at the kitchen table. It was the kind of sandwich Dad used to call a Dagwood, because it had so much stuff piled so high in it, the way Dagwood made his in that Sunday comic strip *Blondie:* a mountain of baloney and cheese and lettuce and what looked like crushed potato chips and pickles and extra bread slices in the middle. Book's chin was yellow with mustard.

The first thing Aunt Sue said to him was "I guess you're eating tomorrow's lunch the same time as your dinner."

Book had too much food in his mouth to answer, but his eyes got wide with what looked like genuine panic. He flinched when Aunt Sue came up behind him, though he was twice her size.

Aunt Sue tilted her head at me. "This is your cousin, Iris. Put down your big sandwich and take her stuff upstairs to the little room."

Book swallowed. He looked me up and down, and then grinned. "Hey, Iris," he said. "Nice to meet you."

I pulled the zipper up higher on my hoodie. "Yeah. You, too."

He followed me out to the truck and grabbed my other soggy

bag. "There's a clothesline," he said. "You can unclip Gnarly tomorrow and hang all your stuff out to dry or whatever. We don't have a dryer. Got a washing machine, though."

That surprised me. Dad and I used a clothesline during most of the year, but we still had a dryer. I wasn't sure I'd ever known anyone who didn't own one.

Aunt Sue wasn't kidding about it being a little room. It had a twin bed, and that was all: no closet, no other furniture, nothing else except a small window. I shivered with claustrophobia. Book dumped my wet bags on the bare wood floor, grunted, looked at me up and down again, then said, "Jeez, nice manners. You're welcome."

I said, "Oh, sorry. Thanks," and he mimicked me: "Oh, sorry. You're welcome again." I think he was trying to be funny. He tromped back down the stairs to his sandwich. I stayed behind and sat on the bed, expecting it to give a little, only it didn't. I might have been sitting on a rock. I checked and there was a big sheet of plywood between the box spring and the mattress.

I heard Aunt Sue and Book downstairs talking about the Whoopie Pies, then I heard a great rustling of the bag and figured it was Book, moving on to dessert. Every breath I took in my closet of a room tasted stale, so I pried open the window and gulped in the cooler night air. Then I dumped everything out of my suitcases—wet clothes in one pile, dry clothes in the other. When I finished, there was no room left to stand, so I lay back on the hard bed and clenched my eyes shut, and stayed like that, trying and failing to pretend that I was somewhere else, until Aunt Sue yelled to me up the stairs.

"You can come down anytime. It's sandwiches for dinner, so you can help yourself."

The last thing I felt like doing was eating, especially if Aunt Sue and Book were still shoveling Whoopie Pies into their mouths. I stepped out of the little room and went down to the kitchen. Aunt Sue and Book both looked up, but without much interest.

"I don't feel very well," I said. "Thanks for coming to get me at the airport and all. I think I'll skip dinner and go straight to bed if that's all right."

Aunt Sue shrugged. "Fine. Whatever. You'll go to school with Book in the morning. You already missed the first three days."

I nodded and went back upstairs. I left my stuff lying on the floor—there was nowhere to put it, anyway—and, after one last look around, pulled the string to shut off the faint overhead light, a naked twenty-watt bulb.

Later, as I lay on that hard bed, the heat and the sadness both pressing down on me, I heard the door slam shut downstairs, then somebody trying to start the truck—once, twice, a third time before it caught. Gnarly launched into a barking fit after the truck pulled out of the yard. I waited for him to stop. After half an hour I started to doubt that he ever would, so I pulled my jeans back on and went downstairs. All the lights were out, but I could see Gnarly in the moonlight, running back and forth again under the clothesline, barking at something in the trees, probably squirrels.

I went outside and squatted in the grass near the clothesline. Gnarly came over and sniffed me, and I let him. After a while he started licking me, which made me smile for the first time since I'd been in Craven County. I lay back in the grass and looked up at the North Carolina stars.

In the silence, I could hear the distinct sound of goats *maa*-ing in the barn. Lying there listening to them made me smile, too. I'd always loved goats—every one of them different from every other one, and all of them goofy and playful. Dad said they bleated in a higher pitch than sheep did—that's how you could tell the difference—and the sound I heard was definitely a herd of goats. I thought about going in to see them, but the barn was dark and I didn't know if I'd be able to find a light. Plus I liked what I was doing—petting this new dog, the way I'd done with hundreds of animals over the years in Dad's vet office. I figured I would save the goats for tomorrow.

Book was snoring loudly from a downstairs bedroom when the mosquitoes finally chased me inside. Even though Gnarly had been peaceful when I left him, he started barking again not long after I crawled back into bed, and he kept me awake for another hour, though I was bone tired and desperate for sleep.

I even tried praying to God that Gnarly would stop, though I wasn't surprised when that didn't work. It hadn't worked when I'd prayed to God to save my dad, either. I wasn't even sure I believed in God anymore. I had confessed that to Reverend Harding the day he came to the hospital and wanted me to pray with him over Dad. He said everybody had their doubts, but it was all right to pray anyway, because you never knew who might be listening, and you also never knew when you might start to believe.

three

I woke up sweating early the next morning, panicked from another dream about my dad. We were together in a dark room. I had been looking and looking for him, and finally found him there, but no matter how much I tried, I couldn't ever reach him—to touch him, to hug him. And I couldn't see his face, either. I was desperate to see his face, and I called to him and called to him: *Just look at me, Dad. Just look at me. Please!*

Aunt Sue was sitting alone at the kitchen table, staring vacantly into a cup of black coffee, when I went downstairs. Beatrice's mom had told me that Aunt Sue worked the graveyard shift as a stockroom supervisor at Walmart, so I figured she must have just come home. I studied her for a minute before I spoke—waiting for her to notice me and smile or offer coffee or do anything that might indicate some sort of kindness.

I finally gave up waiting and said good morning, but she still didn't speak.

“Is it OK if I have some coffee?” I asked.

She studied her mug for another second, then got up and refilled it. “Rest is yours,” she said, gesturing at the nearly empty pot.

I had to wash a dirty mug before pouring myself what was left. Most of the kitchen counters were covered with what I quickly figured out was cheese-making equipment—stainless-steel pots, a mountain of plastic containers, a couple of cheese presses. I looked in the refrigerator for some milk, and it was half full of what appeared to be containers of soft white cheeses. I’d noticed another refrigerator out on the screen porch last night, which I assumed Aunt Sue also used for her cheese-making operation.

Book stumbled in not long after that, slammed a couple of cabinets, then poured half a box of Walmart cornflakes into a mixing bowl. He followed that with several spoonfuls of sugar and most of a half gallon of milk. He practically ducked his whole face inside the bowl while he ate, and I had the impression that he would have taken a nap in there once he finished, except that Aunt Sue thumped him on the head with her coffee spoon and he had to come up for air.

“Goats,” she said. She picked up a two-gallon stainless-steel bucket from the floor and shoved it in front of him, knocking the cereal bowl to the side.

“Why can’t she do it now she’s here?” he said.

They both looked at me.

"Nah," Aunt Sue said. "You show her how this afternoon. I want it done right. Then it'll be her job."

She turned to me again. "You ever milk anything? Cow, goat, anything?"

I nodded. "With my dad. He went to a lot of farms to take care of their animals. Mostly cows, but goats, too."

Aunt Sue yawned. "Book will walk you through it this afternoon. You get the hang of that, then you'll move on to helping make the cheeses for farmers' market."

"OK," I said, happy that I would be working with animals again.

"OK?" She scowled. "Don't you mean to say 'Yes, ma'am'?"

I'd never said "Yes, ma'am" before. No one did in Maine. I apologized to Aunt Sue, though, and said, "Yes, ma'am," though it sounded strange, as if someone else was speaking.

Book headed out to the barn. Gnarly yelped in the backyard, and I jumped out of my chair. I knew a kicked dog when I heard one.

"Don't be going anywheres," Aunt Sue said. "Go get yourself whatever kind of cleaned up and ready you need to be. Y'all got school, and they told me to send you early for the paperwork. I already filled out my part. You got to be there to do yours."

It took all the restraint I had not to run out and defend Gnarly, but I knew I had to get along with Aunt Sue and Book, because where else did I have to go?

So I went to take a shower—and wondered if high school would be as bad as things already seemed to be at Aunt Sue's. I shuddered at the thought, and at the thought of facing it alone. I'd walked or ridden bikes or carpooled with Beatrice to school every day of my life until today, and the prospect of going without her, especially here, at a new school in a new state, left me shaky.

Half an hour later, a small truck pulled into the yard. A guy was driving. Book introduced him as Tiny—they were football buddies—and told me to squeeze in the middle. Tiny, who was even larger than Book, grunted a sort of hello. He seemed nervous, but that didn't stop him from trying to feel my chest with his elbow, pretending to be adjusting the bass on his CD player.

"Hey," I said.

Tiny said he was sorry; it was an accident.

Book just snorted.

Craven County High School was two stories, with walkways on the outside of both stories, but since they'd built it in a geological depression, it sat low to the ground and looked like it was sinking. If there was a town of Craven—and I understood that there was—they didn't put the high school anywhere near it, because all I saw when we got there was the same woods that surrounded Aunt Sue's property.

Book and Tiny didn't even bother to point me in the direction of the office. A couple of their large friends grabbed them in the parking lot, and they dragged one another off toward what appeared to be the gym.

I stopped a small boy with bangs and a giant backpack that looked as if it might cripple him over time. "Can you tell me how to get to the office?" I asked.

"Say what?" he said.

I had to repeat it two more times before I guess he finally understood my Maine accent. In the end he just pointed, as if he wasn't sure I knew much English.

Kids on the first floor hung close to the wall on their way to classes or lockers because of all the guys who leaned on the second-story railing and spit chewing tobacco over the side. I thought I was safely out of their range as I hurried toward the office, but halfway there a disgusting black wad landed on my backpack with a sickening splat.

I ducked into a nearby restroom to wash it off. Three white girls were already in there, sitting on the sinks, smoking cigarettes.

"Excuse me," I said to a thin girl in an oversize army jacket. She didn't move except to blow out smoke and then tap her cigarette ash onto the floor.

"I have to use the sink," I said. She looked me over, shrugged, and slid off.

A second girl chirped at me. "You talk funny. Where you from?"

"Maine," I said. I didn't tell her that she was the one who talked funny. Her "talk" sounded like "towk." Her "where" sounded like "wur."

The second girl offered me a cigarette. "You want one?"

I shook my head. "Don't smoke," I said. "Thanks."

They all laughed. "Everybody smokes down here," the first one said. "It's practically a state law or something."

"What about spitting tobacco?" I asked, nodding toward the brown stain on my backpack. "Is that a law, too?"

"Nah," the army jacket girl said. "More like a sport."

All three girls tossed their cigarettes in a toilet but didn't flush. As they filed out, the last one turned back to me and said, "Welcome to Hell, Yankee."

I shook my head after they left. North Carolina didn't feel like a different state. More like a different planet—one so choked with cigarette smoke that there might not be enough oxygen to sustain normal human life.

I finally made it to the office, and after signing some registration forms, I had to meet with the guidance counselor to pick up my schedule. His name was Mr. DiDio. He was a heavyset man wearing a Hawaiian shirt. He also wore his hair in a ponytail. He had a large Persian rug on the floor of his office and several beanbag chairs. The room smelled of patchouli. He called me "dude."

"Sorry I'm in such a rush here, dude," he said as soon as I sat down—in a real chair by his desk. He handed me my schedule. He had a southern accent like everyone else I'd met, though not as pronounced as the boy with the backpack or the girls in the restroom. "I went through your transcripts already," he said. "There's not a whole lot we have to offer you like the AP classes you had in Maine, but I think we can work out a few things next term, some senior classes maybe. Stuff like that. Let's just start you off in these junior classes and see where we can take it from there."

He stood up. "Meeting with the principal," he said, shrugging and grinning, as if he was in trouble for something, but also as if it wasn't that big a deal.

I reached out to shake hands, but he put his palms together over his heart instead and said, *"Namaste."*

"OK," I said. "I mean, yes, sir. *Namaste.*"

North Carolina felt weirder than ever.

At lunch I saw Book with Tiny and some other large boys who I assumed were football players, but Book didn't say anything, even though I know he saw me, too. The school lunch was something called Hot Hamburgers, which turned out to be grilled hamburger patties on toasted white bread with an ocean of brown gravy poured on top. There might have been canned vegetables under the gravy, too, drowned and dead. It made my vegetarian stomach turn—not that the school lunches back in Maine smelled any better.

I found some vending machines in the hall next to the cafeteria, where I bought Fig Newtons and a Snapple, then I wandered outside and sat alone under a pine tree at the edge of the school property. Other kids were hanging around outside, too, but no one paid any attention to me, not that I expected they would. I didn't particularly mind being invisible, though. It beat being the object of ridicule because of my "accent."

After I finished, I pulled out one of my notebooks and started a new letter to Dad.

I'm not sure I'm in America anymore. I'm definitely not in Maine. I might have to see about taking ESL classes to fit in here and know what anybody's saying. Or maybe SSL classes. Southern as a Second Language. . . .

After lunch I had English. I heard it before I got there—the room was practically shaking from all the talking and yelling. The teacher, Mrs. Roosevelt, was an older black woman with silver hair and a wide face. She wore bifocals that could have hung down on their silver chain in front of her shirt, but she had them stuck up on top of her hair. She asked me my name and directed me to a seat, then closed the door and stood in front of her desk with her arms folded. Everyone hushed.

I thought she'd take attendance, but she didn't. She pointed to a couple of kids in the front row and told them to pass out a stack of books that balanced on the edge of her desk—worn copies of *The Adventures of Huckleberry Finn.* I was surprised they were just assigning it now, in eleventh-grade English. In Maine we had read it in middle school.

"Now, I want you all to look through these books," Mrs. Roosevelt said. "Do you see anything unusual?"

I flipped through my weathered copy and saw black smudges on many of the pages.

Several hands shot up. Several kids shouted. Mrs. Roosevelt nodded at a white boy near the back.

"Somebody went at them with a Sharpie or something," he said. "They scratched over a whole bunch of the words."

Mrs. Roosevelt asked what words.

The hands went down. Nobody shouted this time.

"What words?" Mrs. Roosevelt asked again.

Another boy in the back, a black kid, said, "The N-word, Mrs. Roosevelt. It's anywhere they have the N-word."

"And what's the N-word?" Mrs. Roosevelt asked. She knew, obviously, but she was determined to make us say it, or to make somebody. I knew it wouldn't be me. I scanned some pages. Every reference to *Nigger Jim* was now just *Jim* with one of those black smudges in front of it. A part of me wanted to raise my hand and say how stupid it was—that it made people think even more about the N-word than if they'd just left it alone. I kept my mouth shut, though. I wasn't about to let them hear me say the word *nigger,* or anything else, in my Yankee accent.

"What's the N-word?" Mrs. Roosevelt asked again.

One of the black girls, who sat at the desk next to mine, nodded, and Mrs. Roosevelt nodded back at her. The girl was pretty, with straight black hair pulled back with a red headband. She said, "It's *nigger,* Mrs. Roosevelt."

Mrs. Roosevelt hunted for her glasses, though she didn't put them on, just held them in her hand. "Your homework this week is to read this book. All of this book." Then she nodded again at the girl sitting next to me and said, "Shirelle, will you please turn to the beginning of the novel and read us what Twain wrote there?"

Shirelle did: "'Notice: Persons attempting to find a motive in this narrative will be prosecuted; persons attempting to find a moral in it will be banished; persons attempting to find a plot in it will be shot.'"

"Thank you, Shirelle," Mrs. Roosevelt said. "For tomorrow, I want you to think about that, and come prepared to tell me why Mark Twain wrote it. Also, I want you to write a one-page essay arguing for, or against, the censorship in your copy of *Huckleberry Finn.*"

I looked around. Black kids made up about a quarter of the class. White kids and a couple of Hispanic kids made up the other three quarters. I wondered how any conversation about race, or *Huckleberry Finn,* or anything would go here. Back in Maine, we hadn't had any black kids at my school. I'd never heard anyone use the N-word, and no one had ever blacked it out of a book with a Sharpie.

I was determined to stay angry at Beatrice—not call or write for at least a few days—but as the first day of school wore on and I had no one to hang out with between classes, that determination faded. Talking to Beatrice was too deeply ingrained a habit, and I hoped she'd sent me an e-mail apologizing for how she'd been at the airport. So during study hall after Mrs. Roosevelt's class, I got a library pass and lucked out because I found an empty computer. Signs on the wall listed all the things you were blocked from looking up: sex, of course, and pornography, abortion, murder, homosexuality, birth control, dozens more. I was surprised that nothing blocked me from checking my e-mail, but I wasn't about to ask. My heartbeat quickened when I opened my account: there *was* a message from Beatrice—and it sounded as if she missed me as much as I missed her.

Hey, Iris,
I did the dumbest thing today. I got home and kept wondering where you were, why you weren't home yet, too. I don't know who I'm supposed to do stuff with since you're gone, except Collie, and I'm mad at him.

I had to stop reading for a minute. I didn't want to be the new girl from Maine who everyone knew about because they saw her bawling in the library. I read a poem once called "The Crybaby at the Library," about a boy who starts sobbing in a library because he didn't do his math; he just goes on and on until everything's soaked, all the books swell with moisture, the pages curl up, the ink smears, clouds form at the ceiling. I didn't want to be him.

The rest of the e-mail was just news from school and town. She was mad at Collie because his Facebook page listed his relationship status as "It's complicated." Nate, this boy I went out with for a while, told Beatrice to say hi for him. Coach wanted to start up a fall ball league. She didn't mention her parents, though, and she never said she was sorry. The bell rang before I could write her back, which was probably good because I was still hurt and angry and sad, and couldn't think of anything to say.

four

That afternoon, when I realized, too late, that I didn't know what bus to take, I had to walk the four miles home from school. Two miles on the shoulder of County Road, another two down the canopy road to Aunt Sue's, though I missed her driveway and went an extra half a mile before I realized what I'd done and doubled back.

I was sweaty and tired when I finally got to the farm, but I quickly forgot all that when Gnarly rushed up to greet me, tail wagging like crazy, as if we'd grown up together. I rolled on the ground with him and let him lick my face all he wanted with his big slobbery tongue. I got up and raced him back and forth across the yard, threw him sticks, scratched him and hugged him and rubbed his belly. I'd never seen a dog so happy for the attention—and I was just as happy to be giving it.

Several goats *maa*ed in the field next to the barn, and I wanted to go meet them, but Gnarly didn't want me to go so soon, so I waved to them and kept playing with the dog.

I finally had to take a break, though—to go inside to the bathroom and to get a drink of water. I didn't see or hear Aunt Sue, so I assumed she was asleep. I looked for something to eat while I was in the kitchen, but there wasn't much besides lunch meats and bread: saltines, an apple, cans of green beans and peas and beets. A half-empty jar of peanut butter with traces of old grape jelly and cracker crumbs.

I was just heading for the barn to finally introduce myself to the goats when Book and Tiny drove up from football practice. Book had an enormous Big Gulp in one hand and a 7-Eleven burrito in the other. No books. He headed straight for the barn. Tiny turned his truck around and left.

"Well, come on, already," Book said, waving his burrito at me. "Goats ain't gonna milk theirselves."

He yelled at them in the field and herded them over while I pulled open the barn door. It took a minute for my eyes to adjust to the dim light in the barn, and to see what a wreck it was: dirty goat stalls, splintery wood, a flimsy milking stand, rusty tools, randomly stacked hay bales, phantom engine parts, scrap metal, a chicken coop leaning precariously to one side. Once the goats crowded in, they stayed close together in their open stall and eyed me warily.

Book plopped down into a wheelbarrow with a flat tire, still wearing his padded football pants and sweaty gray athletic department T-shirt, his Big Gulp balanced on his belly. The burrito had disappeared, except for the wrapper. He threw that at the goats, and one of them ate it.

All five were nannies, two of them pregnant. One was obviously due anytime; the other was just beginning to show.

"Those three," Book said, gesturing to the milkers, "their names are Patsy, Loretta, and Tammy. The pregnant ones are Reba and Jo Dee. Mama named them after old-lady country singers. Except for Jo Dee. She ain't old."

Patsy, the smallest goat—or at least the shortest—nodded at me. I nodded back. I could tell right away she was the herd queen. The others bunched up behind her.

"You don't have a buck?" I asked.

"We used to," Book said. "His name was Ruckter, but we couldn't keep him away from the nannies no matter what. He would jump over a fence, dig under a fence, knock down a fence, any which way so he could do the nannies. Plus he had a bad case of goat funk that never let up. So we got rid of his sorry ass, and now we just go out and get us a Rent-a-Buck when we need one."

The slats in the side of the barn let a soft yellow afternoon light leak in. Book told me that I should always milk Patsy first. "She's the boss of the rest of them," he said. "Plus she's Loretta's mom. Once you get Patsy up there, every one of the other ones will go after her. But if you don't get her to do it—or to do anything—the others won't budge a muscle. They will fight you, and you'll have to drag their asses up on that milk stand."

I looked at Patsy again, and she looked back at me in the same way—each sizing up the other. I already knew about herd queens and a lot of other things about goats from helping Dad at Mr. Lorentzen's farm back home. It would have made Dad happy to know I still remembered.

Patsy was a Nigerian dwarf. Her beard nearly reached the ground, thanks to her stubby legs, but you could tell she was strong. Loretta, her daughter, appeared to be half Nigerian, half La Mancha. All the others were full La Manchas—taller, leaner, more American. No ears, or practically none, anyway, which is another characteristic of the breed.

"Mama says Patsy gives the best milk," Book said. "It's fatter than those other ones give, so it's tastiest. But Mama mixes their milk all up, so I don't know how she knows the difference, but she does."

I took a handful of feed and held it under Patsy's nose. She didn't take her eyes off mine as she tongued it out of my hand. She nodded at me again, and then, without my coaxing her, stepped up onto the milk stand.

"You better lower that stanchion down over her neck to keep her there," Book said.

The stanchion was like the thing that keeps people's heads in place on a guillotine, which I'd read about in *A Tale of Two Cities*—not that anybody in Craven County was likely to have ever heard of it.

Something told me Patsy didn't like the stanchion, though,

and that I didn't need it with her. Maybe with the others, who seemed more skittish. But not with Patsy.

She didn't move while I milked her. Just ate out of the feed trough at the head of the stand. She smelled like dirt and hay, and like our barn back in Maine, and like Dad when he came home from his vet rounds to other people's farms.

Dad used to tell me I started out in life loving animals—since the second I was born. He said it was probably because my mom was feeding a hog we had in our backyard when her water broke and she went into labor. Everything happened so fast, she couldn't make it past the barn before I was ready to come out. Dad did the delivery and said it wasn't half as hard as getting a horse to foal. Mom apparently told him it smelled like manure in there and asked him to *please* get her up to the house. Dad told me he threw the placenta into the hog pen for the hog to eat, which my mom thought was disgusting. As soon as I could crawl, though, whenever I was outside, I would try to get into the hog pen with that hog. I liked that story. It was one of the few my dad ever told about my mom.

After I finished with Patsy, I scratched her under her chin. She seemed surprised by that—I doubted Book or Aunt Sue were ever very sweet to their goats—but she quickly relaxed. She closed her eyes. If she'd been a human, she might have even moaned.

After she stepped off the stand, Loretta practically hopped on up. I must have gotten too cocky, because again I didn't lower the stanchion, and I also forgot to refill the feed trough, so once Loretta finished what Patsy had left in there, she pulled away and knocked over the milk bucket.

Book laughed. "Told you. Mama's gonna have your ass now."

"Just don't tell her," I said.

He laughed again. "She'll know. Can't make the cheese if you don't got the milk. Can't sell the cheese if you don't got the milk. Can't do nothing if you don't got the milk. And you don't got the milk." He noisily sucked down the last of his Big Gulp. "Mama says once we turn them pregnant goats into milkers, she can make a couple hundred dollars a week extra from all their cheese. Unless somebody goes around spilling too much."

I put Loretta in the stanchion and refilled the grain trough, and finished up with her milking.

The third milker, Tammy, had slipped back outside the barn. Book finished off his Big Gulp, then said, "Hold on. I'll show you how to fetch her. She likes to be trouble."

I followed him outside, thinking he'd coax her in with grain, but he just screamed at her and shooed her back toward the barn. He kicked her so hard that she stumbled, and before she could fully right herself, he kicked her again.

"Stop!" I yelled.

"Stop, hell," he said. "You want her or don't you?"

I laid my hand gently on Tammy's head, but she shied away, and when I tried to lead her into the barn, she balked and bolted back out into the field.

Book snorted his usual snort. "I ain't going after her," he said. "That one's all on you."

I ended up tricking Tammy back to the barn with a pile of grain on the ground by the door. When she wandered over to inspect it and then eat it, I jumped out from behind her and shoved her inside—and latched the door before she could bolt again. I had to drag her onto the milking stand and dropped the stanchion over her neck right away. Book went back to the house. Patsy and Loretta stayed out in the field. Tammy, defeated, shoved her face into the trough and let me milk.

We had to pasteurize the milk, then stir in the bacteria culture and rennet, which is what turned it into cheese. Book told me how to do it while he sat at the kitchen table. "So this is your job from now on, like Mama told you this morning," he said. "Now what you do is just cover it and let it sit in the fridge or anywhere cool until tomorrow, then you salt it and set it up so you drain off what they call the whey, and then you have your cheese." He pointed to the stack of plastic containers. "Mama spoons it in there, and that's what she sells at the farmers' market."

"You don't add anything else?" I asked him. "You don't smoke it or flavor it or anything?"

Book shook his head. "Mama says it's too much trouble. We're the only ones in five counties that makes goat cheese, and rich people can't get enough of it just like that—just the soft goat cheese. They think it's better than real cheese. More fancier."

Looking around, I figured they could use the money. They didn't have a computer. No answering machine and probably no voice mail — just basic service and a black telephone so old the numbers were worn off the touch pad. They did have a TV and an antenna on top of the house, but no cable and no satellite dish. Aunt Sue had a twenty-year-old VCR that probably ate most of the tapes she brought home from the warehouse.

About the only thing she had for entertainment that worked properly was a small, tinny, food-stained Walmart store-brand CD player. She kept it on the kitchen counter for listening to her country music CDs. Book told me sometimes he snuck his friends' heavy metal on when she wasn't home, but Aunt Sue always knew when he did because she said the nannies heard it all the way out in the yard and it caused their milk to sour.

We had sandwiches again that night. I made mine with white bread, processed cheese, and wilted leaves from a half-brown head of iceberg lettuce, with a dill pickle on the side, which was pretty much all they had that I could eat. Aunt Sue didn't allow us to eat any of the goat cheese or drink the goat milk. I thought about telling Aunt Sue that I was a vegetarian, but I suspected she would give me a hard time about it. Plus if all we were ever going to do around there was eat sandwiches, it probably didn't matter. She and Book both made Dagwoods like the one Book had been eating the night before, with plenty of meat. I felt a little sick watching them wolf it all down.

They talked about the football team, the schedule, the college recruiters, the asshole coaches, the asshole refs, the game coming up this Friday night, the game last Friday night, which must have been before the school year even started, though I didn't care enough to ask. Neither of them asked about my day, which didn't really surprise me. But I thought I should at least make some effort to be friendly.

"So I think I got my schedule lined up OK," I said when they both stopped to chew. "It's not great. I've already taken all of the AP classes they have here when I was back in Maine. They might put me in some senior classes in the spring, though, which could be good."

Book snorted. It seemed to be an involuntary response to just about everything. "Know what *AP* stands for? *Absolute Puke.*"

Aunt Sue didn't laugh, but she did nod, which I supposed meant she appreciated Book's joke.

Then she turned back to me. "Was there anything else you wanted to interrupt us about?" she asked.

I thought about just shutting up. I'd gotten pretty good at it over the past month, biting my tongue around Mr. and Mrs. Stone, and eventually even around Beatrice. But I was getting tired of it. And besides, there was something I had to ask if I didn't want to have to survive every day at school on a diet of Fig Newtons and Snapples.

"I'd like to pack my own lunches for school," I said. "Sandwiches would be OK," I added, which I thought was pretty generous of me, given the limp thing on my plate. "I hope that's not a problem."

Aunt Sue looked as if I'd just walked in the door uninvited. She glanced down at her sandwich, then back at me. Finally she said, "I ate school lunch." She nodded at Book. "He eats school lunch." She leveled her gaze at me again. "You eat school lunch."

She took a bite of her sandwich. "Now, was there something else you needed?"

"No," I said, afraid my face had turned red and they could see that I was embarrassed and angry. "There's nothing."

I made myself finish my sandwich, though every bite seemed to stick in my throat, and I had to drink glass after glass of water to swallow. Then I rinsed my knife and plate and cup and laid them in the drain board.

"Thanks for dinner," I said. Aunt Sue and Book both grunted.

I went upstairs, intending to reread *Huckleberry Finn* and write my essay, but when I shut the door, the tiny room felt too claustrophobic again. I stood on the bed and leaned against the window, drinking in the evening air, listening to the low bleating of the goats—a comforting sound, but not comforting enough to keep me from missing Maine, and Beatrice, and Dad, and a life that wasn't mine anymore. Whatever I might have been hoping for in North Carolina, it wasn't this.

I lay on the bed and curled into a ball and stayed there, and thought about Dad—his gray hair he always let grow too long and unruly, his green fishing cap, which was buried in one of my clothes piles on the floor, his red flannel shirts that always had a tear in them somewhere, his Saturday stubble, his Sunday aftershave, his Christmas-tree coffee mug, which he used year-round. I dug through the piles of clothes until I found his cap, then held it against my chest. I sat hugging it for a few minutes, then pulled out my notebook and started another letter.

Dear Dad,

I milked goats today. I'm surprised by how much I remember about them from Mr. Lorentzen's farm. There are also chickens and guineas, and they have a great dog here named Gnarly. . . .

I finally forced myself to sit up and do my homework, and that helped a little, too.

The phone rang just before Aunt Sue left for work.

"Iris!" Aunt Sue yelled from downstairs. "You got a phone call."

I practically ran from the room to get it. It had to be Beatrice. No one else knew where I was or would think of calling me. I reached for the phone, but Aunt Sue didn't let go right away.

"I don't like calls here," she said. "Keep it short."

"Yes, ma'am," I said.

Beatrice heard. *"Yes, ma'am?"* she said once I had the phone to myself. "What's that all about?"

"It's how they talk down here," I said. I stretched the cord out of the kitchen and down the hall. "Aunt Sue has a lot of rules. I'm supposed to say it, to be polite."

"You aunt doesn't sound too polite herself," Beatrice said. "Telling you to keep it short the first time I even call."

"Yeah," I said. "She's pretty strict. But they have goats here, so that's a plus. And they have a dog."

But Beatrice didn't seem to hear me. "God, I miss you, Iris. There's nobody to talk to up here. I still can't believe you're really gone. How are you? How's the school?"

"Different," I said.

"Different how?" Beatrice asked.

I told her about the girls in the restroom, and the chewing tobacco, and Book's friend Tiny with his big elbows.

"What?" said Beatrice. "They think the Civil War is still going on, *and* they're perverts?"

"Some, I guess."

"Just remind them who won."

"Maybe I'll wait awhile on that."

"Do they have a softball team?"

"I haven't checked. Anyway, it looks like I'll have to come home in the afternoons to milk the goats and do chores."

"Are you kidding me?"

"It could be worse." I didn't want to tell Beatrice how much I already liked the goats—the feel and smell of them. And how much I liked Gnarly, and he liked me. I didn't want her to think anything was good here.

"It's not OK, Iris," she said. "It's child labor. You should complain to someone."

"There's no one to complain to."

"What about a social worker?"

"I don't think I have one."

"Well, when you get one, complain."

"OK."

"OK."

"Good."

"Good."

There was an edge to my voice that surprised me, and I wondered if Beatrice noticed. I didn't want her advice. I didn't need it. I needed her to understand what I was going through, and for her to be torn up with guilt that she hadn't made her parents let me stay.

"So how are your parents doing?" I asked. "Are things any better now?"

"Oh, God," Beatrice said. "*Them.* Who knows? They're parents. They fight; they don't fight. I'm just trying to ignore them."

"So what about Collie?" I asked. "How are things with him?"

"You mean Mr. 'It's complicated'? I think I'm going to start ignoring him, too. But there are plenty of boys up here besides him. Well, maybe not plenty, but some. Nate called me tonight."

"Nate?" I said, surprised. Nate and I had dated for a month back in the spring; I stopped seeing him after Dad got so sick.

"Yeah," Beatrice said. "I mean, we just talked. He heard Collie and I were having a fight, and he just wanted to see how I was doing. That's all."

That edge came back into my voice then—and I didn't

care if Beatrice heard it. "You can't go out with somebody your best friend dated, B."

"I know, I know," she said quickly. "I wouldn't ever do that. You know I wouldn't. Come on, Iris." She sounded hurt.

I knew I was supposed to say something to make her feel better, maybe apologize. But I didn't want to. I didn't know what else to say to Beatrice, though, and she didn't seem to know what to say to me, either.

Aunt Sue ended the conversation for us.

"Hang up!" she shouted from the kitchen.

"I have to go," I said.

"Yeah," Beatrice said in a voice that was already fading out. "I heard. Bye, Iris."

"Bye, B."

five

I didn't want to be crammed into Tiny's truck between him and Book, so I rode the bus the next day. I felt strange at school, silent in a way I'd never been before, and I kept to myself. I ate lunch alone under that pine tree outside, handed in my *Huck Finn* assignment, didn't say anything in any of my classes. But the farm was different—or at least the part that I quickly claimed as mine: the fields and the barn and Gnarly and the goats. I played with Gnarly as soon as I got off the bus in the afternoon. I milked the goats and looked after the chickens and started making the goat cheese. Aunt Sue supervised me the first time, but the process was simple. She couldn't find much to criticize.

"Put in more salt," she said, and that was about it. "People around here like salty. Salty boiled peanuts, salty goat cheese, salty everything."

So I added more salt, which was double the standard recipe I found in one of her cheese-making books for what they called bag cheese—the soft white chèvre that was all Aunt Sue made.

My third day there, Aunt Sue ordered me to clean out the barn, which I'm sure she thought was a lousy job, since neither she nor Book had done it in what looked like years. But I didn't mind the work. I liked having a routine and feeling useful. Most of the goats wandered out in the field, but Patsy stood half in and half out of the barn door, hardly moving, watching me intently as I stacked and cleaned and piled and nailed. I had the impression that she was taking inventory of everything I left in and everything I hauled out. She walked around inside the barn several times once I was done, as if inspecting the job.

"So what do you think?" I asked her. "Good enough?"

She blew her nose on the barn floor, raising a puff of hay dust.

"Forget it," I said. "I've never heard of anybody sweeping out a barn."

If a goat can shrug, then that's what Patsy did. Then she blew her nose again, I guess to make a point. But I still wouldn't sweep.

The other goats, or three of them anyway, rubbed against me as if I was a fence post when I took a break after a couple of hours and went out into the field. Patsy let me scratch her head and under her chin when I milked her, but Loretta, Reba, and Jo Dee loved it anytime, all the time. They liked to play with me, too — wrestling and tag and tug-of-war. Gnarly stayed on the other side of the fence when I was with the goats, watching jealously until I came back out into the yard to pay attention to him some more, too.

The one goat I had trouble with was Tammy. She butted me hard a couple of times when I tried to play with her in the field, and tore a hole in my T-shirt with one of her horns. All the goats except Jo Dee, the youngest, had horns, and though they weren't very long, they could still hurt. Tammy poked the other goats with the pointy ends of her horns sometimes. She never drew blood, but you could tell it hurt. Patsy wouldn't stand for it, though, and tossed Tammy back a couple of times a day just to make sure she knew her proper place in the herd.

One afternoon that first week, when I was busy in the barn, I heard Tammy bleating frantically, and I came outside to find her with her head stuck in the fence. I had to wrestle it around to pull it out, but it wasn't easy. "Just turn your head sideways!" I yelled at her about ten times. "That's how you got it in there in the first place!" When I finally got her loose, I thought she'd be grateful, but she just waited until my back was turned and butted me into the fence.

I got mad at first, but then I thought about how Book had treated her that first afternoon, and I thought about he treated Gnarly. I knew goats liked to play rough, but Book wasn't just rough with the animals; he was mean.

• • •

Book had an away game that first Friday, and it was close enough for Aunt Sue to drive and still make it to her shift at work. She left in the afternoon and didn't bother inviting me along. I didn't mind, because it meant I had the farm all to myself, and after I milked the goats and finished the rest of my chores, I decided to explore the woods behind Aunt Sue's property—a tangle of brush and saplings and hardwoods that eventually gave way to pine forest. Book had told me there was supposed to be a haunted place deep in the forest, ringed with stones, where nothing ever grew and the earth had been scorched by fire. He called it the Devil's Stomping Ground. He was probably trying to scare me, but it just made me curious. I looked for it for a long time, but all I ever found was a nice green meadow, the grass chewed low by deer. It was a serene spot, the opposite of a devil's stomping ground, but I decided to call it that, anyway.

Gnarly trotted along with me, happy as usual to have somebody notice him, and he lay down with me in the cool shade at the edge of the meadow. I petted him for a long time, rubbed his belly, checked him for ticks and fleas.

"You like this, boy? Huh? You like this, Gnarly?" I talked to him the way I'd talked to dogs all my life, and I let the calmness of the Devil's Stomping Ground and being with Gnarly wash over me.

When we got back to the farm, I found Loretta chewing on the rusted end of the downspout from the gutter at the corner of Aunt Sue's house. I had no idea how she'd managed to get out of the pen. Patsy was pressed against the fence watching—more curious than concerned. Goats can eat a lot of stuff, but I doubted rusty downspouts were on the recommended list. Plus I knew Aunt Sue would be mad if she saw any of the goats running around in the yard—or chewing on her gutters. Loretta must have really liked the taste, though, because I had to grab her by her horns and pull to get her back inside the fence.

She quit fighting when I opened the gate, though, and she nuzzled me once I got her in—an unexpected display of affection. That moment, and the sweet afternoon with Gnarly, made me realize how long it had been since anyone had shown me any sort of kindness. I dropped down onto my knees and hugged her back.

Aunt Sue and Book continued to ignore me for the most part. No one asked about school, or how I'd slept, or if I missed my dad. At Aunt Sue's it was chores, dinner, and reality shows on TV. The only things Aunt Sue and Book talked about were goat cheese, football games, and the sorry knuckleheads Aunt Sue worked with at Walmart. Aunt Sue sat on the back steps every morning and evening smoking her cigarettes—one after breakfast, one after dinner, one anytime she drank a beer—and if I happened to walk past, she sometimes nodded, but that was all.

At school, in English, the class got into a discussion about Jim in *Huckleberry Finn*—about what he meant when he called Huck "honey" all the time.

"Mrs. Roosevelt," one kid asked, "do you think Jim was on the down low? You know, like, dude has a wife and kids and all, but he's got a thing for the Huckleberries, too?"

Everybody cracked up when he said that, except Shirelle. She rolled her eyes in exasperation.

"Yeah," a girl said when things quieted down. "I wondered about that, too, if Jim's sweet on Huckleberry. They spend all that time in their nudeness and everything."

Mrs. Roosevelt told them they should keep in mind that people talked differently back in those days, before the Civil War, and what people a hundred years from now would think about the way people talked today.

"I guarantee if they write the book on us, somebody better have a whole bunch of them Sharpies to pass out in the classrooms," said a boy. "Do some Sharpie marking on those books first thing."

Shirelle shook her head. I knew if I was going to make a friend in Craven County, she would probably be the one, but I didn't try to talk to her after class. I didn't try to talk to anyone else at school, either. Things were strained between Beatrice and me—we were e-mailing but hadn't talked in a week, since my second night in North Carolina—but I hoped that would pass, and I still didn't want to be a part of anything here. Except maybe Gnarly and the goats.

One night near the end of my second week, not long after Aunt Sue left for work, Gnarly started barking. I had just fallen asleep, and it woke me up with a start. Maybe it was squirrels, or raccoons, or deer. Maybe he was just barking because he felt like it, because Aunt Sue was gone and he was happy. It didn't seem to bother Book—I doubted anything could wake him up—but after an hour I couldn't stand it anymore. I went outside and found Gnarly running back and forth under the clothesline, so I lay down with him in the grass, which calmed him down. As soon as I went back inside, though, he started up again. I jammed my pillow over my head, closed the window, shut my door, but nothing worked. Finally, after another noisy hour, I went back outside and unhooked Gnarly's leash. I figured he would run around in the field for a while, maybe head for the woods and tire himself out. And it seemed to work, because everything was quiet when I crawled back into bed.

The sun was barely up hours later when I heard someone yelling. I bolted straight up in bed, confused. I'd been dead asleep for the first time since I'd been there. Dreaming about my house in Maine, only it didn't look like my house, exactly. The rooms were empty. I was looking for somebody. Just like in the dream I'd had about my dad. Beatrice was there, but she wasn't who I was looking for. Then Book was there, telling me I forgot to feed the goats, I was supposed to feed the goats, what about the goats?

The yelling that woke me up kept on, finally shaping itself into Aunt Sue's voice: "Who in hell let Gnarly off the clothesline?"

Book ran out of his bedroom and into the kitchen—I heard him even though my door was shut—stuttering so bad it was impossible to understand a word.

I felt sorry for him, so I pulled myself out of bed and stumbled to the top of the stairs. "It was me, Aunt Sue," I yelled down. "Gnarly was barking, and I let him loose."

Aunt Sue appeared suddenly at the bottom of the stairs, glaring up at me. Book appeared next to her.

She said, "Gnarly don't bark at night."

"He started when you left."

Aunt Sue turned to Book. "That true?"

Book shook his head like he was trying to get water out of his ear. "No. Nuh-uh. I never heard him."

Aunt Sue swore again. She disappeared for a second, then reappeared holding two dead chickens upside down by their feet. "Look at what that dumb-ass dog did when you set him loose." She shook them at me, and their blood splattered on her jeans and dripped onto the floor. "You're lucky he went after the neighbors' chickens and not mine." She pointed to the puddle with her boot. "Now get your ass down here and clean this up."

"OK," I said, halfway down the stairs before she'd finished talking. "I mean yes, ma'am."

Aunt Sue shifted both chickens to her left hand.

Then she slapped me.

I stumbled back into the wall and fell to the floor, more from the shock of it than from the force of the blow.

Before I could say anything, before I could make sense of what had just happened, Aunt Sue stormed back outside.

I touched my face and felt blood.

"Don't worry," Book said. "It's just from the chickens."

He grabbed my arm and pulled me up. "Come on, already," he said. "You ain't hurt. She usually hits a lot harder."

Still stunned, I followed Book across the kitchen, and we watched Aunt Sue through the window: she pulled the chickens' heads off, plucked the bodies, then stuffed the feathers and heads and beaks into a trash bag.

Book seemed relieved. "She don't like the neighbors, anyway," he said.

For dinner that evening we had chicken potpie—the first time since I'd been there that it wasn't a sandwich night. Aunt Sue parboiled the chickens, opened canned beans and carrots, boiled some potatoes, and hauled out a couple of frozen Walmart pie crusts. When I finished pasteurizing the goat milk and starting the new cheeses, Aunt Sue called us to eat. Book practically jumped up and down with excitement.

Aunt Sue pulled the chicken potpie out of the oven and set it on a worn pot holder in the middle of the kitchen table, then she scooped out enormous servings onto all of our plates.

She almost seemed happy about what she'd done. Her anger had vanished as quickly as it had come on.

"Dig in," Aunt Sue said, though Book's mouth was already

stuffed full. I picked up my fork and thought about eating the chicken-soaked vegetables just to keep the peace, but my stomach revolted at the thought.

Aunt Sue noticed my hesitation and stopped eating. "Well? What's your problem now?"

"I don't eat chicken," I said.

She gave me a blank look. "Say again?" she said, licking her fork. Book already had his face practically buried in his own potpie and only looked up every now and then to breathe.

"I'm a vegetarian," I said, my voice smaller than I liked it. "Maybe I can just make a sandwich? Or if there are some vegetables left over, I could cook those separately or something."

"Sandwiches have meat," Aunt Sue said.

Book stopped eating long enough to chime in. "Not hers, Mama. I seen her. Iris don't ever put meat on her sandwiches."

Aunt Sue pointed at me with her fork. It was a big fork. All their silverware was big; I don't know why.

"Around here you eat what you're served," she said. "Sixteen years old should have already learned that lesson in table manners."

I didn't say anything, so Aunt Sue tried again. "Looky," she said. "You can fish you out some carrots, and some crust, and there's potatoes in there, too. See those peas? Don't you like peas? Everybody likes peas." She held one up, rolled it between her thumb and forefinger like maybe I hadn't ever seen one before. Like it was one of the great marvels of nature.

I kept my eyes on my potpie while she talked. "Well?" she said. "Don't that sound like a good idea?"

"I can't," I said reluctantly. I didn't want her to hit me again—and I didn't know what might set her off. But I hadn't eaten meat since I was twelve, and I wasn't going to start now, or ever. "It's been cooked with the chicken, so I can't eat it. I'm sorry."

That stopped her cold. I think she'd used up what little store of nice she had in her by then, anyway. "Fine, then. Just fine," she said. "But I ought to point out that since you were the one let out Gnarly, it's kind of like you were the one that got the chickens killed in the first place. But you just go ahead and be that-a way, and while you're at it, you march yourself up to the bedroom we were good enough to let you have all for yourself and you go on and do your homework and go on and eat air for dinner tonight, because you're not getting anything else. Nobody ever did nobody a favor by coddling them, and I'm not about to start now. So go."

So I went.

six

Book knocked on my door a couple of hours later. "Mama says you're supposed to come with me and Tiny. There's a field party and we're going, and she says we have to take you with us."

I hadn't opened the door yet, but I could tell from his voice that he didn't want me to go.

"That's OK," I said. "Thanks for the invitation. I'll just stay here."

Something bumped high against the door. Probably his head. "Mama says you have to. She's having company and doesn't want anybody else here."

That surprised me. I opened the door. Book nearly fell in on top of me. "Damn it, Iris," he snarled. "Give me some warning next time you're just gonna open the door."

He backed out into the hall.

"Who's the company?" I asked.

"Nobody," he said. "Just company."

"But who?" I said.

"Damn, you're nosy," he said. "Is that how all y'all are up there—so nosy like that?"

"Forget it," I said, retreating.

Book waved his hands in front of him. "No. Come on. You have to come with us. Mama'll be mad. Come on. Tiny's outside in his truck. Come on."

I stopped backing up when he mentioned Aunt Sue. I didn't want her any angrier at me than she already was. "Who's going to be there?"

"Just people," Book said. "From school. It's a field party. What do you care? You don't know anybody, do you? You can meet some people. Don't you like to meet people?"

"Not particularly."

He blinked. This clearly wasn't in his plan.

"Iris." He lowered his voice until it was almost a whisper. "You're gonna get me in trouble. So come on. Mama's downstairs. She's waiting."

I told him all right, I would go, but I wasn't happy about the idea of sitting between him and Tiny.

"You can sit in the back, then," Book said. "Tiny's probably got a blanket or something you can sit on."

We heard Gnarly yelping and growling before we got outside. He was lunging at Tiny but could only get as far as the end of his leash and the give of the clothesline. Book laughed.

Tiny grinned his stupid grin. He looked at me, and the grin widened practically to his ears, which looked like question marks jutting out from the sides of his shaved head. Tiny's bigness always surprised me whenever I saw him. Everything about him strained against whatever tried to contain it: the seat of his jeans, the buttons on his shirt, even the flesh of his face.

"I was just showing Gnarly my karate," he said. He made chopping motions with his hands, then pirouetted in a spin kick that just missed Gnarly's face. Gnarly lunged at his shoe.

Book shook his head at Tiny. "Come on, Ninja Turtle," he said. I knelt to pet Gnarly and calm him down, then I climbed into the back of the truck. Tiny's face fell when he saw, but Book just pushed him toward the driver's seat and said, "Let's go."

Twenty minutes later we bounced off the highway and careened down a set of tire tracks that turned into ruts so deep I felt the oil pan scraping the ground. Every bump bounced me hard on my tailbone, and I yelled for them to take it easy. They couldn't hear, though. They had their white-boy rap music cranked up too loud, with the bass set on Headache.

At last we stopped. We were at an open field lit by a fading red sunset and headlights from a dozen other trucks. Book and Tiny parked between a couple of Jeeps, then jumped out and yelled "Craven Ravens rule!" A huddle of other big white boys roared something back that was too southern for me to understand. I stayed next to Tiny's truck, but Book and Tiny headed straight across the field to join a bunch of their friends at another truck that had a keg in the back. When they got there, Book grabbed Tiny around the neck and wrestled him to the ground. Three other guys grabbed Tiny, too, and they piled on top — a mountain of guys, pinning him down. Somebody locked his arms around Tiny's head and held on while somebody else shoved a funnel in Tiny's mouth and a girl poured in a cup of beer. Tiny bucked and shuddered, but they held on. Other guys poured in their beer, too, then the girl moved the wide end of the funnel to the keg and opened the tap. I thought about the waterboarding they did with secret terrorist prisoners overseas.

When they finally stopped and let him loose, Tiny sat up gasping and coughing. He staggered to his feet and swung his fist at someone he must have thought was there. Then he dropped to his knees and vomited. Everybody laughed and yelled, and in a minute Tiny roared and laughed and yelled with them. The sun vanished behind the tree line, and people turned into shadows. They threw sticks and paper into a barrel off the back of another truck and doused it with gas and flicked matches in until one of them caught and the fire exploded ten feet into the sky.

Then they went after Book. The whole mob of them, yelling, singing. Book took off running, out of the headlights and through the field. Somebody jumped into the cab of another truck, and a bunch of them hopped in the back and they took off, too. They turned on floodlights for spotlighting deer, mounted to the truck roof, and the beams caught Book running hard away from them in the thickening dark. Once they had him trapped in the bouncing lights, it took seconds for the truck to catch up. Two guys dove onto Book and tackled him to the dirt. The driver slammed on the brakes, and then more guys piled on, too. They dragged Book over to the truck and then lifted him into the bed. They sat on him as he kept fighting, and drove him back to the circle of headlights, and the keg, and the funnel.

None of the noise sounded like any language I knew or had ever heard. There was the headache bass line from the giant speakers, a screeching rap song that was mostly distortion, the singing boys, the screaming Book, then something like a chant—"Huh-huh-huh-huh-huh-huh-huh!"—as they pried open his jaws, shoved in the funnel, and poured down the beer. This must be what those girls in the restroom meant on my first day at Craven High when they said "Welcome to Hell." I wanted desperately to leave and thought about hiking the ten miles back to Aunt Sue's. And maybe I could just keep going after that—out of Craven County altogether. Out of North Carolina. All the way back to Maine.

But I didn't have a chance to go anywhere. Three football guys came over to Tiny's truck and saw me before I could leave or hide.

"Hey," one of them said. "Know what this is?"

He had unzipped his pants. The other guys laughed. They were all already drunk.

"I'm not sure," I said, trying to be nonchalant, even though my heart was pounding. "But it kind of looks like a birth defect."

The guy with his pants open looked confused, but his buddies laughed even harder. One asked if I would judge their contest. Before I could answer, they all unzipped and took aim at a blue Camaro six feet away. One mostly peed on himself, one made it halfway, and the third hit the Camaro's passenger-side door.

"Congratulations," I said. I knew I needed to stay calm, as if I saw this sort of thing all the time and dealt with these sorts of guys. "That's quite a talent. You could probably get a scholarship for that."

The winner took off his baseball cap and grinned. "Don't I get something right now for pissing the farthest?"

I shrugged. "Yeah. You get another beer. You better hurry back over, though, because I heard they were running out." I waited until they left, then I climbed into the cab of Tiny's truck and locked the doors with shaking fingers to wait out the rest of the night.

I stayed in the cab for the next couple of hours, watching the beer funnels, the waterboarding, the fights, the drunk couples pulling off clothes and grinding on top of one another in dark corners of trucks or the field. Finally, well past midnight, I saw Tiny and Book staggering toward the truck, covered in mud and vomit and blood and beer and, from the smell of it, cow shit. They didn't quite make it, though, before they collapsed on the ground. Book pulled them both up into sitting positions, and he leaned on Tiny for balance. Then he started crying and talking, though Tiny didn't respond. I wondered if he'd passed out. It took a while before I understood that Book was talking about Aunt Sue's "company."

"I gotta leave so he can come over on her like that, at our house? That ain't a date. A date, he takes her out to a movie and dinner and flowers and candy and opens the door. Isn't that a date? Isn't that a date? He thinks a six-pack is a date. That's not a date. Is that a date? Is a six-pack a date? Is a twelve-pack a date? Is kicking Book out of the house a date? Where's Book supposed to go? You think I want to be here? You think anybody cares I'm here? Why are we here? Ah, hell. Move over, Tiny. I gotta lie down, too. Let me lie down, too."

I thought about taking Tiny's truck and just leaving, but I was in enough trouble with Aunt Sue as it was, and knew I couldn't actually abandon them. I climbed out of the cab and tried getting Book and Tiny up, but they were both passed out now and wouldn't budge. They were too heavy for me to drag. "Just come on!" I said, gritting my teeth and pulling on Book's heavy arm. "Just come on." But they were too drunk. It was useless.

Finally I realized that if I wanted to get us home before morning, I had no choice but to ask for help. I chose two guys who seemed to be stumbling less than most—a couple of football players in Confederate caps and practice jerseys.

"Hey, baby," the first one said when I walked up, before I could calm my nerves enough to say anything myself. "I'm Dennis. Like Dennis the Menace."

The second one laughed, as if that was the funniest thing he'd ever heard. "Yeah," he said. "And I'm horny."

Now it was Dennis's turn to laugh. "Nah," he said. "His real name's Donny."

"It's nice to meet you," I said. I pointed to Tiny and Book. "My cousin and his friend are passed out. Could you guys help me lift them into the back of the truck?"

Dennis and Donny looked down. "Is that Book Allen?" Dennis asked. "And Tiny Tankersley?"

"Hell, yeah, it is," said Donny. "Couple of lightweights." He nudged Tiny's head with his boot.

"So can you help?" I asked.

Dennis shrugged. "Yeah, sure." They dragged Tiny through the dirt to the back of the truck while I lowered the tailgate. It took all three of us to lift him in. Then we went back for Book and lifted him in, too.

"OK, then," Donny said when we finished, and he stumbled off.

The other one, Dennis the Menace, hesitated. He wasn't big like Book and Tiny, but he was bigger than me, and drunk. It made me nervous to suddenly be alone with him, but he still caught me off guard when he lurched forward and mashed his face into mine. His hands locked around my waist, and I felt his swollen tongue against my lips, and the raw scrape of his stubble against my chin.

I tried to pull away but couldn't, so out of instinct or

desperation or fear—or all three—I grabbed both his ears and twisted.

"Ow," he whined, breaking his hold to rub them. "That hurt."

I held his face away from mine, my palms pressed hard against his cheeks so his lips pooched out. My heart was pounding, and I struggled to keep my voice from quavering. "Hey," I said. "Hey, Dennis." I was scrambling to come up with something to distract him.

He pried my hands off his face and said, "What?" His breath was so bad it made me tear up. He must have eaten manure.

"Dennis," I repeated. "Hey, Dennis, can you find me a beer? Can you go over there and get me a beer? I'll come over there in a second."

He grabbed my arms, and my panic rose higher. "Come now, baby," he said.

"I will," I said, my heart jackhammering. "I have to pee first, but I'll be right there. Give me a second. We need beers. You let me go pee."

"Yeah," he said. "Beers." And he let go. "Beers," he repeated. He shuffled off toward the keg, and when he did, I jumped into the back of Tiny's truck and fumbled through his pockets until I found the key. It took me three tries to fit the key into the ignition, my hands were shaking so bad. But once I did, I shoved the truck in gear and hit the gas, tearing up a chunk of field as I spun out of there.

• • •

I never thought I'd be happy to find myself back at Aunt Sue's, but tonight I was. The yard light shone a dull yellow, the house itself was dark, and Aunt Sue's truck was the only vehicle in the driveway. Whoever had come over earlier—the company Book wailed about to Tiny—was long gone.

I left the boys passed out in the open truck bed for what was left of the night, at the mercy of the mosquitoes and the pinecone-throwing squirrels. Gnarly came over and nuzzled my hand but didn't bark, because Aunt Sue was home.

I went inside and used the bathroom and got a glass of water, wishing I could take a shower but afraid that would wake Aunt Sue. I was drenched in sweat from lifting Book and Tiny, and from my encounter with Drunk Dennis.

Just then the phone rang, making me jump. Nobody called that late at Aunt Sue's. I snatched it up before it could ring a second time. "Hello?" I whispered.

It was Beatrice.

"Hey, Iris," she said. "Hey. Are you awake?"

She sounded drunk.

A bedroom door opened in the back of the house. Footsteps padded down the hall. Aunt Sue stepped out of the shadows. She had on her Harley T-shirt and gray sweatpants.

"I have to go, B.," I said nervously. "It's too late for you to be calling. You woke up my aunt."

Aunt Sue glared at me with bloodshot eyes.

"Just tell her you'll get off in a minute," Beatrice said. "You have a right to talk on the phone."

"I can't, B.," I said. "I've gotta go. I'll call you tomorrow."

Aunt Sue grabbed my wrist and twisted until it burned. She said, "No, hell, you won't." Then she slammed the phone down so hard that something cracked.

I sat on my bed in the dark for a long time after that, not able to sleep, not wanting to lie down—afraid that if I did, I'd never get back up. My stomach hurt, and I realized I'd hardly eaten in days, so once I felt certain Aunt Sue must be asleep again, I slipped downstairs and rummaged through the cupboards until I found the bread and some peanut butter and honey. I brought the sandwich back up to my room, but chewing it seemed impossible. My mouth was dry, and I could barely swallow. Each bite I did manage to get down felt like a stone dropping inside me. I quit halfway through and pulled out my notebook.

Dear Dad,
Today sucked. Tonight sucked worse.

I crossed that out and started again.

Dear Dad,
It's quiet here tonight. Gnarly's not barking, because Aunt Sue is home and he never barks when she's home. Everybody is asleep except me. I went to a field party. You don't want to know about that. I had a conversation with Aunt Sue about

vegetarianism, which was very interesting. I let Gnarly loose and he killed some chickens, so that didn't turn out so great. I realize this is coming out garbled, and I'm sorry. I'm tired and I should probably just go to bed. But I'm kind of afraid of what might happen once I close my eyes.

P.S. I'm ready to come home.

seven

Aunt Sue banged on my door first thing the next morning. I felt as if I'd just fallen asleep.

She shoved the stainless-steel bucket in my hands and said, "Goats." Then she went back downstairs to her bedroom.

Tiny and Book still lay in the back of the truck, though Aunt Sue must have brought out a blanket, because they had one tangled around their legs, roping them together. Book lay on his side behind Tiny, who lay on his side, too. Book snored on the back of Tiny's neck. They were practically spooning.

Gnarly jumped on me as soon as I got to the bottom step and knocked me down, but I didn't care. I was hungry for any kind of affection, even the rough kind. I let him lick my face until he tired of it, then I scratched his belly and his ears for a while, and then we went in together to milk the goats.

The chickens flapped their wings and hopped up on the fence in the barn to stay clear of Gnarly. I never let him in there, but today I didn't care. I wanted to be around whoever liked me, and Gnarly liked me. I let the pregnant goats in first so I could hug them and mother them. I poured grain in a couple of buckets so they could eat and wouldn't get in the way, and I sang a Joni Mitchell song: "Both Sides Now." Dad told me Mom used to sing Joni Mitchell songs to me when I was a baby, and I had a vague memory of her doing that when I was a little kid, too, before she left. I hated that I didn't remember much more than that.

Patsy ignored me when I held out a handful of grain to her. She shifted her gaze over to Reba and Jo Dee, and I caught on right away. "Sorry," I said. "I know I should have fed you first, but they're pregnant. And they're nicer to me than you are, to be honest about it. I just needed somebody to be nice to me this morning."

I reached closer to Patsy with the feed. "Want this? You still get to be first on the milking stand." She licked my hand clean, acting as if she were doing me a favor, and took her time stepping onto the stand. She gave me a long look, just to make sure I'd gotten her point, before lowering her head into the feed trough.

I aimed the first squirt from each of the goats at Gnarly, and he did somersaults trying to lick the milk off his face. One by one, once I was done with the goats, I scratched them under their chins, and hugged them, and let them out in their field.

Aunt Sue had already laid out the strainer and thermometer and timer in the kitchen. I pulled out the big pots and set them on the stove to pasteurize the new milk and start the cheese process all over again. After that, I went back out to the barn to collect the eggs, feed the chickens, and look for anything else to do to keep me distracted. When I finally emerged from the barn, Book and Tiny were staggering toward the house. Their faces had been chewed raw by mosquitoes. The next time I saw them, their skin was entirely pink, as though they'd poured a whole bottle of calamine lotion on their heads.

I spent the day in the barn cleaning everything I could find to clean that I hadn't gotten to before. The goats all crowded around to watch me, or more likely to see if I'd brought them anything to eat. Once it was clear that I hadn't, they wandered back off into the field. They needed their hooves trimmed, but I figured it would be a battle with Tammy, and maybe all of them, so I'd wait awhile before taking that on. I'd helped Dad trim the hooves of plenty of horses and cows over the years, but they were usually docile, especially compared to goats. Plus Dad was Dad—he could handle any animal, no matter how frightened or hostile. He always knew how to talk to them, how to calm them, how to get them to cooperate. I was just the helper. The sidekick. The daughter who everybody thought was so cute to be tagging along with her dad on his vet rounds. I wished I was still that girl.

Aunt Sue went into town that afternoon—it was Sunday—and she was in a good mood when she came home.

She'd bought a new flat-screen TV. I watched her as she carried it in from the truck.

"They had one of those employee discount sales at the Walmart," she said, though I hadn't asked.

She and Book spent the rest of the afternoon hooking it up, while I stayed outside with the goats and Gnarly.

That evening Aunt Sue cooked greens. Someone had given them to her at the farmers' market the day before. She also heated leftover chicken potpie for herself and Book. It was the second night in a row we didn't have sandwiches, but she hadn't forgotten about my being a vegetarian, because after I ate all my greens, she said, "Ha! I cooked them with fatback. That's what you get for not eating what you're served. And for leaving your cousin out there in the truck like you did last night to get chewed up by mosquitoes."

I pushed myself away from the table and walked quickly to the bathroom, where I brushed my teeth for ten minutes before I felt like I got the taste out.

Aunt Sue kept at it the next couple of nights, too. She made canned vegetable soup to go with our sandwiches. She said it was vegetarian, but I didn't believe her. I tasted it, then put down my spoon.

Aunt Sue cackled.

"Oh, wait. I didn't mention there was chicken broth in there?"

Then she served some nasty gray stuff. "That's called wheat gluten," she said. "It's for vegetarians. It's like a meat substitute. Honest. I got it at the health store. They got one in town."

Book grinned, and I knew something was up.

I poked at it with my fork and smelled it. I shoved my plate away and stood up from the table. It was fried liver.

So I stopped sitting down to dinner with Aunt Sue and Book altogether after that and pretty much lived on peanut-butter sandwiches, which I fixed when Aunt Sue wasn't around, and on whatever canned vegetables and fruit they served at school.

Meanwhile Aunt Sue kept buying stuff. She bought a new CD player, and a microwave oven, and had a satellite dish installed for the big-screen TV.

"How'd we get all this?" Book asked as they pored over the operation manual.

Aunt Sue shrugged. "Raise at work."

I fumed about the tricks Aunt Sue had played on me with the food, and I fumed about the purchases. I knew she had to be using money from Dad's estate—money meant for me. But I kept quiet and kept my head down and just tried to get through each day. I did my homework and went quietly to school. I listened to Shirelle and the others discuss *Huckleberry Finn,* and I kept my mouth shut no matter how much I wanted to join in. I did my chores. I went for long walks in the woods with Gnarly. I petted him until even Gnarly, who needed love as badly as any dog I'd ever known, decided he'd had enough. I wrestled with the goats until half my body felt bruised from their butting and their horns. I caught myself talking to them—Patsy most of all. I wrote letters to Dad. I told him about the Devil's Stomping Ground, Reba's growing pregnancy, how well I'd cleaned up the barn—anything positive I could think of.

And I called Beatrice. Late one night after Aunt Sue left for work. I figured it would be a month before Aunt Sue got the phone bill, and I would deal with the fallout then.

"Hey," Beatrice said as if she'd been expecting the call. "What's going on?"

"I don't know," I said. "Same old North Carolina. What about you?"

"Same old Maine."

"Sounds better than here," I said, keeping my voice low so Book wouldn't hear—though I doubted he'd wake up. It was nearly eleven. "Look, I'm sorry about the other night, when I had to hang up on you."

"Yeah," Beatrice said. "Whatever. I was kind of drunk."

"I wanted to talk," I said. "It's just that my aunt was right there, and everything's been pretty terrible here."

"Terrible how?"

"Well, she hit me, for one thing. She slapped me."

"Damn," Beatrice said, though she didn't sound as angry as I thought she should. "What did you do?"

"What do you mean?" I asked sharply. "What did I do when she slapped me?"

"No, I mean, why'd she slap you in the first place?"

I started to explain about Gnarly barking, and about the chickens he killed, but Beatrice cut me off. "You shouldn't have let out their dog."

"What?" I said. "Are you kidding me? She *slapped* me, B. I can't believe you said that."

She sighed into the phone. "I'm not saying she should have slapped you. But she probably did have a right to be mad."

"You're taking her side?" I said, incredulous.

"Oh, just forget it," Beatrice snapped. "Can we talk about something else besides your aunt and your farm and your goats? Can we talk about what's going on up here maybe? You're so caught up in your own stuff, Iris. Why don't you ever ask about anything that's going on with me? You could ask me about my parents, who aren't even talking at all now, which is worse than when they were fighting all the time. You could ask me about Collie. You could ask me about *my* stuff."

I sat down on the kitchen floor with the phone cord looped around my arm.

"I'm sorry," I said, flattened by all she'd just said. "I didn't know about your mom and dad. I thought maybe things had gotten better with me gone."

"Well, they haven't."

I sighed, already letting go of the idea—faint in the first place—that Beatrice could help me with my problems at Aunt Sue's. "Do you want to talk about it?"

"I don't know," Beatrice said. "Won't your aunt kick you off the phone again?"

"Not tonight," I said. "She just left for work."

For the next hour, I let Beatrice talk—about her parents, about Collie, about whatever she wanted. She'd always done most of the talking, anyway, for as long as we'd been friends. Ironically, it even made me feel better to just be listening to her, to be back in my old familiar role—at least for a little while.

It was after midnight when we finally hung up and I crawled into bed. I was exhausted, my head crusty from lack of sleep—not just tonight, but since I'd been in North Carolina—but I was still wide awake. *Beatrice's parents weren't talking anymore.* I couldn't stop thinking about that and what it meant. The chances of me going back to Maine were more remote than ever, and I felt myself sinking so low that I was in danger of being swallowed by my bed. I finally turned on the light and picked up *Huckleberry Finn.* I flipped through to a favorite passage I'd marked. Huck and Jim are drifting down the Mississippi River, just the two of them, hiding from the civilized world, which seems less and less civilized every time they go on shore. Off the river there's only sadness and trouble: bloody feuds and dead children, grieving parents and lynch mobs, slave traders and murderers, the bloody corpse of Huck's dad, Pap.

But when they're on the river, it's different.

Soon as it was night out we shoved; when we got her out to about the middle we let her alone, and let her float wherever the current wanted her to; then we lit the pipes, and dangled our legs in the water, and talked about all kinds of things. . . . Sometimes we'd have that whole river all to ourselves for the longest time. Yonder was the banks and the islands, across the water; and maybe a spark—which was a candle in a cabin window; and sometimes on the water you could see a spark or two—on a raft or a scow, you know; and maybe you could hear a fiddle or a song coming over from one of them crafts. It's lovely to live on a raft. We had the sky up there, all speckled with stars, and we used to lay on our backs and look up at them, and discuss about whether they was made or only just happened.

It reminded me of Dad, and Maine, and the life we had when I was little—going on vet rounds, visiting farms, playing with animals, hiking through the Maine woods, climbing Mount Katahdin, watching movies about heroic dogs and horses with great heart. It reminded me of Beatrice, too—the Beatrice from when I was younger: playing softball, riding her horse, laughing about boys, casting off in our sea kayaks to explore hidden coves along the coast.

I finally fell asleep remembering all of that. None of it existed anymore, but I hoped I could dream about it and have it be mine again at least for a little while, for whatever was left of the night.

eight

Aunt Sue bought a new truck that weekend. It was fire-engine red. She hadn't told us she was getting it, just drove it into the yard when she came back later than usual from the farmers' market. She parked next to the back steps and practically needed a ladder to get down.

Book scratched his big head. "How'd you get this, Mama?" Aunt Sue didn't answer at first, but Book kept asking until she said, "It's from the estate."

"What estate?" I said, but I already knew the answer.

"Your dad's," she said. "They appointed me the executor, or I guess they said it was the execu*trix,* and I figured we needed a new truck. See? It's got a king cab."

I thought again about all the things Aunt Sue had bought lately, supposedly from her big raise: the high-definition TV, the new CD player, the satellite dish. And now this hulking pickup. How much of Dad's money had she spent?

The truck especially was a slap in the face. I hated big polluter trucks and SUVs, and Dad did, too. When I was little, he called them "P of the P," which stood for "Part of the Problem," and I grew up yelling that out to him every time I saw one. "Dad! Dad! It's a P of the P!" If it was a van with a really big family—four kids, two parents—he said that was an exception. Same thing if it was a working truck, like the one we had. But he hated them otherwise.

Aunt Sue could have fit all her stuff for the farmers' market in a hatchback. There was no need for her to have a truck the size of the Tundra.

If she'd wanted to get to me, she'd finally succeeded. My dreams about Maine ended as soon as I woke up the next morning. I was never going back there to live. I knew that now. Beatrice's dad didn't come home from his office some nights; she thought he might be staying in a motel; she wondered if he was having an affair. Their lives were falling apart, and that meant there was never going to be room for me there again.

And what did I have here, in North Carolina, at Aunt Sue's? Redneck field parties, a prisoner's diet, an aunt who hit me, and the money my dad had made pissed away—stolen—on things he detested.

The more I thought about it, the more worked up I got. I was too angry to sleep, and lay awake for hours just shaking with rage. I finally got out of bed and got dressed. I went outside and looked at the truck. I kicked the bumper. I even spat on the windshield. Gnarly, maybe sensing my hostility, lifted his leg and peed on one of the rear tires. "Good boy," I said, and scratched him behind his ears. I paced around the yard and the field. I glared at the truck.

And just like that, I knew what I needed to do. I marched back into the house and rooted through the giant silverware drawer in the kitchen until I found an ice pick way in the back. Then I flattened every one of the tires on Aunt Sue's new Tundra, including the spare.

A small part of me was scared, afraid I'd get caught in the act, afraid of what Aunt Sue would do when she found out. But mostly I felt exhilarated, like I had that night with Beatrice on the seawall. Once I was done, I practically danced over to the barn to tell the goats. Patsy woke up and nodded at me sleepily. The chickens clucked.

I went back outside and lay with Gnarly in the grass, the way I had my first night in Craven County. I looked at the stars and wished I'd paid more attention when Dad tried to teach me the constellations. The Big Dipper, the Little Dipper, the North Star, Cassiopeia—those were the only ones I remembered. Finally, just before sunrise, I let myself into the house, crept up the stairs, and collapsed on the bed.

Aunt Sue stormed up to my room a couple of hours later. She didn't say anything, just grabbed my hair, pulled me out of bed, and slapped me hard across the face again.

She yelled at me: "I know it was you, you ungrateful little bitch!"

At first I stood frozen in the middle of the room while the world circled around me, or maybe I was the one doing the spinning while everything else stood stone still. My face burned. My eyes teared up, but I swore I wouldn't cry. Whatever she did to me now, it had been worth it.

"You had no right to buy that truck," I said, struggling to keep my voice even. "Or any of that other stuff. That wasn't your money. That was my dad's."

"You're damn wrong about that," she said, leaning her face so close I could smell her cigarette breath. "Plus you got no say in the matter. And you shit-sure better believe you'll pay for those tires."

"No, I won't," I said. I'd been looking for some trace of my mom in Aunt Sue since I got to Craven County—not just in how they looked, but in who they were—and I guessed I'd finally found it. Not the mom I liked to remember, singing Joni Mitchell and reading me books in a big overstuffed chair by a south-facing window in streaming sunlight, but the other one—the one who might turn angry all of a sudden without your knowing why, the one who Dad said hit me when I was five and left a dark bruise. The one who walked out on us not long after that.

"Oh, you'll pay, all right," Aunt Sue said. "I'll see to that. I will not allow anybody to break bad in this house."

She ordered me to stay in my room for the rest of the day, except to use the bathroom. Book brought up a jug of water and a couple of sandwiches he left on a plate outside my door. Both had baloney on them, which I peeled off and threw out the window. At least there was lettuce, and a little cheese.

I wrote Dad a letter, but I didn't mention getting slapped again. I thought he'd rather just hear about the truck.

Dear Dad,

You would have been proud of me last night. I flattened the tires on a disgusting P of the P.

I did homework, exercised on the floor, and spent hours looking out the tiny window at the barn and the goats. Book must have been the one to milk them, and from the sounds of things—the bleating and complaining—the girls weren't happy about it. I bet they wondered where I was, and why I wasn't there, and why brick-handed Book pulled so mean and hard on their teats.

I couldn't let myself think about that too much, though, so I started reading the new book Mrs. Roosevelt had assigned, *Their Eyes Were Watching God.* It was pretty depressing. The heroine, Janie Starks, marries a man who is nice to her at first but then gets jealous and won't let her hang out on their front porch and visit with anyone. When she finally finds a man she truly loves, the guy gambles away their money. Then there's a hurricane, and a flood. Then Janie's man gets bitten by a rabid dog, so she has to shoot him. The man, not the dog. It breaks her heart.

It was a short novel for all that, and after I finished reading, I lay on the floor with my legs up on the bed and cried until my eyes ached. I felt as if my insides had been hollowed out.

Aunt Sue finally let me out Monday morning for school. We didn't speak. She acted as if nothing had happened, but I was seething again by then, determined to do something. I had seen stacks of papers—mostly bills—balanced on a spindly table in the downstairs hall. I waited until she left for work that night, then rifled through until I found the paperwork for the truck. There were loan documents and payment forms and an authorization letter from a lawyer who I assumed must be the guardian, or estate lawyer, or something.

I skipped the bus after school the next day and hiked into Craven, which was a regular Mayberry, with wide streets downtown, an old Belk department store, smelly diners, offices with striped awnings. The guardian's office was wedged between two taller buildings, and had a redbrick facade, just like everything else in Craven. The ceilings were so low and there was so much dark wood paneling that it could have been the inside of a log cabin. I waited half an hour before the secretary walked me back to see the lawyer. His name was Mr. Trask, and he looked like a beaver. His black suit coat even stuck out in the back like a big beaver's tail when he stood up to greet me.

I introduced myself, or started to.

"Oh, I know who you are, Miss Wight," he said, easing himself back into his black chair. "I have heard from your aunt. All about the situation."

"'The situation'?" I wondered if Aunt Sue had already told him what I'd done to the Tundra—if that's the situation he meant.

"Yes," he said. "And what brings you here today?"

I sat in a straight-backed chair. "I came to talk about the truck."

Mr. Trask blinked several times, as if adjusting to the dim light. "If you're asking whether your aunt had approval for the purchase of the truck from the estate—a forty-percent down payment—then the answer is yes." He pulled a folder from a desk drawer and thumbed through the papers. "Miss Allen needed reliable transportation to care for you at her farm. It was a reasonable use of the estate funds. She will be responsible for making her own monthly payments on the balance."

"But shouldn't I get to have a say in what she buys, since it's my dad's money?" I asked.

Mr. Trask blinked again. "You aunt is your legal guardian. If she chooses to consult with you, that's her decision. She did consult with me—about the purchase of the truck, and about the other purchases as well."

"But why did you approve those?"

"Quality of life," he said, with what I assumed was an attempt at a smile. His mouth seemed to rise a little on his face. "*Your* quality of life," he added.

"But I don't need any of that stuff. I don't want any of it."

Mr. Trask didn't respond. He just rubbed his teeth with his finger, like a toothbrush.

"Is there anything else?" he finally asked.

"Yes," I said, though it was clear whose side he was on. "Aunt Sue hit me. Twice."

Mr. Trask steepled his fingers and looked at the ceiling. "I was made aware of the incident—of both incidents," he said. "My understanding is that there was some provocation. An act of vandalism."

I slumped back in my chair. Whatever anger or self-righteousness I'd come in with had vanished. "She shouldn't be allowed to hit me, or steal my dad's money, no matter what," I said weakly.

Mr. Trask ran his tongue over his teeth. "A foster parent has every right to discipline a child, Miss Wight," he said. "These acts of vandalism on your part, should they continue, will require us to take matters before the Juvenile and Domestic Relations authorities. We are all sympathetic to your loss. But that does not give you license to be disrespectful. Or to vandalize."

"Weren't you supposed to meet with me?" I said, grasping for something, anything. "Check up on me? Make sure I was OK? Isn't that your job?"

He folded his hands on his desk.

"Is there anything else, Miss Wight?" he asked again.

• • •

It took two hours to hike out to Aunt Sue's; once I got there, I went straight to the barn to milk the goats. I'd just gotten Patsy up on the milking stand and laid my cheek against her warm side when Aunt Sue came in. She stood in the open barn door, backlit by what was left of the afternoon sun. Mr. Trask must have already called her, though she didn't say a word. I stayed as far away from her as I could while I milked Patsy, then Loretta, then Tammy. Nervous Reba, more anxious all the time as she got closer and closer to kidding, must have picked up on my anxiety, too. She kept nuzzling me, rubbing against me, gently butting me.

Aunt Sue was still standing in the door when I finished, and I was a wreck, waiting for her to say something, or do something, wondering if she was going to hit me again. Wondering what I could do to stop her.

Loretta and Tammy went back outside through their stall door, and Reba surprised me by following them out. Patsy stayed. She stood next to me, actually between me and Aunt Sue.

Aunt Sue finally spoke. "I know where you been," she said. "Don't you even think about trying to make a federal case out of this-here with anybody else. You're lucky I don't have you already locked up in the juvie detention for that little vandalism of yours. You step out of line again, and you better believe we'll be considering that option. You understand me?"

I put my hand on Patsy's shoulder. I didn't say anything.

"There better be a 'Yes, ma'am' coming out of your smart mouth," Aunt Sue said.

My jaw tightened so hard it ached, but I managed the "Yes, ma'am." She'd been blocking the door, but now she stepped to one side to let me pass. I couldn't help flinching as I walked by her, and I could practically feel her smug grin burning into my back. Patsy came with me. I stayed in the field with her and the others until long after dark.

I e-mailed Beatrice the next day at school, and she said all the right things when she wrote back—how sorry she was, and how terrible she felt, and how hard all this must be. Things were better between us since that night I called and let her talk, but she was still a thousand miles away, and besides a little sympathy I figured there was nothing she, or anybody, could do to help.

I started a letter to Dad but couldn't think of anything to say after the salutation. So I drew a picture of our old house, and our old barn, and our old hog, who Dad never had the heart to have slaughtered. It was a pretty nice picture. I tore it into tiny scraps when I finished and fed the scraps to the goats.

nine

We had to write an explanatory essay that week in English on the topic of our choice, and Mrs. Roosevelt assigned us all to small groups to read and discuss our drafts. I ended up with Shirelle, a cheerleader, a kid with a mullet, and a Goth kid whose first name was Littleberry.

I'd noticed him in class before, always wearing an oversize army jacket, usually sitting in the back but sometimes at different desks, which bothered some people who were used to being in the same seat every day. A few told him to move, but he wouldn't unless Mrs. Roosevelt made him. He wasn't very big—a couple of inches taller than me, maybe. Still, I thought he was kind of cute, except for the way his bottom lip stuck out, as if he was pouting.

Shirelle took charge as soon as we circled our desks, which didn't surprise me. "OK," she said. "Here's the order. We'll talk about mine first, then yours, then yours, then yours, then yours." She pointed to each of us as she spoke. I was last, which was fine with me. Maybe we'd run out of time before it was my turn.

Shirelle had written her essay on "How to Play Zone Defense in Basketball." The kid with the mullet wrote his on "How to Crop and Cure Tobacco." The cheerleader, whose leg was in a cast, wrote hers on "How to Stunt." Littleberry's was on "How to Care for a Head Wound." The cheerleader complained that it was gross, and Littleberry got defensive.

"Well, I wanted to write about 'How to Survive a Zombie Attack,'" he said, crossing his arms over the front of his army jacket. "But Mrs. Roosevelt wouldn't let me. And anyway, mine is personal, so shut up about it, *Lucy*." He practically spat her name, which for some reason hadn't registered with me when I was reading her essay.

"Whatever," Lucy said, crossing *her* arms.

"Enough," said Shirelle. "Let's move on."

With a glance at the clock, I read aloud my essay, which was on "How to Build a Pet Crematorium."

The winter before Dad died, the smokestack cracked on our old crematorium behind the barn, and we decided to build a new one. It was so cold, the ground frozen so hard, that people couldn't bury their dogs or cats or hamsters in their own backyards the way they usually did, so they called us. Just about every day when I got home from school, Dad had me driving out somewhere to pick up another body. Beatrice went with me sometimes but didn't like it and usually begged off. I didn't like it, either, but I'd seen and smelled a lot worse stuff than a dead Great Dane with his head locked inside a block of ice.

Dad designed the new crematorium and ordered all the parts and applied for all the permits, but he was already coughing a lot back then, especially out in the cold, so we had to hire some guys to come in and do the job. Dad called it a comedy of errors: first the steel beams for the interior of the furnace fell off the guys' pickup truck onto the highway and clipped the bumper on a bus. Then the hoist bent, so we had to rent a forklift for the heavy materials. Then one of the guys burned himself welding and had to go to the hospital.

They finally finished, though, and Dad and I fired up the furnace right away. By then the bodies were literally piled up. It would have been convenient to just stoke it full of animals, but most people wanted to keep their pets' ashes, so we had to cremate them one at a time and then collect what remained into little urns for the owners. I was the one who swept out the ashes, because I didn't want Dad to be around all that dust. But it turned out that the ashes weren't just dust. There were also tiny shards of bone, teeth, beak, hoof, and claw you could see if you looked close enough.

We kept the crematorium burning off and on for most of a week to catch up on the backlog of corpses. That frozen Great Dane was the hardest because he wouldn't fit, and Dad had to break the dog's legs so we could fold them in with the body. It almost got to the point where I didn't mind all that death, and sometimes when I went with Dad to deliver an urn, I was actually surprised that the owners cried, that the urns represented something sad to them. Some of them wept so hard they couldn't even speak. One old lady, once she got her voice back, said she wished there was a way she could be cremated, too, and have her own ashes mixed with her bird's.

The bell rang just as I finished, so I didn't have to listen while the group critiqued my essay. I stuffed my notebook in my backpack and was out of my seat and out the door before anyone else. Even so, Littleberry caught up to me halfway down the hall.

"Hey, Iris," he said. "Hold on a second."

I kept walking, but a little slower. He grinned. "So I really liked your story," he said. "Man, that business with the Great Dane, that was just sick. I totally dug it."

"Thanks," I said. "I guess. It was just what we had to do."

I stopped at my locker to drop off my books.

"So what I was wondering," he said, "was if maybe you might want to hang out after school. Talk about pet crematoriums or something."

I shut my locker and turned to look at him. He actually blushed.

"You want to go out with me?" I asked, just to be sure.

He grinned a little wider. "Or just hang out or whatever."

I was tempted to say yes, partly because he was cute and I was lonely, and partly because I was curious about his head-wound essay. But then he spat a black stream of something into a paper cup. I'd thought he was just holding a drink all that time, but now I realized he was chewing tobacco.

"I can't," I said, trying not to stare at the cup, and trying not to show him how disgusted I was. "But thanks."

He drummed his fingers on his notebook. "Well, what about tomorrow? You want to hang out then? I have an extra helmet. We could go for a ride."

"You have a motorcycle?"

He looked down. "Not exactly. It's more like a motor scooter, I guess. A Vespa."

He seemed even cuter to me in that moment, all embarrassed about his scooter. It almost made up for the tobacco and the spit cup. Almost.

But I couldn't go, anyway, and it wasn't just the dip. "I'm sorry, Littleberry. I just can't," I said. "I have chores every afternoon. I have to milk our goats."

His mouth dropped open—enough for me to see black goo between his lip and gum. "Goats?"

"Really," I said, looking away.

"OK, Iris," he said. "I guess I better get to class. I'll see you around." And he left.

I thought about Littleberry later that afternoon while I milked the goats. He *was* pretty cute, but I couldn't imagine kissing someone who chewed tobacco. Not that I was thinking about kissing Littleberry. I wondered if he'd ask me out again and decided that if he did, and if he got rid of the dip, and if I could get away from Aunt Sue's, I might just say yes.

Aunt Sue piled on the chores after the truck incident, but I felt as if I'd gotten off easy. She didn't hit me again, or try, though I found myself flinching for the first couple of days whenever she walked past, wondering if she might.

First I had to haul an extension ladder out of the barn and clean the gutters on the house, which took a couple of afternoons and left me covered in mud and roof gunk. It was nice to work out my arms and shoulders, though, which hadn't gotten much use since I quit summer softball back in Maine, except for throwing with Beatrice in her backyard. Two blue jays dive-bombed my head when I got too close to their nest, which was tucked under an eave at Aunt Sue's house where the bird-blocking had pulled loose. Another time I had to stop because Tammy got her head caught in the fence again, and Loretta, who must have come over to investigate, got hers stuck, too.

After the gutters, Aunt Sue ordered me to paint the barn with a half dozen old cans of leftover paint in four different colors.

"Are you sure you don't want to paint it all one color?" I asked her tentatively. "It wouldn't cost that much for barn paint."

Aunt Sue sniffed. "I don't give a good goddamn what colors the barn is," she said. "That's usable paint, so you use it."

I spent that afternoon painting the front of the barn red. The wood was so old that it soaked up the first coat, the red barely visible, so I would definitely need a second. I still had some red left over when I finished, though, and some green and some blue and some brown, and I decided I'd paint a life-size goat on the side door of the barn before I finished painting the back and sides. I used Patsy as my model—a front view of her, looking straight ahead—and once she saw what I was doing, she even stood still for a while as if she was posing. I could tell she liked it. They all did. I had to sit in front of the painting while it dried, then stack up sawhorses so the goats wouldn't get too close and rub it off.

I wished I had someone else to show it to besides the goats—I even thought for a second about asking Littleberry if he'd like to come out to see it. I finally settled on Gnarly, but he just wanted to play, happy to be allowed out in the field.

Still, things weren't too bad overall for most of that week. I spent the next two afternoons finishing the barn, and liked having the work to do. I got an A from Mrs. Roosevelt on my crematorium paper. Littleberry waved from across the room when I saw him in class. We didn't talk, but he smiled said "Hey" when we passed in the hall.

I should have known Aunt Sue wasn't going to let me off that easy, though. She went into my bedroom one afternoon when I was out in the barn and tore it apart until she found my money—two hundred dollars I had saved from working at the L.L. Bean outlet back in Maine, and what was left of the two hundred dollars Mr. Stone had given me on the way to the airport. I hadn't bought much with it besides those Whoopie Pies for Aunt Sue and Book, and the airport parking, and Fig Newtons, Cheetos, and Snapples at Craven High. The Cheetos were for the goats.

I stormed out of my room when I found out what had happened, but I only made it halfway down the stairs before I pulled up short. Aunt Sue and Book stood waiting at the bottom, with identical sour expressions on their hard faces. My legs shook so much that I had to hold on to the railing.

Aunt Sue spoke first. "You can call it a down payment on a new set of tires."

Book crossed his oak-branch arms over the front of a grass-stained practice jersey.

"Well," Aunt Sue said, "was there something you wanted to say?"

My legs were trembling bad, but I was furious and couldn't stop myself. I said, "You can both go to hell."

Book started up toward me, but Aunt Sue put a hand on his arm, almost smiling. "Let her be," she said. "She ain't nothing but talk."

That made me more furious, but I felt helpless, too. They turned and went into the kitchen for their Dagwood sandwiches. I sagged to my bottom in the stairwell and stayed there, deflated, in the gray half-light between upstairs and down.

That Saturday, Aunt Sue had a double shift at Walmart, so she made me take her place selling goat cheese at the farmers' market. She came home from her graveyard shift early that morning, just as I finished milking the goats, and ordered me to help her load up the truck with coolers and table and awning and sign.

She didn't speak the whole way into town, and I didn't, either. Even when we got to the farmers' market, she didn't say much, except to tell me where to set up, in what I assumed was her usual spot—next to a middle-aged Hispanic couple, the Gonzaleses. Aunt Sue said they were from Mexico. She grunted at them, which didn't seem very friendly. I couldn't tell if she didn't like them or if she was just in a rush to get back to Walmart.

"I won't be back to get you until this afternoon," she said after we put up the awning over the card table and hung her sign. "I know every container of goat cheese in these coolers, and I know exactly how much money you better have when I get back, so don't go getting any ideas about spending any."

I realized I'd come without any food or water, and I asked about that. Aunt Sue thrust a water bottle at me, but nothing to eat. Then she handed me a metal box with fifty dollars in fives and ones. "I know how much is in there, too," she said. "It's for your change."

Shortly after Aunt Sue left, a little girl climbed out of the Gonzaleses' truck, which was parked next to their stand. She sat on a crate of green peppers and rubbed her eyes as if she'd just woken up. She was maybe six or seven years old. She had dark hair and dark eyes and was wearing a threadbare cotton dress. Mrs. Gonzales cut up an apple into slices and handed it to her on a paper towel. The little girl watched me while she ate, and I smiled at her and watched her back.

I tried to make conversation with the Gonzaleses, who seemed friendly, but they spoke very little English, and I only knew a little high-school Spanish—though enough to learn that they were from Honduras, not Mexico. They had one of the busier stands at the farmers' market—three wide wooden tables loaded with peppers, beans, cucumbers, tomatoes, and apples—and they were in constant motion, weighing and bagging, restocking their tables, dragging produce crates out of their truck, and stuffing money into a shoe box that served as their cash register.

Every fourth or fifth customer they had also stopped at Aunt Sue's stand. Some asked for a taste, but since Aunt Sue hadn't said anything about samples, I was reluctant to open a container to give them any. Plus I didn't have a knife or plates to serve it with or on. I didn't have anything except the cheese itself and the money box.

Some customers seemed outright suspicious when they saw me. "Where's Sue Allen?" an older woman asked, as if I might have murdered Aunt Sue in order to take over her farmers' market stand.

I remembered the manager's instructions when I worked at the L.L. Bean outlet and smiled politely. "She had to go to work," I said. "I'm her niece."

"Is this still her goat cheese?" the woman asked, even though the sign over the stand said SUE ALLEN FARM GOAT CHEESE in large block letters, and it was the same sign, and the same awning, and the same card table that Aunt Sue had used since I'd been in North Carolina — and that she'd probably used for years.

"Yes, ma'am." I said, still smiling. "Same cheese."

She bought five containers. Several others who stopped — and who asked about Aunt Sue — also bought multiple containers of cheese. I assumed these were regulars, though only one, a thin woman in a peasant blouse who wore her hair in two long braids, engaged me in anything like a real conversation.

"I didn't know Sue had a niece," she said. "Are you just here visiting, or do you live in town?"

"I live here now," I said, though I didn't like admitting it. "I'm actually from Maine."

"Oh, I love Maine," the woman said. "My husband and I used to go there in the summers. We always camped at the state park in Camden. Have you been there?"

I nodded and started talking enthusiastically: "Camden's just an hour away from my hometown. I must have hiked all the trails there a hundred times. My softball coach drove our team up there last year before the season started and made us do training runs up that two-mile road from the park entrance to the top of Mount Battie."

The woman smiled. "And what brought you down here?" she asked.

"My dad died," I said matter-of-factly. And then I stopped short, dismayed by how casually I'd just said it.

The woman must have seen the look of regret, or sadness, or confusion on my face, because she reached across the card table just then and put her hand on mine. "I'm so sorry, dear."

After she left, the Gonzaleses' little girl came over and offered me a slice of apple. I knew she spoke English better than her parents — she would sometimes translate for the customers or for her mom and dad — and I wondered if she'd heard the exchange and felt sorry for me. I hoped not.

"Thanks," I said, and I smiled at Mrs. Gonzales, who was watching.

"Isabel, ven acá." Mrs. Gonzales gestured the girl back over to their stand and handed her a whole apple, a Gala, to bring to me as well. I said *"Gracias"* this time and ate that, too — especially grateful for it, since I hadn't had breakfast.

Isabel hung out with me for a while after that. We talked about her school — she was in first grade; her teacher's name was Mrs. Hanak; her best friend was a girl named Ainsley; her favorite subject was lunch. And then for the next hour, between sales, we played rock, paper, scissors. When she won she punched me lightly on the arm. When I won I tickled her until she couldn't stop giggling and yelling, "*¡Basta ya! ¡Basta ya!* Stop! Stop!"

Business tapered off around noon, and by one o'clock nearly all the stalls were closed and almost everyone was gone. The Gonzaleses were some of the last people to leave, and I wondered if they might have been waiting until Aunt Sue came back for me. But eventually they couldn't wait any longer. Isabel hugged me, and I thanked Mr. and Mrs. Gonzales for the apples, while they thanked me for entertaining Isabel. As they pulled away in their truck, Mrs. Gonzales leaned out the window and said, *"Vaya con Dios."*

Aunt Sue didn't show up until after three, but I didn't mind, except for being away from Gnarly and the goats for so long. I'd brought my school copy of *Their Eyes Were Watching God* and re-read it while I waited alone in the Sue Allen Farm Goat Cheese stall. A few people wandered through the park next to the farmers' market, which was near downtown. There weren't any more customers, though, and even if there had been, I didn't have anything left to sell. I had made two hundred and fifty dollars—and was sure I could have done even better if I'd had more cheese, and if Aunt Sue was ever willing to put out samples to attract new customers.

I was surprised by how much I'd enjoyed being at the farmers' market. I liked the Gonzaleses and I liked the customers—even the cranky ones, but especially the woman who'd been to Camden. I liked having something useful to do, even if it was for Aunt Sue.

ten

Aunt Sue came up to my bedroom the evening Reba went into labor. It was a Friday. Book had an away game all the way up in Elizabeth City, too far for Aunt Sue to drive to watch the game, even though she had the night off from work.

She hesitated at my door and looked around, mostly at the floor, where I had my piles of books.

"Go into town and buy a tub of K-Y Jelly," she told me. Then she said, "You do have a driver's license, don't you?" She'd never seen me drive, never asked me if I wanted to drive — which, once she bought the Tundra, I wouldn't have wanted to, anyway.

I nodded. "From Maine."

"Well, good enough. Here's the keys. Reba's gonna deliver tonight, and I need that K-Y. She's got multiples. They get tangled sometimes, and you got to go in and untangle them, turn them around, things like that."

I didn't say anything.

Aunt Sue said, "You know where the Walmart is out on County Circle Road? The one where I work. They have it there. Get the kind with the pump. That's the size I need. Now, get going."

I thought about saying no, and telling her I wouldn't be caught dead in her damn P of the P, but instead I got up, took the keys, and pulled on my hoodie. "The only reason I'm going is for Reba," I said, but Aunt Sue had already turned away. She beat me downstairs, and by the time I reached the truck, I saw her, or the shadow of her, disappear into the barn. She had already shooed the other goats out into the pen from the stalls. Reba started bawling inside the barn, and the rest of them jerked up their heads and crowded by the fence, trying to hide behind Patsy. Gnarly started barking, even though Aunt Sue had walked right past him, so he knew she was home.

The truck seemed too big for the road, and I shoved everything I could find underneath me so I could sit high enough to see: Aunt Sue's Walmart jacket, some of Book's recruiting pamphlets from college coaches. Even then I felt as if I was straining to peer over the steering wheel and could barely follow the lines on the road.

A tall, geeky clerk with long sideburns was the first one I saw at the Walmart. He leered at me when I told him what I wanted. I said, "It's for a goat." He smiled a pervert smile and raced off—he said to find the pump tub of K-Y Jelly back in the storeroom, but probably to laugh about me to his buddies.

Five minutes later, he thumped it on the counter and said, "You think this'll be enough?"

"It's for a goat," I said again, my face burning. "She's pregnant." I should have just not said anything, because that cracked him up, too.

Aunt Sue had Reba lying on her side in a stall when I got back. She was sitting with Reba, bent over so their foreheads nearly rubbed together. I thought Aunt Sue might have been saying something, maybe even singing, but whatever she was doing, she stopped as soon as I walked in. I'd never seen her be tender to the goats, and it surprised me. The one naked bulb hung from its electrical cord from a rafter overhead and cast long shadows. Reba was mostly hidden in one of them.

I set the K-Y tub down on the milking stand and went into the stall.

"What now?" I asked.

Aunt Sue shrugged. "Wait."

"How long?"

"Long as it takes. Why? You got to be somewhere?"

I didn't say anything else. I wasn't crazy about spending so much time with Aunt Sue, but I refused to leave Reba. She'd been her usual self the past couple of days—following me around, rubbing against me, lifting her head so I would scratch under her chin, eating all the Cheetos I brought from school. Now she was shaking all over, her breathing getting heavier and heavier, and her eyes were open wide, giving her a worried look.

Aunt Sue stood up. "I'm going outside for a smoke."

I took the opportunity to sit closer to Reba, who laid her head in my lap.

"It's her second time," Aunt Sue said, sounding gruff, but not entirely convincing. "She knows what she's doing." Then she left the barn to have her cigarette.

The next couple of hours passed like that — me continuing to hold Reba, rub her, talk to her, while Aunt Sue alternated between smoking outside and standing watching in silence inside. Finally, around midnight, something happened with Reba. She shifted in a certain way; her breathing quickened; her nostrils flared. She made low, guttural sounds.

Aunt Sue said, "Here we go." She pumped K-Y Jelly into her hands and smeared it up her arms, then she knelt behind Reba, spread Reba's legs wide apart, and slid her hands inside. Reba started bawling hard, and pushing. "Hold her," Aunt Sue said, and I held her, my arm locked around her neck.

"I can see the first one," Aunt Sue announced. She pumped more jelly on her hands and went in again. "They're tangled up, like I thought."

Reba struggled against me as Aunt Sue worked her arms up inside and wrestled the first kid around. The struggle went on for half an hour. Sweat poured down my face. I wished I'd taken off my hoodie because I was roasting in it, holding on to

Reba. Both of us panted, pretty much together. I said things, dumb things, but the stuff you always say in those situations: *Hold on. It'll be OK. Almost there.*

"Would you shut up already," Aunt Sue barked. "She's a goat, in case you forgot."

Aunt Sue grunted again, pulled hard, then leaned against Reba and pulled harder. The first kid popped out and Aunt Sue fell backward, still holding it in her hands. She dropped the kid right away and went back for the other one, but a second kid slid out on its own, and a third one followed almost immediately.

"I'll be damned," Aunt Sue said. "Triplets."

She gestured with her bloody arms at an open cardboard box nearby. "You can let go of Reba now. She's done. There's milk bottles right over there. You go ahead and give those kids one each."

"You're not going to let them nurse at all?" I said. "What about the colostrum?" I knew from attending deliveries with Dad that colostrum in the mother's milk helped immunize newborns against infections.

Before Aunt Sue could answer, though, something else slid out of Reba. The bloody mass of placenta. Everything was happening fast with this kidding. Reba shrugged herself around and looked at it for a minute. Then she started eating it.

I'd seen a lot of stuff with Dad, but I had to admit to being nauseated at that. I did what Aunt Sue told me, though. I grabbed the box of bottles and an old blanket and drew all three of the kids into my lap. They were all slick from the births, but I hardly cared as I hugged them to me. They were smaller than I'd expected—maybe because they were triplets—but each one was a perfect miniature of Reba. They stared up at me with huge liquid eyes and *maa*ed feebly. Two took the bottles right away; the last one I had to coax, but pretty soon he sucked, too. For the first time since coming to Craven County—for the first time since my dad started coughing, really—everything seemed perfect.

Aunt Sue wiped down Reba with an iodine solution. Then she started talking. It took me a minute to realize she was answering my question about the colostrum.

"I'm guessing you didn't notice," she said, "but every one of these kids is a male—a billy." She almost sounded angry.

"Yeah?" I said, though I had a sinking suspicion about where she was going.

"So they're not good for but one thing, and that's their meat. I'll fatten them up for a couple of weeks, maybe a month, then do the slaughter when they're bigger but the meat's still tender. So there's no sense wasting good goat milk on them. We'll get them on grain in a couple of days. Till then the bottles will do just fine."

My heart sank—the perfect moment gone just like that—as she stalked outside to let the other goats back in for the night. I figured it must have been two in the morning by then. Patsy came in and stood behind me. She laid her head on my shoulder to check out the new kids. The other goats surrounded Reba, settled into the straw, and soon went to sleep. The kids sucked for a while, then stopped and looked up at me with those liquid eyes again. I wished they wouldn't, because I couldn't help falling in love with them when they did. I offered them their bottles again, and they blinked, and then sucked again, off and on until the milk was all gone. They staggered around a little on their wobbly legs, and I crawled on the barn floor with them, to catch them when they fell and lift them back up until they were too tired to stand. I gathered them into my lap again and tucked the blanket around us. They *maa*ed softly for a while, and then one by one they fell asleep.

Aunt Sue didn't come back. An hour later a truck pulled up to the back porch. It was Tiny and Book, back late from their away game, and whatever party they'd been to afterward. The door slammed, and the porch light cut off.

I stayed in the stall with the kids all the rest of the night. After a couple of hours, the billies woke one another again and bleated hungrily. I was out of bottle milk, so I gently massaged Reba's udder and squeezed just enough from her teats to refill the bottles for the kids. Their little bellies swelled, and they soon fell back asleep.

The kids gave me a reason to look forward to coming home from school each afternoon. They were all I could think about most of the time, and even if Littleberry had wanted to ask me out again, I never gave him the chance—rushing out to get on the bus the second the bell rang. We had to keep the kids separated from Reba during the day—I let her out in the field after the morning milking; they stayed in the barn. But once I did the afternoon milking, they could all play outside together. Reba couldn't get enough of them then, nudging them around in the close-cropped grass, letting them butt her with their hard little heads. I followed along, waiting my turn, and when Reba needed a break, I took over.

Their favorite game was when I pushed on their foreheads and they butted back until they practically couldn't stand up anymore. They would probably have butted one another to death if Aunt Sue and Book hadn't burned out the buds where their horns were supposed to grow. I hated seeing that—the tool Aunt Sue used was like a soldering iron, and she did it just a week after they were born—but I hated it even more the following Saturday when they castrated the kids.

I'd gotten up early as usual that morning and gone out to the barn to do the milking and play with the goats and Gnarly. When I brought in the milk to pasteurize it, Aunt Sue and Book walked out without saying anything. I didn't think much of it, though it was early for Book to be awake the morning after a game, until I heard one of the kids bleating frantically.

I dropped everything and ran back outside. Book was sitting on the barn floor, holding one of the billies in his lap with his big, rough hands. Aunt Sue was binding the kid's scrotum tight at the base with a thick rubber band. Everything happened fast.

"Don't worry," Aunt Sue said before I could protest what they were doing. She let that kid go and grabbed another. "It only hurts for a minute. Everything gets numb and they can't even tell when it falls off."

The first kid staggered away from them over to me, dazed. I picked him up and held him close to me; he was trembling.

Aunt Sue might have been telling the truth, but I didn't believe her. I'd never helped Dad with neutering or castrating any of the animals he worked with, so I didn't know much about it, and didn't *want* to know. But I could tell by the kids' straining eyes, their plaintive bleating, and their stumbling around that they were scared and confused.

Afterward, Book told me I couldn't call them billies anymore.

It was an hour after the castrations. The kids were still hanging close, bumping against me, as if I could protect them from what had just happened. We were sitting in the grass near the fence. The kids wobbled away from me a little ways and then wobbled back. Reba looked on mournfully.

Book was in the backyard washing the new truck, which I continued to make a point of spitting on every time I walked past.

"Once they don't have their nuts, you're supposed to call them wethers," he said. "When they're wethers, they don't smell so bad as a regular buck. Plus they fatten up quicker." He smacked his lips. "That'll be some tasty meat. Too bad you don't eat any, but more for me, I guess. Me and Tiny, last year the two of us ate an entire goat one time. We cut strips of a lot of it, wrapped it in bacon, and fried it. Called it Billy-in-a-Blanket."

"You mean *wether,*" I corrected him.

"Yeah, well," he said, "it just sounded better to say it that way."

"Because of the alliteration," I said.

Book kicked at a chicken that was trying to sneak past. It squawked and jumped out of the way. "Some damn times," he said, "I don't know what the hell you're talking about."

It wasn't as if I didn't know people ate meat, and it wasn't as if I didn't know where it came from. I'd seen plenty during those vet rounds with Dad, including this slaughterhouse outside our town where they stunned calves with sledgehammers then hung them upside down on giant hooks and sliced through their throats. And that was nothing compared to what they did at the chicken plant.

But I felt protective of the wethers. I still gave them bottles sometimes when Aunt Sue wasn't around. She wanted to fatten then up with grain, but they still liked to nurse, and I loved holding them while they did. They followed me everywhere, even on my walks in the woods behind the house, all the way out to the Devil's Stomping Ground. They knocked one another silly in ferocious butting contests. They hopped everywhere. They danced when I came home from school.

I knew Aunt Sue had plans to slaughter them in a few weeks or a month, but I had plans as well—to keep them alive.

Which was why I named them:

Huey, Dewey, and Louie.

eleven

Beatrice called me a couple of weeks after the kids were born. It was a school night. Aunt Sue had just left for work, thank God. Book had fallen asleep on the couch, still clutching the remote control. I sat on the floor in the hall off the kitchen, which was as much privacy as the phone cord would allow me.

We hadn't talked or e-mailed in a couple of weeks, and I wanted to tell her about the kids, but we barely got through our hellos before Beatrice cut in with her news.

"I thought I was pregnant," she blurted out.

"You *what*?" She hadn't told me she and Collie were having sex. She hadn't told me she wasn't a virgin anymore. How could I not know these things?

"Yeah," she said. "I mean, I'm not. I never was, I don't think. But I was worried for a while. I missed a period. My breasts sort of swelled a little, and they ached. But then I started bleeding. It might have been a miscarriage, or it might have just been a really heavy period."

"When?" I said. "When did all this happen?"

"Last week," Beatrice said. "I didn't tell Mom. But I did go to the Planned Parenthood in Camden. They said I was OK."

"*Are* you OK?" I asked.

"Yeah," she said. "I guess. I mean, I'm glad I'm not having a baby." She laughed weakly.

"I'm so sorry, B.," I said, not sure what else to say.

"Yeah," she said. "It was hard not having you here. I had to figure everything out by myself."

"So you didn't tell Collie?" I asked her. "He didn't know, either?"

"About the baby scare? No way. Anyway, we broke up."

"Sorry about that, too, B.," I said, but this time I didn't feel it as much. For some reason the news about her and Collie shocked me as much as the news about Beatrice maybe being pregnant. I was struggling to understand it all—why I was only hearing about this now, how she could have cut me out of so much of her life.

"It was a while ago," she said—though how long could it have been, really? "But it's no big deal. I've been out with a few other guys. You know."

No, I didn't. "Who?"

"Just some boys," Beatrice said. "Some stupid boys."

I wanted to press her for details—was it Brady Jenerette? Eric Wilburn? *Nate?*—but decided to drop it. I wasn't sure

I actually wanted to know, and I doubted she would tell me, anyway. I hesitated, then changed the subject.

"So what was it like?" I asked.

"What was what like?"

"The sex," I whispered, as though Book might wake up and hear me from all the way in the living room.

"Oh," Beatrice said. "That." She laughed. "Nice at first. I mean, they were boys, and I guess they didn't exactly know what they were doing, and I didn't, either, not that it's that hard to figure out. And they said all these sweet things, about how beautiful I was, or how hot I was, and how crazy they were about me. You know, all that clichéd bullshit." She paused, and I wondered what she was thinking. It wasn't so long ago that I didn't have to wonder—I just knew.

"I liked it while we were doing it," she said eventually, "even though it was kind of messy. And I liked it afterward, the holding—or I guess the being held part."

"And then what?"

"Oh, you know," Beatrice said again. "Then you get dressed, and they're in a hurry to leave, and you kind of are, too, because you don't quite know what to say next, or to talk about. And then you see them at school and it's awkward, and you want them to call, and they don't, or you call them and they don't call you back. And your best friend has moved away and isn't allowed to talk much on the phone, and your parents still aren't speaking to each other, or to you, and the next thing you know, you miss your period and think you might be pregnant."

I opened my mouth to say something to comfort her, to tell her I wished I could have helped her through all that. But then I thought about how she hadn't been there for me, and how she hadn't even asked how I was doing. So I just told her I was glad she was OK now, and I told her I missed her. It sounded automatic, and it sounded automatic when she said it back, "I miss you, too, Iris."

I lay awake for a long time that night after we hung up. I stretched out on my bed and felt my abdomen with both hands, trying to imagine being pregnant. I'd always been so thin, though. Where could there possibly be room for a baby? I wondered what it must have been like for my mom when she was pregnant with me, as young as she was then — not much older than Beatrice. Or me.

I felt my rib cage, which stood out now that I was lying down. I cupped my breasts and thought of them swollen. Not Victoria's Secret swollen. More like the nannies' pendulous udders, hanging low with all that milky weight.

Being pregnant had made Reba and Jo Dee skittish sometimes, and more dependent on me. Otherwise, though, they went on about their goat lives just like the others: foraging in the field, eating their hay, bumping and butting and climbing and sleeping. So what was the big deal about being pregnant?

Other than the fact that once you had your kid, if you were human, it was supposed to change the whole rest of your life.

I guessed it hadn't changed my mom's life, though, and I kept thinking about her that night, imagining her pregnant with me, and wondering what it must be like for her now, to have missed out on being my mom. Wondering what must have broken inside her, and how badly, for her to have left the way she did.

twelve

One night in October, Aunt Sue made Book and me leave the house again because her company was coming over. It was a Friday, but the football team was off that week. Book's face turned a dark shade of red, and he flattened his giant sandwich down on his plate.

Aunt Sue narrowed her eyes. "Was there something you wanted to say about something, Book?"

He didn't look up, just hunched his shoulders protectively over his plate, as if he was worried she would hit him. "No, ma'am."

They were at the kitchen table. I was across the room on a stool, eating a saltine and an apple.

Aunt Sue nodded. "All right, then. I expect y'all to be gone by seven."

Book scooted his chair back. "I don't want her along," he said, pointing at me without looking at me.

Aunt Sue shrugged. "So have Tiny drop her off in town and pick her up later."

"Couldn't I just stay here?" I asked. "I could just hang out in my room, or out in the barn with the goats. I could bring a space heater out there."

Aunt Sue looked in my direction, though not exactly at me, as if she couldn't be bothered to bring me fully into focus. "Oh, you're going to town," she said. "There's no discussion about that."

I sat in the back of Tiny's truck again, though it was cold during the ride. They dropped me off at a mall, which surprised me. I hadn't realized Craven County was big enough to have a mall, or a parking lot as massive as the one surrounding it — a black ocean of a parking lot, with the cars and trucks huddled together close to shore.

I had no idea how I would spend the next four hours. I didn't have any money. I didn't know anybody. I didn't have anywhere else to go, or a way to get there even if I did.

The mall doors swooshed open just then, before I could go inside, and Littleberry stepped out, along with two other guys and two girls, none of whom I recognized. One of the guys lit a cigarette and handed it to one of the girls. They were all dressed in standard-issue black on black, plus Doc Martens, except for Littleberry, who had on duck boots, which made me smile, even though I could tell with just a glance they weren't L.L. Bean. He separated himself from his friends when he saw me.

"Hey, Littleberry," I said.

He pulled off his black wool hat, freeing a wild mass of black, curly, Jim Morrison hair. His bottom lip looked normal, so I guessed he was dip free. "Hey, Iris. I never seen you here before."

"First time," I said. I looked past him into the gaping mouth of the mall: Gap. Disney Store. Sbarro. Claire's. Starbucks. Dick's Sporting Goods. JC Penney. "Looks like a retail dream come true."

Littleberry grinned as if he was proud of his mall. Maybe he was. He pulled his knit cap back on. I wasn't sure why he'd taken it off in the first place. "Hey," he said. "We're gonna go smoke a blunt. Wanna come?"

I considered my options. I had only smoked once before, and it had given me a headache. But that would be nothing compared to what four hours in the mall would do to me. Plus, I kind of liked the idea of hanging out with Littleberry.

"Sure," I said. "Thanks. That sounds great."

"Awesome," Littleberry said. I followed him and his friends across the vast parking lot, past the scrum of cars and trucks, past the security lights, and past the emptiness after that, until we reached a berm topped with a wall of pines. It was already dark where we were. We scrambled up the berm, even deeper into the dark, and sat in a line with our legs hanging over the side, looking back at the mall.

"Feels like the end of the world," said one of the guys, who looked like Opie on *The Andy Griffith Show.*

"End of the mall," said the other boy.

"Same thing," said Littleberry, sitting next to me. He busied himself with a little penknife, disemboweling a cigar. I felt a little nervous, sitting so close to him, and I wasn't sure why. His arm rubbed against mine while he worked, but I didn't mind. He smelled like fresh pizza.

"The first time my mom brought me to this mall was when she bought my confirmation dress," said one of the girls.

"You're a Catholic?" said the other girl.

"Yeah. A lapsed Catholic," said the first girl.

"What does that mean?" Opie asked.

The other boy said, "It means she lost her virginity in like the fourth grade."

"Shut up," Other Girl said. "It just means she doesn't go to Mass anymore."

The guy who wasn't Opie asked Lapsed Catholic if she'd ever been molested by a priest, and she told him to shut up, too.

Opie said, "Hey, you know Mr. DiDio, the guidance counselor? I heard he used to be a priest."

Littleberry gave a last lick to the cigar paper to seal up the blunt. "Nah," he said. "Mr. DiDio, he's not Catholic. He's, like, a Buddhist. I bet he'd smoke this blunt with us if we asked him to. I mean, if nobody would find out and all."

From what I remembered of my one brief meeting with Mr. DiDio, my first day of school, I had to agree.

Littleberry struck a match and handed me the joint. I took a small hit, but it made me cough so hard that I nearly fell off the berm.

"You OK, Iris?" Littleberry asked, his hand hovering over my back, ready to give it a helpful slap.

I nodded vigorously even though I kept coughing. I finally managed to pass the joint on to Opie. Opie took his hit, then passed it on to Lapsed Catholic, who gave it to Not-Opie, who handed it to Other Girl. Each one took a hit. It went around three times, and then Littleberry swallowed what was left.

"Littleberry ate the roach," Lapsed Catholic said.

Somebody laughed, but it wasn't me, even though I thought it was kind of funny. I guessed I might have been high. I couldn't be sure, though, since I'd never been high before. Some minutes must have passed without my being aware of it, because the next thing I knew, I had my shoes off and was clapping them together for no particular reason except that I liked the sound.

I'm not sure how softball came up in the conversation, but it did. I said I loved softball. Somebody said we should play. Littleberry and Other Girl and Not-Opie left. They said they were going to Dick's Sporting Goods to get equipment. They vanished somewhere into the black parking lot. Opie and Lapsed Catholic and I lay on our backs and looked up through the pine branches to the smoky sky. Three jets went past in precision formation, leaving vapor trails that looked like scars, but then dissipated slowly, imperceptibly. Stars managed to break through the clouds.

I asked them why Littleberry knew so much about head wounds.

"Oh, yeah," Opie said. "You mean that thing he wrote for his class, that thing about his dad? He showed me that. That was sick."

I kept studying the vapor trails. "That was about his dad?" I asked, surprised. "It didn't ever mention his dad. Just how to treat the wound. The bandages and gauze and shaving around it"—I gestured at the sky—"and the discharge and infection, and antibiotics and saline solution."

"Had to be his dad," Opie said. "His dad was in one of those wars, like Afghanistan, and a bomb blew a hole in his head. A chunk of his skull came off or something. I heard his brain leaked out. Some of his brain."

"Ew," Lapsed Catholic said. "That's not even true. He's got all his brain. There's just the wound, and some kind of trauma. He has to go to the VA hospital at Camp LeJeune a couple of times a week. They're having a hard time getting it to heal up. He can walk and everything. They just have to keep changing his dressing where it won't heal."

"Well, that's kind of like his brain leaked out," Opie said.

"Maybe," said Lapsed Catholic.

I wasn't sure how the two of them went from that conversation to making out, but they did. I got lost for a few minutes, feeling bad for Littleberry and his dad, and wondering what happened to the vapor trails I'd been watching earlier.

Lapsed Catholic and Opie stopped making out as abruptly as they'd started.

"Hey," Opie said—to both of us, "check this out," and then he rolled down the berm. He landed hard on the pavement at the bottom. I heard the splat.

"Oh, man," he moaned. "My elbow."

Lapsed Catholic and I burst out laughing like it was the funniest thing we'd ever seen. Soon we heard Opie laughing, too, from down there on the ground.

We were still laughing when Littleberry and the others came back, which could have been a minute later or an hour. Not-Opie pulled something out of his long coat. It was an aluminum softball bat. He held it high over his head as if it was a sword. *Excalibur* or something. I slid down the berm and asked if I could see it. I felt so good holding it that I nearly started giggling. I choked up on the handle a little and took a couple of loose swings. I hadn't had my hands around a bat since July, when I quit the select team in Maine. I positioned my feet, laid the bat on my shoulder, choked up on the bat again, and swung a few more times. The bat weight was good for my size, though I generally preferred something shorter.

"We got these, too," Littleberry said. He held up some balls. The others did, too. Regulation softballs—some white, a couple orange—and baseballs, and even a few rubber T-balls.

"Where'd you get all this?" I asked.

Littleberry laughed. "Borrowed it."

I didn't know what to think. My dad would have been disappointed in me for having anything to do with stealing. Then again, he would have been disappointed in me for smoking the blunt, too.

"Pitch one to me," I said.

"Which one?" Littleberry asked.

"Doesn't matter."

"OK." He lobbed one of the orange softballs at me, underhand. I cocked the bat, rotated my hips around, let shoulders and arms and bat follow through, and crushed it—deep over the berm and through the pines.

Somebody whistled.

"Another one," I said. "A fast pitch this time. And step back more. I don't want to kill anyone."

A white softball came at me, faster, but still with some arc. I cracked it straight back at whoever pitched it—Opie, maybe—and it hit him hard in the thigh. He yelped in pain, which made us all laugh.

Littleberry pitched the next one, a baseball, overhand, and I fouled that one off. He threw another baseball, harder, and I blasted that one into the trees just like the first softball. In Maine I'd been a singles hitter, a spray hitter. A contact batter. I didn't have much power, but I always put the ball in play. Coach had me second in the lineup, so I bunted a lot, to move our leadoff hitter over. I worked hard on my sprinting; I killed myself getting out of the box and down to first. I beat out a lot of throws, too, even when they played the infield in.

Tonight, though, I was a power hitter. They kept firing balls at me, all of them overhand now, each guy trying to throw harder than the others. None of them had strong arms, though, and I murdered every pitch—I was just *crushing* them—except one so far over my head I would've needed a ladder. After five minutes, maybe not even that long, they ran out of stuff to throw, and everybody just stood there.

I leaned on my bat and smiled. It was the most fun I'd had in months. Since Maine. Since before Dad died.

I raised my hand to wipe the sweat from my brow and realized I was crying, too, even though I had a big grin on my face. It was a surreal moment.

"Wow, man," Littleberry said, finally breaking the silence.

We all continued to stand there in the middle of the perfect night.

This time Opie spoke up. "Y'all want to fire up another blunt?"

We didn't get the chance, though. Lapsed Catholic yelped, and we all turned to see the blipping blue light of a security van lumbering toward us across the now-empty lot.

Littleberry yelled, "Haul ass, everybody!" I dropped the bat and immediately wished I'd kept it, but didn't have time to go back for it as we all scrambled over the berm and ran off into the night.

Littleberry had his motor scooter parked on the other side of the mall. Everybody else scattered in different directions, but he said he'd give me a ride out to Aunt Sue's, so we snuck back around to his Vespa and hopped on. The trip had taken fifteen minutes in Tiny's truck, but the scooter was old and slow and had a top speed of thirty-five, so going home took half an hour. I leaned to the side to see the road in front of us and was surprised by all the wildlife that was out: a turtle and a raccoon, even a fox in the high grass on the side. I knew it was supposed to be cold, but I didn't really feel anything. It was a nice change.

Finally we turned onto the long driveway down to Aunt Sue's. It occurred to me that Littleberry might want to kiss, or make out, or whatever, and that that's probably why he offered to drive all the way out here. I thought about how I hadn't kissed a boy in a long time, and I leaned a little closer against Littleberry on the scooter.

Halfway down the driveway, I heard a loud grinding coming from the direction of the farm—tires spinning through deep gravel. I saw headlights, then a car suddenly careened around a blind corner and was heading straight at us—a big silver Lincoln Town Car. Littleberry swerved off the driveway as the Town Car roared past, and we nearly fell over. Immediately after that, we heard the *pop-pop-pop* of a rifle and saw bullets kicking up rocks in the drive where we'd just been. Somebody was shooting at the car, which had now vanished behind us into the night.

Ahead of us, outlined in Littleberry's headlight, Aunt Sue had come around the blind corner. She had on a T-shirt and boxer shorts, but no shoes. Her hair hung wild around her face and she was panting. She held a rifle, now just in one hand. She was cursing, but it was as if she was running out of gas. Her voice got gradually lower, until finally she stopped altogether. She lowered the rifle and looked dazed. I wondered if she even realized we were there.

I waited a minute. Littleberry and I both held our breath. She didn't move.

"Aunt Sue?" I said tentatively.

She turned her head and looked at us dully. Littleberry reached back and blocked me with his arm. "Stay behind me," he whispered.

"Why?" I whispered back.

"For protection," he said.

"Oh, please," I said, pushing his arm away and climbing off the Vespa.

"Aunt Sue?" I said again. She still hadn't moved. Finally she shook her head, looked down at the rifle, turned, and walked back up the driveway to the house.

Littleberry was shivering. "Now what?" he whispered. "You're not going home, are you?"

I thought about the look on Aunt Sue's face, just before she wandered off: drunk, and sorrowful.

"She wasn't shooting at us," I said, sounding braver than I felt. "It was just her company."

I started walking toward the house. Littleberry puttered beside me on his scooter.

"You don't have to come," I said, hoping he would. "I don't need protection."

"Yeah," Littleberry said. "Only my dad always told me to be polite and walk a girl to the door. And make sure she gets inside OK."

"What if her aunt has a gun and is shooting at cars?" I said.

Littleberry laughed. "He left that part out."

He was still shivering.

"Are you cold?" I asked.

"Nah," he said. "Just scared." That made me smile. I'd never heard a boy admit to being scared.

"You think she's scary now," I said. "You should see her when she's not drunk."

"Book Allen's mom, right?" Littleberry said.

"Does that explain anything?"

"Well, you don't mess with Book," he said. "Not even when we were little. I can tell you that."

The Vespa coughed out when we got to the back porch.

Gnarly was on his chain and hiding under the Tundra. He came out when he saw me, and I hugged him and petted him. He seemed nervous, maybe frightened by the gunshots, and whatever else had happened here tonight with Aunt Sue and her company.

"You want me to come in with you?" Littleberry asked, probably hoping I'd say no.

I'd been pretending to be braver than I actually felt, but I couldn't keep it up at the thought of Littleberry leaving now, before I went inside. "Yes," I said. "Thanks."

We tiptoed up the back steps, eased the door open, and waited.

We heard snoring coming from the living room.

"Is that your aunt?" Littleberry whispered. I nodded. We slipped inside, crossed the kitchen, then peeked into the living room. Aunt Sue lay half on and half off the couch, the rifle beside her on the floor. I stepped past a broken lamp, also on the floor, and a neat line of a dozen beer cans on the coffee table.

"You want me to put a blanket on her or something?" Littleberry asked. I shook my head, though I did pick up her legs and shove them onto the sofa. I unloaded the gun and put it in a closet. Dad had kept a rifle at our house—also a .22, which he only brought out to put down injured animals in the wild—and made sure I knew how to use it and take care of it.

Book wasn't home yet, and I wondered if he might be looking for me back at the mall. Probably not. He and Tiny were probably out at another field party and too drunk to remember to go get me from the mall.

I walked Littleberry back outside. I couldn't imagine he'd try to kiss me now, after everything that had happened. He probably just wanted to take off as quickly as he could, and who could blame him?

But Littleberry stopped at the bottom of the steps and grinned. "Kind of a fun date, huh?"

"Were we on a date?" I asked, surprised.

He shrugged. "A secret date."

"You mean like nobody knows about it?" I said.

"Yeah," he said. "Just us."

Gnarly poked his head out from under Aunt Sue's truck to see what was going on. The goats *maa*ed softly from the barn.

Littleberry heard it, too.

"And them," he added.

Dear Dad,

I met a boy.

I hadn't written Dad a letter in a while, so I thought I'd have a lot to say. But once I got that part out, I wasn't sure what else to write. I didn't want to tell him about Aunt Sue hitting me, or about her stealing my money. I might have told him about taking batting practice at the mall, but I didn't want to mention getting high, or Littleberry and his friends "borrowing" the bat and balls from Dick's. I was glad I had something good to tell Dad for once, and I hoped I'd have more soon. But I figured he didn't need to know *everything*.

thirteen

I had just walked up to the house the next morning after milking the goats when I heard Aunt Sue's muffled voice on the other side of the kitchen door.

"I want to go ahead and butcher up them kids this morning," she said. "Get the rifle when you're finished breakfast. Be sure you shoot them in their brain."

"No!" I shouted, slamming open the door, my heart pounding wildly. I threw the bucket on the counter, and milk sloshed over the side. "You can't!"

Book looked up. He had a mouthful of his usual cereal. Aunt Sue was packing coolers for the farmers' market.

"Keep your mouth shut and finish your chores," she said. "You don't get a say in the matter."

"But—but you said you'd wait a month," I stammered. I'd thought I had another week to work out a way to save them. "You said you wanted to fatten them up. They're still so little."

Aunt Sue just looked over at the spilled goat milk on the counter, dripping onto the floor. Then she looked back at me dismissively. "Clean up this mess."

But I had to save the kids. That's all I could think about. I had to hide them somewhere before Book came out with the gun.

"I have to get the eggs," I said, backing away. "I'll do it when I get back."

"Like hell you will," Aunt Sue said. "You'll do it right now, like I said."

I didn't respond. I just stared at her, continuing to back out of the kitchen and then out the back door, letting it slam shut behind me as I ran down the steps and sprinted over to the barn.

I didn't have long. Book would have to find bullets for the gun, plus he and Aunt Sue both had hangovers, so they were moving slowly, but I still didn't have much of a head start. My plan, such as it was, had been to see if Aunt Sue would let me get a job after school so I could buy the kids from her. Then I would ask the Gonzaleses or someone else at the farmers' market to take them in.

But there wasn't time for that now. I could tell by the stony resolve in Aunt Sue's voice that she just wanted the kids dead. She probably didn't even care about the meat. So for now I had to get them away from the farm before Book found those bullets. I'd figure out the rest later.

I grabbed a length of rope off the wall as soon as I got to the barn, shaking the whole time. I tied loops around Huey, Dewey, and Louie the best I could, then dragged them off through the field behind the barn. Patsy escorted us to the fence, which might have helped keep the kids calm. She calmed me down some, too, and I finally stopped shaking. I rubbed her head and thanked her, then I lifted the kids over the fence one by one and led them into the woods. Gnarly came with us.

The other goats *maa*ed behind us—Reba loudest of all. I heard them from deeper into the brush when we waded in to find the trail. Gnarly came with us.

Soon I heard other sounds—Book cursing and Aunt Sue yelling, "Iris! You don't bring back those goddamn goats, it's your ass!"

A gunshot echoed through the trees, and I stopped cold. Was it just a warning shot, or had Aunt Sue killed one of the other goats in her rage? I thought of the nannies back there with no one to protect them and turned to go back, but after a few steps I stopped. Aunt Sue wouldn't shoot a nanny. She'd never give up the milk, and the money. She must have been shooting to scare me. And it worked. I snapped the ropes taut and pulled hard. The kids stumbled forward. We ran.

We only stopped once on the way to the Devil's Stomping Ground—at the faint remnants of a creek. It was hot out, and we were all thirsty. The kids, panting heavily, shoved their long noses between rotting limbs and gray rocks and found enough water to keep them going. Gnarly, too. I went upstream until I came across a pool with a sandy bottom, really more of a puddle, but at least it seemed clear. It was so shallow I couldn't scoop any out, so I had to lie down on my stomach and stick my face in and drink like the goats.

Something crashed through brush far off behind us. Birds fled from nearby trees. I grabbed the goat rope again and we plunged farther into the woods, not stopping for another half hour until we reached the Devil's Stomping Ground and the still-green meadow.

I felt safe there, protected in a way I couldn't explain. I let the kids go free, and the first thing they did was hop around the perimeter. Gnarly stayed next to me, helping me supervise, and he kept watch when the kids stopped hopping and got down to the serious business of eating everything they could find: bark, leaves, grass, branches. My own stomach rumbled. I hadn't brought food, water, anything. I sat on the ground, my heart still racing. I closed my eyes and made myself breathe slowly, deeply, to calm down and to clear my head. I'd saved the kids from immediate danger, but now I needed a new plan. I couldn't leave the goats here by themselves. There were coyotes around, maybe even bears. But I couldn't take them back.

After an hour the kids finished eating and collapsed into a little goat pile, the sun burning as the day inched ahead. I lay with them at the edge of the meadow, half in shade, half out under an empty blue sky.

I thought about my dad, what he would say, what he *had* said when he was alive: "It's wrong for an animal to have to suffer, Iris. As long as how we put them down is humane, though, I think God understands that it's just the way of the world."

Dad wouldn't tell me I was being foolish, trying to save the wethers, but he'd remind me about all the things I already knew—that keeping them was a drain on Aunt Sue's resources, that she couldn't afford to keep them as pets, that she probably did need the meat, that a neat shot to the brain was quick and nearly painless, if you aimed just right.

That all made sense. Dad always made sense. But I still couldn't get past what I knew would be Reba's suffering at the loss of her kids. The trauma to the other goats. The trauma to me.

And you couldn't always count on every aim being true.

We crept back to the farm that night, lucky for a full moon to guide us down the faint trail from the Devil's Stomping Ground. I grew more and more anxious the closer we got—even though I knew Aunt Sue had a Saturday night Walmart shift and wouldn't be there. The only plan I'd come up with so far, and it wasn't much of a plan, was to find something to eat, get enough sleep to clear my head, and spend the night out in the barn so I could be there in case Aunt Sue came home early and tried to hurt the kids. In the morning I would try to convince Aunt Sue to sell them to me, and then see if someone from the farmers' market had a field where I could keep them. But I knew it was more of a dream than a plan. Aunt Sue had already stolen all of my money, and I didn't have a job, so even if she was willing to sell them to me, how would I ever pay for them?

The Tundra was gone, and the lights were off in the house, but I still kept as quiet as possible as I let the kids inside the barn. I couldn't stop the other goats from bleating loudly once they saw us and then mobbed us when I opened their stall. Reba practically cried with happiness to see her three boys. They nuzzled her for a few minutes and tried to latch onto her teats, but came up empty. Her udder was slack, meaning she'd been recently milked. I hoped Book hadn't been too rough with them. I filled the grain trough, and Huey, Dewey, and Louie gave up on Reba and dove right in.

I hooked Gnarly onto his chain on the clothesline, checked his food and water, and then went to check on things in the house. The back door creaked when I opened it, but no one was snoring, so Book must have been gone somewhere, too. I breathed easier, at least for the moment. It felt like a temporary stay of execution. I was certain Aunt Sue would hit me again—or try—the next time I saw her. I also knew that I wasn't going to back down. I was going to save the kids no matter what it took.

I turned on the kitchen light, made a sandwich, fished half an apple out of the bottom of the refrigerator, and filled a water bottle. Aunt Sue had hidden the .22 in another closet, but I found it, and this time I didn't just take out the bullets; I removed the firing pin, too.

I brought my sleeping bag out to the barn and crawled in, exhausted, making sure I had the pitchfork close by in case I needed it for protection. Patsy got up from her stall and settled in next to me in my corner of dry straw. I slid as deep inside my bag as I could go, and fell asleep to the thrumming of her heartbeat and the faint whistling of her breath.

Aunt Sue kicked me awake Sunday morning. I grabbed my side and struggled to sit up inside my hopelessly twisted sleeping bag.

"That didn't hurt, did it?" she said with obvious sarcasm. "I just meant it to be a nudge."

I pulled hard at the zipper, but it was stuck. I looked frantically for the goats and reached for the pitchfork. Only it wasn't there. Aunt Sue had it.

"Don't worry," she said, leaning it against the wall behind her—away from me. "All your little wethers are still here. We don't like to put anything to slaughter until after breakfast here at the Allen family slaughterhouse."

She was still being sarcastic, but now she sounded different. Playful, almost. I wasn't sure I'd ever heard Aunt Sue joking around before. It made me uneasy, but when I counted heads, the goats were all still there, like she'd said: the triplets, Reba, Jo Dee, Tammy, Loretta. Patsy stood next to me, her gaze fixed hard on Aunt Sue.

It was barely light out. Aunt Sue was still wearing her Walmart jacket and had her hair pulled back, the way she wore it to work. She must have just gotten home.

"Where's Book?" I asked, shimmying free of the sleeping bag.

"Inside," Aunt Sue said. Then she said, "All right, look. I thought it over last night. You're in love with them wethers, fine. Isn't so much meat on them that it makes much difference to me, anyways. You done a lot of work around here, I admit it. So you want them, you have to find some other home for them. I won't allow them to stay here and eat all my grain under any circumstance. You do that, get them gone this week, and I won't have Book put them to slaughter."

I should have been more suspicious. I figured Aunt Sue would be furious about yesterday and would take it out on me and the wethers. But my head hurt, and I ached from sleeping on the hard barn floor, even with straw as a cushion. I was tired. But mostly I just really needed to believe that everything would be OK. That the kids would be OK.

"Do your milking," Aunt Sue said. "Then go get cleaned up. You smell like goat."

They waited until I finished milking the goats, and brought in the milk, and pasteurized it on the stove. They even waited while I took a shower. They waited until I dragged myself upstairs to put on clean clothes and lie down on my bed, bone tired.

I had only been there a few minutes when I heard the stairs creak. I sat up, wondering if Aunt Sue had decided to lecture me after all, or worse. But the next thing I heard was the click of my bedroom door being locked, then whoever it was retreating back down the stairs.

It's OK. It's OK, I told myself, my heart suddenly pounding in my chest. *I took out the firing pin. They can't shoot without the firing pin.*

I heard terrified bleating from out in the yard, and I jumped on my bed to look down through my little window. Book was dragging Dewey into the field, then tying him to a post. Aunt Sue stood nearby, shielding her eyes from the low, accusing sun. She looked up at my window, and then handed Book the rifle.

He aimed at Dewey's face, but Aunt Sue stopped him. She pointed at the base of the skull and Book aimed again. I banged against the window. *"No! Don't!"* I screamed, despite what I knew about the gun. I couldn't stand seeing Dewey staked down, so helpless and afraid. But either they couldn't hear me or they chose to ignore me, because Book pulled the trigger.

Nothing happened. Book looked at the gun and tried a second time, and again nothing happened. But now both he and Aunt Sue were cursing loud enough for me to hear them, and I knew Dewey was still in trouble. I climbed off the bed and threw myself at the locked door until my shoulder went numb. I ran back to the window and this time forced it open. I watched Book disappear into the barn. Aunt Sue was inspecting the .22, and she must have realized what I'd done, because she snapped her head around and glared at my window. Her mouth twisted menacingly, but before she could say anything, Book stormed back out of the barn with a shovel.

"Book!" she yelled at him. "Don't you do it!" But he headed straight toward Dewey without slowing.

"Book, no!" I screamed, and watched with horror as he lifted the shovel high over his head, swung down, and slammed it into the hard front of Dewey's skull. Dewey stumbled forward, but the rope pulled taut and jerked him back. He went down on his front knees.

Book lifted the shovel again—and I screamed at him again: "I have the firing pin! I'll fix the gun! Just don't club him to death!"

He paused, and I held my breath.

"Please!" I shouted.

But then Book sneered and swung the edge of the shovel like an ax at Dewey's neck. That brought Dewey down on all his knees. I was screaming and crying again, my fingernails biting into the window frame. Book swung the shovel again, and Dewey's head fell limply to one side, his neck broken. But he was still alive. I could hear him panting and bleating faintly.

I turned and vomited on the bed.

All I could think was that he was still alive. He was still alive, and it was my job to save him. Somehow I would save him.

I threw myself at the door again, but it still wouldn't give. I heard Book shouting, but it was all just noise. I heard the cacophony of other goats, bleating wildly. Desperately I turned back to the window and somehow managed to squeeze through the tiny frame. I tumbled out onto the roof and looked at the scene below.

Book was jumping up and down on Dewey, trying to crush his ribs. Blood gushed from Dewey's mouth, and his eyes strained so wide that the capillaries burst. "Stop, Book! Oh, God, *stop*!" I yelled as I slid down the roof and dropped twelve feet to the ground. I must have twisted my ankle because it gave out when

I tried to stand, but I didn't feel any pain. I limped as fast as I could toward Dewey and Book. Aunt Sue stood off to one side, transfixed at the sight of what Book was doing.

I grabbed the shovel where Book had tossed it aside, and screamed as I swung the flat side of it at Book and hit him hard across his broad back. He fell off Dewey, but Aunt Sue grabbed me before I could hit him again.

"You bitch!" Book roared at me, his face purple with rage. He lunged, but Aunt Sue pulled me away.

She roared back at him, "Enough, Book! Enough! Sit your ass down!"

He sat in the grass, just like she told him to, next to Dewey and a spreading pool of blood. Aunt Sue let go of me, and I dropped to my hands and knees. I couldn't look at Dewey anymore. I couldn't breathe.

I squeezed my eyes shut as hard as I could, to block out all of what had happened, all of what they'd done.

But I could still see Dewey, being crushed to death by Book. And I could still hear him screaming in pain. Screaming for me to help him.

I vomited again.

fourteen

The Craven County Animal Control officer showed up an hour later. The neighbors must have heard what was going on, even though they were a couple of acres away. Aunt Sue and Book met the officer when he pulled up in his truck and parked in the backyard. I had gone inside the barn, once I could make myself walk, and was sitting in one of the stalls with the goats, paralyzed and numb. But they were close enough that the goats and I could hear their conversation.

"Book here," Aunt Sue told the officer, "he accidentally backed over one of the wethers with the new truck. That's likely what the neighbors heard. He couldn't believe he'd done it and he yelled about it some."

I stormed outside in a new rage.

"That's a lie!" I yelled. "That's a goddamn lie. Book killed him on purpose. He beat him to death."

The Animal Control officer looked at me, then at Aunt Sue.

Aunt Sue said, "Well, Book had to just go on ahead and put the goat out of its misery. Some smart-ass took the firing pin out of the twenty-two." She nodded at me.

"Oh, God," I said. "You people are so horrible."

The Animal Control worker lifted his hands and looked at Aunt Sue again. "Ma'am, if we're going to get through this . . . ?"

Aunt Sue told me to go inside the house.

"I won't do it," I said. "Somebody's going to hear the truth about this."

"Ma'am," the Animal Control guy said again to Aunt Sue. She shrugged and nodded to Book. He grabbed my arm and dragged me over to the back porch; I fought him every step of the way, but he was too strong. If I'd had the shovel again in that moment, I was sure I would have killed him.

After the Animal Control guy left, Aunt Sue came over to the porch. She snatched the front of my T-shirt, her fist knotted in the fabric so tight I couldn't pull loose.

"You pushed Book to do what he did," she said, spitting her words. "I don't know who the hell you think you are, but meat is meat, and we don't waste it, and when it's time to kill the wether for the meat, then it's time, and you stay clear out of the way."

She dragged me back over to Dewey. I tried peeling her fingers off, but she just clenched tighter. "Look at it," she ordered, and gripped my chin until I did. Immediately my eyes flooded with tears. "That meat's no good anymore," Aunt Sue snarled. "So you get the shovel and you bury what's left of that goat out in the woods. And deep, you understand? I don't want wild dogs or coyote showing up around here."

I finally looked up from Dewey. "You're both murderers," I said to Aunt Sue. "You as much as him."

She raised her hand to hit me, but this time I didn't flinch or duck. I just stood there, glaring at her, daring her, and I guess she thought better of it. She turned and went inside. The truth was that even though it broke my heart to see his mangled body, I was glad to be the one to bury Dewey. I didn't want her or Book touching him.

I found an old blanket in the shed and wrapped his little body in it and laid him in the wheelbarrow. He was so battered that he didn't look like Dewey anymore. New blood flooded from his mouth when I moved him, covering my arms. I fought the urge to vomit yet again. I had to be calm and strong for the other goats, who had massed together to watch. Reba *maa*ed the loudest and the saddest. Huey and Louie ran in crazy circles, lost without their brother. Patsy stood next to me while I worked.

My anger was already evaporating, though. It had sus tained me for the past hour or so, but now I was afraid that if I stopped moving, I might never start again.

It took a long time to negotiate through all the brush, my ankle throbbing with each step, but we finally made it back to the Devil's Stomping Ground: Patsy and Gnarly and me. Loretta and Tammy and Jo Dee stayed back at the farm with Reba and the two boys. I dug a nice grave at the edge under a dogwood tree.

We sat there together for a long time. It got colder and darker. Not from night — it was too early in the day — but from storm clouds rolling over. Finally Patsy let me know that it was time.

Leaving that place was hard. Something had broken inside me, something I doubted I would ever be able to fix.

Aunt Sue was gone when we got back. I went inside and stripped the blanket and sheets off my bed. I rinsed them in the sink, then threw them in the washer. I went back to the barn with the goats after that, and fell into a feverish sleep. I dreamed something heavy was pressing hard on my chest, crushing me. I dreamed I was drowning.

Monday morning I got up early, hours before Aunt Sue and Book. It was barely light. I milked the goats, who seemed as deflated and as lost as me. I said good-bye to Patsy and the others, then led Huey and Louie out of the barn, across the field, and into the woods. Ten minutes later I let them go. I didn't have a plan to save them — they wouldn't survive on their own, I knew that — but anything was better than letting them die at Aunt Sue's. Huey and Louie busied themselves pulling strips of loose bark off a fallen pine tree. I headed back to the farm.

I didn't go inside the house. I didn't eat, didn't change clothes or grab my backpack, anything. I just walked out to the road to wait for the school bus. A thick morning fog enveloped me like the ones that I remembered rolling off the black Atlantic back in Maine.

The bus came after a while. I got on, and it lumbered down Cocytus Road, cautiously through the thick fog, eventually to school.

I got off and just stood outside until the bell rang. I didn't want to be there. Other than Aunt Sue's, though, I didn't have anywhere else to go.

I was sitting in homeroom when Huey showed up. I spotted him through the dirty classroom window, his face deep into what passed for a flower garden in front of the school. I couldn't imagine how he'd found his way there through the tangle of woods behind Aunt Sue's. Soon all the kids were pressed against the window, pointing and laughing at Huey.

I walked up to the homeroom teacher, Miss Geller. "That's my goat," I said.

She just looked at me. We probably hadn't spoken since my first day of school. "Your goat?"

"Yes," I said.

She called down to the office and they said to send me to the principal, so I went. The secretary stopped me when I got there. "The principal said you can go outside and catch your goat first," she said. "Then come back and he'll speak with you then." She handed me some rope. "It's from the janitor."

Huey didn't move from the flower bed when I walked outside, except to lift his head and *maa* softly. I led him over to the flagpole and tied him up there. I sat with him for a little while—talking to him, rubbing his head, scratching under his chin, trying not to think about what would happen next—until one of the office assistants came out to tell me I had to go back inside.

The principal, Mr. Fenstermaker, said he'd already called Aunt Sue, and my heart sank. I was out of ideas. I didn't know how to save Huey. I didn't know how to save myself.

I was sitting alone on a bench outside Mr. Fenstermaker's office when Aunt Sue pulled up in the red Tundra.

She walked past me without speaking. Mr. Fenstermaker closed the door and they talked for a while; then they came back out, and she signed me out of school.

"Come on," she said to me in a voice I recognized—trying to sound nice, the way she'd sounded when she tricked me about not killing the kids.

I helped her tie Huey down in the back of the truck, then I climbed into the passenger seat. We didn't speak while Aunt Sue drove out of the school parking lot. When we got onto the highway, she backhanded me across my face, but she didn't say anything then, either. Neither did I.

It hurt, but I barely flinched. I'd been expecting it. I pressed my hand against my cheek, just for a second, then opened the window and spat out blood.

Once we got home, Aunt Sue told me to put Huey in the field and to muck out the barn. I knew I wouldn't be getting off that easy, though, with just a slap and some chores. Part of me dreaded what I knew was coming. Another part of me, the part that had broken when I buried Dewey, didn't care.

Louie had wandered back home on his own, and he danced around Huey as soon as they saw each other, as if Huey had been gone for days. I did what Aunt Sue said, and stayed with the goats for the rest of the morning and into the afternoon.

I was doing the second milking, late in the day, when I heard Tiny's truck pulling into the backyard, bringing Book home after football practice. The anxiety I'd managed to keep at bay flooded over me, and I trembled as I patted Tammy's udder to release the last of her milk. She lifted her head from the grain trough, as if sensing something was wrong, and *maa*ed nervously. I hugged her side until she calmed down and until I did, too—long enough to finish.

As soon as Tiny left, Aunt Sue dragged Book out to the barn to find me. She was carrying a dark towel and the first-aid kit.

"Come on," she said in an icy voice. "We're going for a drive over to the lake. I don't want the neighbors hearing any of this."

fifteen

I saw the newspaper article two days later. That was how long they kept me in the hospital after the beating. They left out my name, but I knew that wouldn't matter. Everyone in Craven County — everyone who knew Aunt Sue and Book — would know it was me.

There were a lot of other things that didn't make it into the article: How I almost didn't feel anything after the first time Book hit me. How it was as if I was outside my own body, watching as he picked me up and threw me to the ground. How Aunt Sue had to keep yelling at Book to make him do it, and how he cried and cried the whole time. How Aunt Sue might have cried, too, when she sat me down afterward and opened up the first-aid kit. But I was having too hard a time seeing through my swollen eyes to be sure.

Another detail that didn't make it into the paper was how nice Aunt Sue acted afterward—nicer than she'd ever acted toward me. She put clean sheets on my bed and brought aspirin up to my room. She brought me soup, too—Campbell's vegetarian vegetable—which she heated in a mixing bowl, with the empty can next to it on the tray, to prove it was what she said it was.

She must have known they'd gone too far.

They said the reason I was in the hospital was for observation, which just meant that they didn't know what else to do with me now that Aunt Sue and Book were in jail. I was in a semiprivate room—just me and one other girl. The girl in the other bed had been in a car accident and was in a coma. Her parents took turns staying with her in the room. They sat next to her bed and cried a lot. I was jealous of that girl.

A social worker named Mindy came each day and asked me a lot of questions. She said my name every time she spoke: "How are you feeling today, Iris?" "You're looking better, Iris." "I'm here to help you, Iris."

The first thing I did after she introduced herself was ask about the goats. "Are they OK? Do you know if anyone's taking care of them?"

Mindy said she didn't know, but she'd be sure to follow up on that. She asked me if there was anyone I knew in the area who might be willing to take me in, or if there was any family left other than Aunt Sue. I told her I wanted to move back to Maine and live with Beatrice and her family. I knew that wouldn't happen, but I didn't know what else to say. Mindy took down the information, but all she would tell me was, "We'll see, Iris."

My head still hurt from the assault, and I worried that my hair wouldn't ever grow in again in the back where Book had grabbed it in his fist and torn it away. My face was cut and bruised, with my left eye still swollen shut. I couldn't lift my left arm above my shoulder; I worried that the pain would make it hard to milk the goats, once I got out of the hospital. Every part of me felt too heavy to move, and even going to the bathroom was a struggle, so mostly I just lay in bed and watched Animal Planet and tried not to think about anything. When I did go to the bathroom, I stared, horrified, at the mirror, hardly able to recognize myself. I had always been a small person, but now I looked even smaller, the angles of my face sharper, my skin translucent, the bones visible underneath. My hair hung dull and limp to my shoulders.

Sometimes I caught myself crying, without realizing I'd even started. The television screen would turn blurry, and I'd feel tears on my face. The front of my hospital gown would hang low, damp, the fabric clinging to my skin. But the crying didn't end when I finally noticed. It kept on, and the sadness of everything—the awfulness—swept over me so deep, the current so strong, that I thought I might actually drown. At times I even thought I wouldn't mind drowning. It scared me to think that way, though, so I kept turning up the sound on the TV.

• • •

Mindy came and got me on my third day in the hospital. "No word yet from your friend in Maine, Iris," she said. "No one has answered at the phone number that you gave me, and they haven't returned calls. But we found a very nice couple for you to stay with while we sort things out."

I was sitting in a chair by the window, though the window was too high to see out of. I'd been watching the coma girl instead. Every now and then her hand trembled. The nurses left it out on top of her sheets, so her parents could see.

"I do have some news about your goats, though," Mindy said. "I spoke with Animal Control, and they'll be going out to your aunt's farm periodically to check on them."

"How often is 'periodically'?" I asked doubtfully.

"I'm not sure," she said. "Let me see what I can find out."

A nurse rolled in a wheelchair for me. I lifted myself in, mostly numb to the pain in my shoulder and my face. Mostly numb to everything.

Mindy gave me a copy of the newspaper just before we left the hospital. "I'm sorry, Iris," she said. "I thought you should know."

At first it seemed as if I was reading about someone else, but by the time I got halfway through the article, I was almost too nauseated to continue. I felt Book's fists all over again. Heard Aunt Sue screaming curses at me, egging Book on.

I pulled myself out of the wheelchair, staggered into the bathroom, and threw up over and over until I had nothing left but bile.

• • •

It took us ten minutes to get to the foster family's house, which was in the town of Craven. Mindy chattered away about what nice people they were, and how safe and comfortable I would be. I wanted to tell her that I didn't care. But just the thought of speaking made me tired, so I stayed quiet.

The family's name was on the mailbox—the Tutens. There was a shiny brown leather reclining chair by the road next to their trash. Everything else looked the same as every other home on the street: square yard, brown grass, no trees, brick house, black shutters, minivan.

Mindy knocked for a full minute before Mrs. Tuten finally answered the door. She was a heavy woman with graying hair, maybe in her late forties, and had an odd face, with more of a snout than a nose. A couple of white puffs hung in her limp brown hair. I looked closer and saw that they were the Styrofoam peanuts you use for packing.

Mindy smiled and said hello to Mrs. Tuten, then gestured toward me. "This is Iris, who we spoke about on the phone. Iris Wight."

"Hello," I said.

"Goodness. Hello, hello," Mrs. Tuten said. "I'm sorry it took me so long to get the door. It's been an awful day. I just got back from the animal hospital." She sniffed when she talked, quick and shallow, like animals do when they see strangers.

Mindy put her hand against the small of my back and nudged me inside the house, or tried to. But I balked. Mrs. Tuten noticed.

"It's the smell, isn't it?" she said. "Don't worry. You'll get used to it. It's not as bad as it seems. It's just our ferrets."

I recoiled. Mindy hadn't mentioned any ferrets. I hated ferrets. Dad had, too. He said they were in the same family as polecats and weren't made to be pets.

"How cute," Mindy said. "Did you know Iris's father was a veterinarian?" she asked Mrs. Tuten. "And Iris tells me she just loves animals."

Mrs. Tuten beamed. I dragged my backpack inside past her and plopped down on the couch in the living room, exhausted. The pain meds were wearing off. My shoulder and ankle throbbed. My scalp ached. And I smelled the acrid odor.

Something furry swam around my legs, which I assumed was one of the ferrets. I didn't look down, though. If you ignore an animal, it usually goes away. The same with people. Mindy sat next to me. She was kind of heavy, and we sank so deep that our faces were almost at the level of our knees. I felt as if I was sitting in the school office, waiting to see the principal.

"That's Hob, our little boy," said Mrs. Tuten, pointing. She hovered over me and Mindy with a couple of glasses of ice water. I wanted to dump mine on the ferret, but I set it down on the end table instead. Mrs. Tuten scooted over with a quilted coaster. Everything in the house seemed quilted. It was very neat and homey, except for that ferret smell, and the Styrofoam peanuts. There were more peanuts stuffed between the couch cushions.

Hob kept swimming around our legs, with the occasional detour under the couch and behind the curtains. That's where he was when the second ferret hobbled into the living room, one leg encased in a splint.

"There she is," said Mrs. Tuten. "That's Jill. Her leg got caught in the springs of Mr. Tuten's recliner."

"The chair out by the street?" Mindy asked. There was an empty space in the room next to the couch, and four small indentations in the carpet where the chair legs must have been.

Mrs. Tuten nodded. "I've told Mr. Tuten and told him and told him, 'Check the springs before you lean back in your chair.' Poor Jill got a hairline fracture of the femur this morning. We're lucky it wasn't worse."

Jill studied us intently from her spot on the rug. She had a Styrofoam peanut clinging to her fur to match the ones in Mrs. Tuten's hair. Hob left the curtains and went over to sniff the splint. It was almost tender, but it didn't last long. All of a sudden Hob jumped back, arched his spine, flared his nostrils, and strained his eyes so wide you could see white all the way around his little black irises. Then he started thrashing his head from side to side as if he was possessed.

This went on for about a minute, until I thought his head would fly off. Then he stopped, rose up on his toes, arched his back even higher—so high he practically folded himself in half—and started hopping wildly, sideways, over and over, a foot in the air each time. Jill tried to do the same thing—the arched back, the flared nostrils, the crazy eyes, the thrashing head—but fell down because of her splint. Hob kept going, crashing into a chair leg, then into a wall, then tripping over his own feet. He panted, hissed, and clucked like a chicken.

Mindy drew her legs up onto the couch, shoes and all. Hob slammed into mine, but it didn't hurt, so I didn't move. Mrs. Tuten pulled out her cell phone and aimed it at him. "Oh, this is wonderful! I have to get this. Mr. Tuten will love seeing this."

"What is it?" Mindy asked.

"It's called a weasel war dance," Mrs. Tuten said.

"But these are ferrets," Mindy said.

Mrs. Tuten kept filming. "It's just what people call it. The thing that they're doing with their backs—that's known as a piloerection. And the noise—that clucking—that's dooking."

Mindy had her legs pulled so far up on the couch that it looked as if she was trying to bite her own ankles. "Dooking?" she said.

Mrs. Tuten smiled. "They do it all the time. Well, not all the time. Mostly they sleep. This is just a special thing, because we have visitors and they're excited. We don't ordinarily have visitors. They're usually the most active at dawn and dusk."

"At dawn?" I said, finally breaking my silence. "When people are still sleeping?" Mindy looked at me sympathetically.

Mrs. Tuten said, "Yes, that's right. And at dusk. They're what you call crepuscular."

"What does that mean?" Mindy asked.

Mrs. Tuten shrugged and smiled again. "It means they're the kind of animal that sleeps most of the day but are most active at dawn and dusk."

I turned the word over in my mind: *crepuscular.* It sounded like an oozing infection. And that other word, *piloerection,* sounded creepy and perverted.

Hob finally stopped. He might have knocked himself out. Jill had exhausted herself as well trying to keep up on her bad leg.

Mrs. Tuten shut off her phone and picked them up. She draped Jill over her shoulder and let Hob hang limp over her arm.

She smiled at me. "Wasn't that something?" She reached for my backpack. "Well, now that the show is over, how about we take you back to see your new bedroom and get you all settled?"

The bedroom smelled like potpourri—there was a bowl of it on a little pink desk—which was even worse than the stink of the ferrets. Mindy took a quick look around, then gave me a side hug. "Don't worry, Iris," she said. "Everything is going to be fine."

Mrs. Tuten pointed out the closet, a dresser, the desk. "These are all for you, Iris. You can put your things wherever you'd like. Hanging clothes here in the closet. Folding clothes in the dresser, of course. Your school things on the desk."

Then she went into the kitchen to sign some papers.

"I had an aunt who used to keep ferrets," Mindy said. "They really are supposed to be very nice and cuddly."

"They're illegal in New Zealand," I said. Dad had told me that. "The government brought them there to kill rabbits, but since they don't have any natural predators, now they're killing off all the wild birds."

Mindy patted me on the back. I hated when people did that, and I decided if she told me to "Hang in there," I was going to do something violent.

"Hang in there, Iris," Mindy said.

I bit down hard on the inside of my cheek.

Mrs. Tuten came back in the bedroom and handed over the papers to Mindy. She patted me on the back, too. "I'll have to show you where we keep the ferrets' food. It's right out through the kitchen in the laundry room. Their litter box, too. And it's just about time for their laxative. We need to give them that. They ingest a lot of their own fur and have a hard time expelling it."

Mindy made a face behind Mrs. Tuten's back as we walked her to the front of the house. She said she would call me the next day to check on things. The door made a dull, solid sound as it closed behind her. My heart sank, and I felt heavy again, the same way I'd felt in the hospital.

Mrs. Tuten led me to the laundry room. My feet moved themselves. The rest of me wanted to crawl into bed. I usually held animals close to me when I helped Dad give them medicine or if they needed shots. I couldn't bring myself to do that with the ferrets, though, with their crusty fur and their stench, so I held them out to Mrs. Tuten at arm's length as she rolled their laxatives in peanut butter and poked the pills into their weirdly grinning mouths.

I stepped in poop twice, because even though ferrets can be trained to use a litter box, they don't always remember it's there. Mrs. Tuten pulled two identical ferret leashes off a nail by the door—little H-shaped harnesses that buckled over their front shoulders and around their front legs.

She handed them to me, and I slipped them easily onto Jill and Hob, even though they wouldn't stop squirming.

"You're a natural," Mrs. Tuten said. "I can see you grew up around animals. It really shows. I think we'll make this one of your jobs in the afternoons."

"Putting on their leashes?"

"Well, yes." Mrs. Tuten scratched Hob and Jill behind their ears. "And taking them for their walks around the neighborhood. But we do have to keep them on their leashes because they're so friendly. They're so trusting. Almost foolishly so. We have to watch out for them constantly, to be sure they're safe out there in the world."

I couldn't help thinking about the goats back at Aunt Sue's farm while she talked, especially the wethers.

They had trusted me to take care of them. I had let them down.

sixteen

I met Mr. Tuten when he came home from work—a small, round man in a white shirt and striped tie. Mr. Tuten worked at the Department of Transportation; he talked a lot about problem intersections. We had dinner—beef Stroganoff with cooked carrots on the side—but I had a hard time focusing, and they kept having to repeat everything they said to me until eventually they just gave up. I didn't bother mentioning that I was a vegetarian. I couldn't eat, anyway.

I finally just excused myself and asked if I could take a shower.

"Why, of course you can," Mrs. Tuten said. "I already laid out a bath towel and a hand towel and a washcloth for you on your bed. And there's new shampoo I bought for you already in the shower on the tray. Be sure to put down the bath mat. It's hanging over the side of the tub. You'll see it."

I thanked her before she could give me any more instructions, or offer me a loofah, or soap on a rope. Hob and Jill followed me to the bathroom and seemed disappointed when I didn't let them in. I thought I'd feel lighter without my clothes on, but I didn't. I felt damaged and ugly. I found bruises on my side and legs where I hadn't noticed them before. The hot water stung at first, especially on the back of my head, but I let it burn over me until I realized I was crying again.

They let me use their phone later that evening to call Beatrice. I tried a couple of times, but nobody answered or called back. I hadn't e-mailed Beatrice, or spoken to her on the phone, in two weeks. I wondered if her parents had gotten Mindy's message, and what they would say when they did. Did Beatrice know about the assault at the lake, or the arrests? Did she know I'd been in the hospital, and that now I was staying at the Tutens'? Did she know anything about what had happened to me?

After the Tutens went to bed, I poked through the kitchen until I found a grocery bag. I dumped the potpourri in it and buried the bag under a pile of blankets in the closet. A row of faded yellow bears marched in stenciled formation around the tops of the walls, with "The Teddy Bears' Picnic" lyrics stenciled underneath in flowery script.

I turned off the light but couldn't fall asleep. Maybe it was the lingering smell of the potpourri, and the ferrets. Maybe it was missing the safety of the hospital. At three in the morning, I found a pen and notebook and tried to write a letter—my first in a week.

Dear Dad,

Things didn't work out so well with Aunt Sue and Book. They're in jail. They kind of beat the crap out of me. They killed one of my goats—one of the little ones; his name was Dewey. I was in the hospital for a few days, and now I'm living with ferrets. I miss Patsy and Loretta and Tammy and Reba and Jo Dee and the wethers. I hope they're all right. The social worker says Animal Control is taking care of them, but I don't trust Animal Control. I worry about them all the time. I miss Dewey. I miss you.

I miss you.

I miss you.

I went to sleep with the light on but woke up a few hours later, sweating through my clothes. I kicked off the blanket but kept sweating and turning, trying to get comfortable on the pink twin bed for what seemed like hours. The fever finally broke, but that left me trembling from the cold, shaking so hard that it hurt. I wrapped myself back in the sheets and blanket and somehow fell asleep again.

The ferrets woke me at sunrise, dooking at the door.

Mindy was waiting for me the next afternoon when I got back from my first ferret walk. It was a Thursday, but I hadn't gone back to school.

She stood on the front steps with Mrs. Tuten. It looked as

if they'd been there for a while. Mindy asked if I wanted to go for a walk, and right away I didn't like the sound of things.

"I just did," I said.

"Without the ferrets, then," she said.

I took in Mindy's outfit. She was wearing a tight calf-length skirt and high heels. Not ideal for walking. I handed the leashes to Mrs. Tuten and shoved my hands as deep as I could get them in the pockets of my black hoodie. It was cold, and I hugged myself but didn't like feeling my ribs. One time Dad had to put down three horses that an old farmer had starved nearly to death. It wasn't on purpose; the farmer had Alzheimer's and had hung on to his farm too long. I wondered if I was starting to look like those poor horses. Maybe someone would put me down, too.

We walked a couple of blocks before Mindy began talking. I should have been icing my ankle; my limp got worse, but Mindy didn't notice. She shivered without her coat and wobbled along beside me in her high heels.

"The reason we haven't been able to reach your friend or her mother is because they've been staying in Portland with relatives. I believe there's a younger brother with them as well. The father is still living in the house, but he's not answering the phone. The school put me in touch with the mother. There's been a separation."

I stopped. "Are they getting a divorce?"

"I don't know," Mindy said. "That has to be a possibility."

"When did they get separated?" I asked.

Mindy shook her head. "I'm afraid I don't know that, either, Iris."

"Then what *do* you know?" I snapped, but I didn't wait for her to answer. "Just give me the phone number in Portland," I said. "I'll call Beatrice myself."

"I can't do that, Iris," Mindy said. "You'll have to be patient. I gave Beatrice's mother the Tutens' phone number, and I'm sure your friend will call you as soon as she can. Things are just very difficult for them right now. I know this is sad for you, and I'm so sorry, sweetie. I really am."

She tried to put her arm around me, but I stepped away from her. She thought I was sad, but it wasn't that at all. I was angry—at Beatrice *and* her parents. How could they not appreciate everything they had? How the hell could they throw it all away? And for *what*?

Mindy tilted her head to the side sympathetically and said those damn words again: "You just have to hang in there, Iris."

I stared up at the sky through the mostly bare branches of a sickly elm tree. Cirrus clouds were racing south on fast-forward—so fast it made me dizzy. I counted to ten. Out loud.

It didn't work, though, because I was just as furious when I looked back at Mindy—with her doe eyes and tilted head and mousy brown hair and too-tight skirt and ridiculous high heels.

I stepped farther away from her toward the street. She reached for me, as if she thought I was going to jump in front of a car, but I pushed her away with my good arm. "If you ever say that to me again," I said, "I will find out where you live and I will put ferrets in your bed."

Mindy recoiled. "I'm only trying to help, Iris," she said.

She sounded so wounded, so pitiful, that I almost felt sorry for her. But I also wanted to kick her.

"I just can't hear that anymore," I said. "It doesn't help. Getting me back to Maine, and somewhere to go back *to*—that would help. Getting me away from the Tutens and their ferrets—that would help."

Mindy shuddered, and I realized why she'd wanted to go for the walk. It wasn't so we could be alone. It was because she couldn't stand the ferrets and would rather totter around the block on high heels with no coat on and get frostbite and blisters than go inside the Tutens'.

"I'm sorry, Iris," Mindy said, retreating back into her social-worker voice. "We'll have to wait and see what happens with your friend and her family, but that doesn't appear to be a viable option. And I'm afraid we can't change the foster-care placement just because the family has unusual pets."

I pointed at Mindy accusingly. "But *you* don't like them. *You* won't even go in their house."

"It's not me we're talking about, Iris," she said. "You have to give it a chance. The Tutens are very nice people, and they're happy to have you with them."

"You have to get me out of there," I said.

Mindy seemed to be shrinking. "I'm sorry, Iris," she said again, "but there's nothing I can do."

A detective came to the Tutens' Friday morning. He wanted to know what I might have done to provoke Aunt Sue and Book. He already knew, of course, but he wanted me to say it. So I told him about how I let the goats out, and how Huey somehow found his way to the school.

He nodded. His name was Detective Weymouth, and he looked like a marine—tall, buzz-cut, ramrod straight. We were sitting at the Tutens' kitchen table the day after Mindy's visit. Mrs. Tuten made him black coffee, which she served in a white bone china cup and saucer. He took a sip and winced, so I guessed it was either too strong or too weak. Or maybe flavored. My dad hated flavored coffee, and so did I.

Mrs. Tuten excused herself, and Detective Weymouth got down to business.

"Miss Wight," he said, leaning in. "Your aunt gave a long list of complaints against you. She called it her Bill of Particulars."

"Like what?"

He pulled a sheet of paper out of his briefcase. I recognized Aunt Sue's spidery handwriting. He read:

1. Wasted food on a working family tight budget.
2. Let dog loose to kill neighbor chickens.
3. Took Book to underage drinking party.

4. Vandalized family weapon used for self-defense. Second Amendment protection.
5. Stole food after hours against orders.
6. Stole and hid goats meant for family meat.
7. Talked back to grown-up, disrespectful, with cursing.
8. Made late-night long-distance telephone calls, not allowed.
9. Used ice pick to vandalize and destroy tires on new truck—all plus spare.
10. Assaulted Book Allen with shovel.

"So that's it?" I said. "Just the ten?"

Detective Weymouth didn't change his expression. "Were there more?"

I shook my head. "I don't know. Maybe. Does that mean it was OK for Aunt Sue to have Book attack me?"

"No, no," he said. "This is just part of the investigation. We need to know all the circumstances, and we need to anticipate what sort of case they might make in their defense when it comes before the grand jury."

That caught me off guard. Somehow I hadn't thought about this turning into an actual legal case, or going to a grand jury, or to a trial. What would happen to Aunt Sue and Book? What would happen to the farm? As much as I didn't want them to hurt me anymore, I didn't want to be responsible for sending them to prison.

But what was the alternative? They couldn't go free after what they'd done — and after what I'd already told the authorities. There would have to be a trial, but how could I possibly stand up in court, in front of Aunt Sue and Book, and tell a roomful of people what had happened? Just thinking about seeing them again made my heart race, my hands sweat —

Suddenly I couldn't breathe. I pushed myself back from the table and tried to stand up.

"Easy, now," Detective Weymouth said. He stepped behind me and guided me back to my chair. "Here's some water. Drink this." Mrs. Tuten walked into the kitchen just then, which made me wonder if she'd been listening the whole time. She laid her cool hand on my forehead. I closed my eyes, but that made me dizzy again, so I opened them. I took a sip of water.

"You're in a cold sweat," Mrs. Tuten said. Then, to Detective Weymouth: "Should we let her go lie down and talk about this tomorrow?"

"It's OK," Detective Weymouth said. "I have enough."

I raised my head from where I'd been resting it on my arms.

"Two things on that list are lies," I said.

Detective Weymouth paused. "All right," he said. "Do you want to tell me what they are?"

"I didn't take Book to an underage drinking party," I said. "He took me to one. And I hit Book with the shovel because he killed one of my goats. He stomped him to death."

The detective and Mrs. Tuten looked at each other.

Neither one said anything. One of the ferrets popped up on

Mrs. Tuten's shoulder, and Detective Weymouth jumped back as if he'd been attacked.

"My apologies," Mrs. Tuten said. "That's just our little pet, Hob."

Detective Weymouth scanned the room for more pets. I excused myself and stumbled into the bedroom.

I slept for the next fourteen hours, and had three dreams.

In the first dream, Beatrice and I were practicing cartwheels in a meadow in Maine, only the meadow changed after a while into the Devil's Stomping Ground. Dewey was there—he'd come back to life—and I was so happy. But then I got frustrated. I could make it onto my hands, but I couldn't cartwheel. I fell over each time. Beatrice kept saying, "It's easy. It's easy. See? Watch me." And I kept getting madder and madder.

In the second dream, I was sitting with Nate, the boy I had dated back in Maine. We were in his car up on Mount Joy, where couples went to make out. He was trying to convince me to have sex with him.

"No," I said. "My first time isn't going to be in the backseat of a car."

"Then where?" Nate asked.

"I don't know where," I said. "Nobody ever knows where these things will happen. You can't know this, just like you can't know when you'll die."

"Oh, yes, you can," he said. "Scientists can tell you when you're doing to die. They told your dad. He knew. He told you."

"He didn't tell me," I said, horrified. "He didn't know. Nobody did. They thought it would be different. They thought he would get better."

Nate shook his head. "Everybody knew," he said. "He must have told you."

I shoved him against the door. I didn't understand how he could be so sure. He was just a stupid boy. I cried and cried and cried.

The third dream was the most disturbing. I was on a beach in Maine. A thick fog had rolled in off the Atlantic. I was looking down on the beach from somewhere higher—I couldn't tell where—and I could see all these bodies of people that I knew. Only their features had changed, so they were themselves but not themselves. Then I heard my name.

"Iris!"

I turned toward the voice. It was my mom, and she was angry.

Suddenly I was a little girl again. She grabbed both my arms and shook me. I hung from her fists, limp. If she let go, I would fall on the rocks and it would hurt.

"Iris!" she shouted again, and she kept shouting my name: "Iris! Iris!"

And then she started hitting me.

seventeen

Mrs. Tuten drove me to school on Monday. Most of my injuries had faded. I wore my dad's fishing cap to cover the missing hair. Mrs. Tuten had called the school office and gotten permission from the principal for me to wear it during my classes. I wasn't limping too badly anymore, but I still couldn't lift my left arm all the way. Mrs. Tuten must have known that I was anxious, because when she let me out of the car she said, "Everything will be all right, Iris. I promise." I didn't know how she could make a promise like that, but I didn't say anything. Jill and Hob pressed their noses to the back window and watched me leave.

"Wave to the babies!" Mrs. Tuten called out. "They want you to wave!"

I waved.

I was supposed to go to the principal's office first, but I went to my locker instead to drop off all my stuff. Someone had spit tobacco juice all over the front of it and the combination lock. They had also carved *#91*—Book's jersey number—into the green paint.

I didn't bother telling anyone. I just got paper towels from the restroom and borrowed spray stuff from the janitor and cleaned it up myself.

The principal was meeting with someone, so I had to wait on a bench outside his office. I kept nodding off. I shouldn't have been so tired still after sleeping so much the day and night before. I finally just lay down on the bench and put my head on my backpack and closed my eyes. I must have looked so peaceful that no one thought to wake me, because the next thing I knew, the bell was ringing. I sat up, disoriented. I had no idea how long I'd been asleep, or what period it was, so I just wandered down the hall to English.

I sat in the back behind a couple of girls, neither of whom looked familiar, but I fell asleep again before I could figure things out. I woke up at one point and realized that they were discussing a new book—*I Know Why the Caged Bird Sings*—but then I dozed off again until the end of class, which was when Mrs. Roosevelt finally realized I was there.

"Iris?" she said. "Iris?"

I lifted my head. Everyone else was gone. I had drool on my cheek, and I wiped it off with my sleeve. "Yes?"

"Why are you sleeping here, honey?" she asked.

"Was I asleep?" I said. We seemed to be talking in questions. "Is class over?"

"This isn't your class, Iris," she said. "Your class meets after lunch. Are you all right?"

I sat all the way up and hugged my backpack. "I'm sorry, Mrs. Roosevelt. I've just been so tired." My cheeks burned with embarrassment.

Mrs. Roosevelt said, "I think you ought to go see the nurse. Do you know where the nurse's office is? How about if I walk you down there myself?"

I was too tired to protest. The nurse let me crawl onto a crisp white cot and go back to sleep for the next hour. She woke me up when the bell rang for lunch.

I smelled hamburgers well before I got near the cafeteria, so I veered off and found the vending machines instead. Mrs. Tuten had given me a couple of dollars. I bought my usual Fig Newtons and Snapple, then found a secluded spot under the stairs. I slid to the floor and leaned against the dirty wall to eat. I was invisible, and I didn't mind it at all.

I had my actual English class after lunch, though Mrs. Roosevelt led the same discussion of *I Know Why the Caged Bird Sings* that I remembered, at least in part, from that morning. The main difference was Shirelle.

"I don't get it, Mrs. Roosevelt," she said. "First Janie Starks in *Their Eyes,* and now Marguerite in *The Caged Bird.* Why does the black woman always have to be the victim? And why does the black man always have to be the one abusing her? It's like, both these books are written by a black woman, but they have all the bad stereotypes about black people. All the white racist business in here, you know that stuff used to happen and all, because some of it still happens today. But Marguerite's daddy, and her mother's boyfriend, and that boy she lets get her pregnant—why do they all have to be such sorry people, and do the terrible things they do to Marguerite?"

Mrs. Roosevelt said that the book was based on the author's life, so she had to be honest in writing her memoir.

Shirelle fidgeted in her seat. She clearly wasn't happy with that answer.

The discussion didn't go on for too long, though, because Rasheed jumped in. He wanted to know if Marguerite was supposed to be a lesbian, even though she had sex with a boy to try to prove she wasn't.

I looked over at him when he asked that, and when I did, I saw Littleberry. He mouthed the words "You OK?"

I shrugged. I hadn't seen him since the night of the mall, the night of Aunt Sue and her company and her gun. So much had happened since then—and not all of it had been in the paper.

Mrs. Roosevelt gave us a homework assignment at the end of class. We were starting another composition unit, and she wanted us to try writing a one-act play. Littleberry was still looking at me, wanting to talk, but the minute the bell rang I grabbed my backpack and bolted from class. Shirelle called out to me as I was leaving, but I didn't turn around to see what she wanted. I didn't want to talk to anyone. I wanted to remain invisible.

eighteen

DINNER AT THE TUTENS'

A One-Act Play by Iris Wight

Setting: A stupid house in Stupid Town. Ferrets swarm over all the furniture. They run into walls and fall down.

A middle-aged woman hovers over the stove, cooking Hungarian goulash. She frowns when she thinks nobody is around to see her. Otherwise she smiles so wide it has to hurt her face. She wears an apron that says, What part of IT'S MY KITCHEN don't you understand?

A teenage girl sits on a bed with a disgustingly frilly bedspread in a yellow bedroom next to the kitchen. She wishes she had an iPod so she could listen to the Clash, or the Kinks, or Modest Mouse. She is trying not to gag at the disgusting smell of potpourri, which lingers stubbornly, though she is grateful that it mostly masks the even more disgusting smell of ferret musk and poop, and of Hungarian goulash.

Middle-Aged Woman (calling out toward the bedroom): Oh, Iris!

Teenage Girl: Yes, Mrs. Tuten?

Middle-Aged Woman: It's almost dinnertime, and Mr. Tuten will be home any minute. Can I get you to take care of the litter box?

Teenage Girl looks up to heaven and asks God to kill her, please. Nothing happens. God hasn't been answering her prayers for a while now. She gets up off the bed, goes into the laundry room, scoops ferret turds into a bowl, and brings them into the kitchen. Middle-Aged Woman thanks her, takes the bowl, and studies the turds. She stabs one with a toothpick and lifts it to her nose. She sniffs, nods, returns the turd to the bowl, and hands it back to Teenage Girl. Teenage Girl exits.

Cue sound of toilet flushing.

Middle-Aged Man enters the house. Happy ferrets leap into his arms, and he kisses and greets them: Oh, Hob! Oh, Jill! I missed you. Did you have a good day? Did you miss Daddy?

Middle-Aged Man puts ferrets back down, then shouts into kitchen: Honey, I'm home!

Teenage Girl is reminded of Jack Nicholson in The Shining;

makes mental note to write "Redrum" all over the walls with her own blood after Middle-Aged Woman and Middle-Aged Man go to bed. Or, better—ferret blood.

Middle-Aged Man and Teenage Girl both enter the kitchen and sit at the dinner table.

Middle-Aged Man: Well, well, well, well, well. And how are my favorite girls in the whole world today?

Teenage Girl wishes she didn't have to answer, especially since she's only been living with Middle-Aged Man and Middle-Aged Woman a week, but knows he'll keep it up until she says something back: Fine, Mr. Tuten.

Middle-Aged Woman puckers lips and blows kiss at Middle-Aged Man from across kitchen.

Middle-Aged Man, puckering lips and blowing kiss back: And is that Hungarian goulash I smell?

Middle-Aged Woman, smiling even wider, which Teenage Girl didn't think was possible: Yes, indeedy.

Teenage Girl: Is it vegetarian?

Middle-Aged Woman: It's mostly vegetarian.

Teenage Girl: What does that mean?

Middle-Aged Woman: There are vegetables in it.

Teenage Girl: Oh, God.

Middle-Aged Man: Language—language.

Teenage Girl, getting up: Any crackers and cheese?

Middle-Aged Woman sets humongous soup tureen in middle of kitchen table and ladles out three bowls of Hungarian goulash. Whatever is actually in it is anybody's guess, since it's all black. Teenage Girl, returning to the table, pushes hers away. Middle-Aged Man and Middle-Aged Woman dig in. Teenage Girl nibbles on crackers and cheese like a malnourished rat.

Middle-Aged Man: Any homework tonight, Iris?

Teenage Girl: I did it in study hall.

Middle-Aged Woman: And what were your assignments?

Teenage Girl: Algebra. Read two chapters for Government. Write a one-act play for English.

Middle-Aged Man: A one-act play! That sounds like fun. What about?

Teenage Girl: Living here.

Middle-Aged Woman, taking her turn at the interrogation: You wrote about living here with us?

Teenage Girl: Yes. It's called *Dinner at the Tutens'.*

Middle-Aged Man, taking his turn again: Tell us about it.

Teenage Girl: It's a tragedy.

Middle-Aged Man and Middle-Aged Woman, together:
Oh, dear!

Teenage Girl: I mean, it's a comedy.

Middle-Aged Man and Middle-Aged Woman, together again:
How wonderful!

Cue ferrets.

nineteen

It felt almost good to be angry those first few days back at school—which I was when I had to deal with the ferrets, and when I had to write something for school, and when I kept not hearing from Beatrice—because I was scared and depressed most of the rest of the time.

Some of my teachers pulled me aside to tell me how sorry they were about what happened out at the lake, but I excused myself as quickly as I could and hid in the back of whatever classroom I was in. I made sure not to make eye contact with Shirelle or Littleberry in English. I sat near the door so I could slip in at the last minute when the bell rang for the beginning of class and dash out when class was over. My arm was better but still ached, and I still limped when I was tired, which was just about always. I made sure to wear my hat or keep my hoodie up all day.

Someone spit on my locker again, and someone ran into me twice in the hall. It was too crowded to see who, and I didn't bother lifting my head to look. I flinched, clutched my books tighter to my chest, and hurried to my next class, where I sat with my back to the wall. I was sure all the football players hated me because of Book. I hid under the stairs at lunch.

On Friday of that first week back, I saw those two guys from the field party, Drunk Dennis and Donny. They looked surprised to see me at first, but their expressions quickly hardened. I started hyperventilating and worried I might faint, so I ducked into the restroom.

Two girls were leaning against the sinks, smoking. I wondered if they were the same girls from my first day at Craven High. "What's the matter, girl?" one of them asked. She took my arm and helped me sit down on the floor next to the far wall. "Here," she said. "Put your head down between your knees or something. I think that's what you're supposed to do."

"She doesn't got any color in her face," the other girl said.

I tried to tell them I was OK, but I couldn't speak.

"It'll be all right in a minute," the first girl said.

"Yeah," the other said. "It'll be all right."

I stayed that way for a couple of minutes, until my breathing turned normal again and I stopped shaking. Then I lifted my head and the girls helped me to stand. They threw their cigarettes in a toilet.

"You OK now?" the first girl asked.

"Yeah," I said. "Thanks for helping me."

"You're that girl, ain't you?"

I nodded.

They didn't ask me anything else, and I was glad.

I spent the next hour in the nurse's office, curled up on the cot again under the thin white blanket.

The school counselor, Mr. DiDio, called me in to see him that afternoon. He was the one who had contacted the police a week and a half before, when I showed up at school after the beating.

I went down for the appointment during English. Mr. DiDio had on rope sandals and loose-fit jeans and a Hawaiian shirt—which might have been the same thing he was wearing when I saw him the day after the beating—and he was sitting cross-legged on the Persian rug on the floor of his office.

"*Namaste,* Iris," he said.

"*Namaste,* Mr. DiDio."

He smiled a big Buddha smile. "You want to sit on the floor?" He waved at a couple of beanbag chairs he had on the rug, one in the shape of a ladybug. "Or we can do the desk-chair thing if you want," he added.

"Floor's OK," I said, surprised that they let him do that sort of thing in Craven County, North Carolina. I felt the rug with my fingers and liked it right away—the tight weave, the detailed patterns in gold and silk threads, the hard and the soft of it. Afternoon sun angled through the high window over our heads.

“So,” he said. “How are things going?”

“Fine. Great.”

Mr. DiDio nodded. “That’s cool. That’s cool.”

He uncrossed his legs, and then recrossed them the other way. “Well, the thing is, I spoke to your foster-care worker, Ms. Moran, and she filled me in on what’s been happening. Plus your English teacher, Mrs. Roosevelt, showed me the play that you wrote for her class. And I heard from the nurse that you’ve been down in her office a couple of times.”

I studied the patterns in the rug. How could I tell him, or anyone, about Aunt Sue and Book? About Beatrice? About Drunk Dennis and Donny? About the goats, who I still worried about all the time, even though Mindy kept assuring me Animal Control was taking care of them? About Dad? About everything? How could I even begin? And what if I did open up to Mr. DiDio, and couldn’t ever stop?

So I just shrugged. “Hasn’t been my best week, I guess.”

He tapped the tips of his fingers together. “Are you seeing a counselor or a therapist or anything?”

I nodded, but then shook my head. “Not yet. Mindy—Ms. Moran—said she was going to line something up.”

He changed the subject. “Mrs. Roosevelt says she thinks you’re a gifted student, based on your writing. She says you don’t speak up very often in class. Even before what happened . . .”

I shrugged again and traced the patterns with my finger, over and over. One direction smoothed the fibers down; the other lifted them up. I swept the rug with my open hand, too.

"So are you sleeping?" Mr. DiDio asked. "Eating? Exercising?"

"Yeah to sleeping. Too much sleeping," I said. "No to the other two things, unless you count Fig Newtons and walking ferrets on a leash."

"Ah, yes," he said. "The famous ferrets."

I asked Mr. DiDio if he'd ever heard of a piloerection, and he said no. He looked at the door, probably wondering if he should have kept it open.

"How about dooking?" I asked.

"No," he said. "Not that, either. Why?"

"They're just ferret terms."

Mr. DiDio's face relaxed. He smiled a grim smile, leaned forward, and put his hands on his knees. "You've been through a lot, Iris. More than someone your age should have to go through, and I'm sorry. I just want you to know that it's OK to let yourself fall apart sometimes. And I'm here if you need to do that, and need a safe place to do it, and a safe person to do it with."

I thanked him and told him I would keep that in mind. I could tell he wanted to hug, but I didn't want anyone touching me. Besides, there were pretty strict rules against that sort of thing, even in Maine.

Mr. DiDio and I uncrossed our legs and stood up from the rug. We shook hands. That's as close as we got.

Beatrice finally called that night. "Oh, God, Iris," she said. "What the hell is going on? Mom said you were living with a foster family. That you got attacked by your cousin and your aunt and were in the hospital."

"Yeah," I said. It was weird. For two weeks I'd wanted nothing more than for Beatrice to call me and ask me how I was doing and listen to me complain. But now that she was actually on the phone, I didn't really feel like talking. "A lot's happened since the last time we talked."

"Are you OK now? Are you safe and everything?"

"Yeah," I said. "I'm OK now. I'm living with this family, the Tutens. And I'm back at school."

"Oh, God, Iris," Beatrice repeated. "I'm so sorry. I'm so sorry my stupid parents screwed everything up so you couldn't have just stayed with us. None of this would have ever happened."

I pulled a blanket off my bed and wrapped myself in it. I had to change the subject. The last thing I wanted was Beatrice bringing up what might have been—what was *supposed* to have been.

"What about you?" I asked. "I heard you were in Portland. Are *you* OK?"

"I don't know," Beatrice said. "I guess I'm OK. I'm sort of still in shock."

She said her dad had been having an affair. He confessed it to her mom.

"I didn't even have time to call you when it happened," Beatrice said. "Mom woke me up at about two o'clock in the morning. We practically had to carry Sean downstairs and throw him in the van. We drove down to my grandparents' in

Portland. Mom wouldn't let us talk to Dad or call anybody for a couple of days. I just watched TV and went for walks. Sean acted like we were on a big vacation, but when Mom said we weren't going back home, that she and Dad were separated, he wouldn't stop crying."

"So what now?" I asked.

"I already transferred to Portland High," she said. "The Bulldogs! Can you believe that? And they already have a starting pitcher, so I'll probably have to play right field or something."

"Have you seen your dad at all?" I asked.

Beatrice erupted. "Forget him, Iris! He cheated on my mom. Forget him. I wish he'd just leave. Just totally leave, so we wouldn't ever have to have anything to do with him again."

As angry as I was at Mr. Stone, the thought of Beatrice not talking to her dad made me sad.

"I don't know, B.," I said. "Your dad used to come to all our games. He drove us to tournaments and stuff. He was our coach in seventh grade."

"So what?" Beatrice said. "So the hell what?"

I couldn't figure out why I was defending Beatrice's dad. He'd always been nice enough to me, but I knew that didn't really mean anything. He had lied to my dad about keeping me in Maine. He had lied to his own family, lied to Beatrice's mom.

Beatrice lowered her voice. She whispered into the phone. "I think my mom is cracking up, Iris. I really do. She's on these anti-anxiety pills, and sleeping pills. She's in her old bedroom that she grew up in when she was a girl. I even caught her holding her old dolls."

Just then I heard Mrs. Stone's voice in the background. Beatrice muffled the phone for a minute, and when she came back on, she said she had to go. "My mom needs me. We'll talk more later."

I sat for a long time with the phone still in my hands. I'd forgotten where it went, which room the cradle was in, and didn't think I had it in me to get up and look. I probably could have felt the earth move under me if I hadn't been so numb—shifting tectonic plates, Maine separating from the rest of America, sliding off into the Atlantic, migrating toward some other continent, falling farther and farther away from me all the while.

twenty

On Saturday I asked the Tutens if I could go out to Aunt Sue's farm to check on the goats. I hadn't seen them in almost two weeks. I was frightened at the thought of being out there again, but I missed the goats terribly and couldn't stop worrying about them—no matter how many times Mindy mentioned Animal Control.

Mrs. Tuten said no, she was sorry.

"Your aunt's house is private property, Iris. You don't live there anymore, and Mindy said it's not allowed. We thought she already told you."

I tried arguing with Mrs. Tuten, but she wouldn't budge. Mr. Tuten looked at his shoes the whole time and didn't say anything. The ferrets circled nervously, then Hob bit my shoe. I kicked him off and went to my room. Now that I had decided I was ready to go back to the farm, I was desperate to be there. The goats needed me. I couldn't let them think I had abandoned them, too.

And nothing—not the Tutens, not Mindy, not Animal Control—was going to keep me away from them any longer.

My chance came the next day, a Sunday, when the Tutens went to visit Mr. Tuten's great-aunt, who lived in a nursing home in Kinston, an hour away. They invited me to go, but I said I had to catch up on some homework, so they just reminded me to please look after the ferrets and said that they would be home in time for dinner.

As soon as they left, I filled the ferrets' bowls, then went into the backyard. Mr. Tuten had a work shed out there, which I'd never been in. I pulled the door open, hoping to find a bicycle I could ride out to the farm, though I was determined to walk if I had to. I found what I was looking for right away, leaning under a dusty blue tarp—an old three-gear bike that probably hadn't been ridden in ten years. The chain was rusty, but the gears still operated OK. The back brake didn't work, but at least the front brake did, mostly. I adjusted the seat to my height. The frame was too long, but there was nothing I could do about that. The tires were flat. I searched some more and found a pump. Miraculously, both tires held air.

It took me an hour to get out to Aunt Sue's farm. My ankle hurt from pedaling, and holding on to the handlebars made my shoulder ache. I ran out of breath easily and kept having to stop and rest. I refused to turn back, though. Pedaling got harder once I made it to County Circle Road, just outside the city limits. There were steeper hills but nicer scenery. More trees, less concrete. Finally, I turned onto Cocytus Road, a winding canopy road with hardly any cars.

The barn doors were wide open when I got there, and Patsy was standing next to the fence, as if she'd been waiting for me the whole time I'd been gone. I threw myself over the fence and hugged her and hugged her, and then the rest of them, too. I kissed their faces, let them butt me, danced with them in their pen, tried to chase Huey and Louie—who had grown so big! Just in the time I'd been gone! I curled up with them in their stall, nestled down in dry straw. Huey chewed on my shirt, and I let him. I pulled both of them on top of me, burying myself in a blanket of goats. Jo Dee had gotten bigger with her pregnancy and kept trying to nose the boys out of the way so she could nuzzle me and so I could hug her and scratch her chin the way she liked.

Patsy stepped back to let the others have their time with me, but she stayed close, too.

"I'm so sorry," I whispered to her. "I'm so sorry I left."

I could tell by her eyes that she understood and that she forgave me.

Gnarly wasn't tied to the clothesline, and I was just wondering why I hadn't seen him when I heard crazy barking out in the field. I wondered if he'd been roaming free all this time, and if so, how many of the neighbors' chickens he might have killed. I pulled myself out from under the goats but only made it as far as the barn door before he showed up and threw himself onto me.

I staggered under his weight, then sat on the ground so we could wrestle while the goats looked on. We played for ten minutes, and I talked to him the whole time. I told him about the ferrets. I growled when I described them and Gnarly growled, too. I told him about the Tutens, and Mindy, and the football players, who I assumed were the ones who spat on my locker. Finally I had to stop. The goats wanted their turn again, so I checked on Gnarly's food and water bowls by the back steps—both were half full, so at least Animal Control had been doing that much right—and went back in the barn.

I could tell by how swollen the goats' udders were that Animal Control hadn't been milking them, or at least hadn't done it lately, so I got buckets and cleaning rags and grain and coaxed the goats into the barn. Jo Dee attached herself to me, even more anxious in her pregnancy than Reba had been. I hugged her some more and let her stay close during the milking.

I milked Patsy first, of course, and she nodded approvingly, but I moved Reba up to second because she was the fullest, since she'd kidded most recently. Even knowing that, I was surprised by how much she gave. After Reba it was Loretta's turn, and finally Tammy, who didn't seem as cranky or aloof as usual, but almost happy to see me. During each milking I pressed up against the goats' warm sides with my face and shoulder. They were patient with me, and sweet, and the bucket nearly overflowed.

I led the goats outside afterward, back into the warm sun. The kids kept jumping higher and higher, and even tried to do backflips. I'd never seen them so excited. I rolled on the ground and they rolled, too. And butted me, and kept butting, knocking me down and down and down. I let them. And at some point I started crying. I let them push me over, and lick my face, and steal my tennis shoe, and every time I thought I was done crying, I cried some more.

Eventually I started singing to them, too. Dad used to sing "Hush, Little Baby" when I was little, but he changed it to "Hush, little *Iris,* don't say a word. Papa's gonna buy you a mockingbird." So I sang that, but faster, and louder, to hear myself over all the bleating and barking. Soon it was more like shouting—*And if that diamond ring turns brass, Papa's gonna buy you a looking glass!*—and then something came over me and next thing I knew, I was full-on shouting at the top of my lungs, until I was hoarse and my throat burned and I was so out of breath that I thought I would faint.

But I kept shouting—*And if that looking glass gets broke, Papa's gonna buy you a billy goat*—and the song got harsher and harsher until I was rasping it out, and the goats backed away from me and *maa*ed nervously, crowding together over by the fence. Still I kept shouting:

"AND IF THAT BILLY GOAT DON'T PULL—
AND IF THAT CART AND BULL TURNS OVER—
AND IF THAT DOG NAMED ROVER DON'T BARK—
AND IF THAT PONY CART FALLS DOWN—"

And then I lost my voice.

I stood there silent, waiting for something to happen. The goats watched me from a distance. Even Gnarly had backed away and was hiding under Aunt Sue's truck. I'd never gone crazy like that before and didn't know what was supposed to come next. There was nothing left inside me. Finally Patsy came back over and nudged me with her head.

I lay down in the middle of the field, as if that's what she'd just told me to do—and maybe it was. I closed my eyes and let the last of the afternoon sun burn my face.

After a while the other goats came back. Jo Dee lay beside me in the short grass and rested her head on my stomach. She felt heavy and warm. The others inched over, too, and hovered nearby.

We stayed there until the sun touched the tops of the trees and it got cold out. I fed the goats again, and then I headed toward the house, Gnarly at my heels.

I found the key to the back door where Aunt Sue always left it, under a concrete block by the steps, and went inside to pack up some of my clothes. I looked inside the refrigerator and made myself a sandwich with some cheese and wilted lettuce and a couple of dry, white Wonder Bread heels. I opened the door to Aunt Sue's room. She kept it so dark in there—lights off, thick curtains drawn—that I couldn't see anything, and for some reason I didn't want to turn on the light. I fumbled through things on top of her dresser—pictures, a hairbrush—until I found some money. I counted it in the hall. Twenty-five dollars in neatly folded bills. I put it in my pocket.

Book's room—which I'd never been in, either—was surprisingly neat and clean. He had an East Carolina University Pirates football poster on one wall and a Carolina Panthers calendar on another wall. That was pretty much it—Book's plan for his life: college and then the pros. His bed was made, clothes all put away, shoes and cleats lined up neatly on the floor. I kicked them all into a pile in the corner, then left.

The mail was all bills.

As I walked back through the kitchen, I saw the truck keys hanging on a hook by the back door, and I grabbed them. I didn't think I had it in me to ride the bike back to the Tutens'. As awful as the truck was, Aunt Sue had bought it with my dad's money, and that meant it was mine. Gnarly barked and barked while I loaded the Tutens' bike into the back of the truck. Lifting it was hard. My shoulder ached. The excitement of being back with the goats had given way to exhaustion.

I shut the tailgate. "You take care of the goats," I said to Gnarly. He looked sad, but I didn't waver. I said it again, as a command: "Take care of the goats."

I hugged Patsy and the others, then hugged Jo Dee a second time. I told them I'd be back tomorrow and pulled myself into the cab with my good arm. I adjusted everything I could find to adjust—seat, mirrors, steering wheel tilt—but it still felt too big for me.

I parked on a side street a couple of blocks from the Tutens' and rode the bike back to the house, my bag of clothes balanced on the handlebars. I was so hoarse and tired and sore that I just wanted to crawl into bed, but that wasn't going to happen: either I had miscalculated the time or the Tutens had come home early.

They were already back, and waiting for me in the living room.

twenty-one

"Please sit down, Iris," Mrs. Tuten said. She and Mr. Tuten and the ferrets had the sofa, so I took a straight-backed chair by the front window. Mr. Tuten had one hand over Hob and the other hand over Jill, as if they might attack me if he didn't hold them back.

Mrs. Tuten looked at her watch, but that was just for dramatic effect. She already knew what time it was. "You've been out?"

"Yes," I said.

"You didn't leave a note," she said.

"No."

"Do you want to tell us where you've been?" Mrs. Tuten asked. "And what you have in your bag?"

I kicked the bag lightly. I'd planned to smuggle my things in and hoped they wouldn't notice the new additions to my wardrobe. "These are just some of my clothes," I said. "I went out to my aunt's farm. I needed to feed and milk the goats, and check on Jo Dee, the one that's pregnant."

Mrs. Tuten's face reddened. "I see," she said. "So despite what we told you yesterday, you decided to go anyway."

"I'm sorry," I said. "But I had to."

"Whether you had to or thought you had to, all that is beside the point," Mrs. Tuten said. "Mr. Tuten and I were very clear when we said no. That's your aunt's private property. It's considered trespassing for you to be out there."

"But nobody's really taking care of the goats," I said. "Nobody's been milking them. The barn doors were left wide open. I doubt the Animal Control officer has been out there more than once or twice."

"I'm sure it will all be taken care of," Mrs. Tuten said. She looked at Mr. Tuten, then back at me. He kept petting the ferrets. She did all the talking.

"Iris," she said, changing the subject, "how did you get out to the farm?"

"I took a bike. I found it in the shed." I didn't mention Aunt Sue's truck. They'd probably think my taking the Tundra was grand theft auto.

"You did not have permission to do that," Mrs. Tuten said, wringing her hands. "This is not a good way for us to be starting out. We need to be able to trust you. We simply cannot have this."

Mr. Tuten leaned forward. "We need you to understand—there can be no more trips out to your aunt's farm."

"Please," I said, the panic making my voice quaver. "They need me. I'll walk out there. I'll feed them and milk them and come straight home. I'll do whatever chores you want here. I'll keep walking your ferrets. But I have to see my goats. I have to take care of them. Please."

And in a smaller voice I said it again: "Please."

There was a long silence. The ferrets climbed out of Mr. Tuten's lap and came over to inspect my legs.

"We're sorry," Mrs. Tuten said. "If you're going to stay here with us, you're going to have to abide by our rules."

I trembled with frustration and anger, but fought to hide it.

"We'll need you to promise," Mrs. Tuten said, "that you won't go back out there. To the farm."

"It's just that we're responsible," Mr. Tuten added, apologetically. "We don't want anything to happen to you."

I stared at their shoes for a long time. Then I told them I understood, and I told them I wouldn't go back out to the farm. It was a lie, of course; there was no way in hell I was going to stop taking care of the goats. I just had to figure out a way to do it without the Tutens finding out.

Mrs. Tuten and Mindy took me downtown the next day after school for an appointment with the guardian, Mr. Trask, though I didn't want to see him—then or ever.

Mr. Trask didn't look at me when the receptionist showed us into his office. He spoke to Mindy while Mrs. Tuten and I just sat and listened. For ten minutes they discussed me as if I wasn't there: my condition, my situation, my placement options—which didn't seem to exist, except for the Tutens'.

"And as for the estate," Mr. Trask said, finally shifting his gaze my way, "everything was liquidated after Miss Wight's father's death. Her aunt was fully authorized to make expenditures."

He turned back to Mindy. "As I have explained to Miss Wight before."

"How much is left?" I asked. "You didn't tell me *that*."

He continued addressing Mindy. "The balance is forty-two thousand five hundred and eleven dollars"—he paused—"and thirteen cents. Social Services can draw from the account to pay the foster-care stipend to the Tutens, and a small allowance for incidental expenses for Miss Wight—clothing, school lunches, that sort of thing. The rest will transfer to Miss Wight on her eighteenth birthday. This is not an account to which Miss Wight will have access otherwise until that time. And I suppose it goes without saying that Miss Wight's aunt, Miss Allen, has lost her executorship of the estate."

Mindy asked about the status of the cases against Aunt Sue and Book. Mr. Trask said he wasn't directly involved—Book and Aunt Sue both had court-appointed lawyers—but he understood that they had a preliminary hearing in a week, and he expected that the case would go before the grand jury.

"Will they be allowed to get out on bail?" I asked. "Why aren't they already?"

Mr. Trask leaned back in his chair. "It is my understanding that Miss Allen was unable to make her bail, or her son's. You do understand that the state is treating this as a very serious felony."

"What do you mean 'treating it'?" I said.

He leaned back even farther. "I simply mean that it is a very serious felony. That's all."

"But you said 'treating it,'" I said, leaning toward him until I was practically out of my chair. "Don't you think it's serious, what happened?"

Mrs. Tuten laid her hand on my arm. We were sitting in matching straight-backed chairs next to each other, about a mile away from Mr. Trask on the other side of his desk.

"Of course he does," she said in a tone I hadn't heard before—as if she were giving Mr. Trask an ultimatum.

Just before we left, I asked about going out to Aunt Sue's farm. Mrs. Tuten seemed surprised that I brought it up, but it was all I had been thinking about.

"Now, Iris," she said. "We have already discussed this."

"I know," I said. "I just wanted to see if it was possible."

Mr. Trask was unequivocal, though: No, I couldn't go on the property. And no, I couldn't tend to the goats or Gnarly.

My heart sank, but only briefly. Because I was going back to the farm no matter what.

twenty-two

Tuesday morning I pretended to take the bus to school but ducked around the corner from the Tutens' and drove the truck instead. I parked in the student lot, then snuck out of study hall later in the day and raced over to the farm, ten minutes away. I felt as if I'd been holding my breath the whole time I was away. Gnarly's dish was empty — I doubted Animal Control had been there — so I got busy right away, feeding Gnarly, giving grain to the wethers, gathering the eggs, milking the goats. I pasteurized the milk and started some new cheeses — out of habit, and because I didn't know what else to do with the milk.

The goats hated that I rushed through everything; they wanted to play. Tammy butted me in the side, hard, after I let her off the milking stand. I yelled at her but immediately felt bad about it — and bad about having to abandon them again so soon. I thought Jo Dee was going to batter down the gate trying to follow me out of the field when I had to leave.

I nearly got in trouble for being late to English class, but I said I was having my period and Mrs. Roosevelt let me in. Littleberry was watching me as I sat down at a desk by the door. He gave me a crooked smile, as if he knew something was up. I didn't look at him again the rest of class.

I continued to slip off to the farm the rest of that week and into the next—sometimes leaving during study hall, sometimes during lunch. Twice I skipped homeroom and first period. I figured the Tutens wouldn't find out about the tardies for a while.

The goats were always happy enough to see me, but I could tell they didn't understand why I came and went so quickly, why I didn't stay, and why I milked them only once a day. Tammy attacked me a couple more times, even after I freed her head yet again from the fence. Jo Dee, whose pregnant belly hung so low that she practically dragged it through the grass, pressed herself so close to me that my jeans took on her goaty smell. I was afraid the Tutens might notice it, so I starting leaving a pair of jeans in the truck to change into and out of, just for the farm.

There was trouble with Gnarly, too. I didn't want to tie him up to the clothesline, even if he could still run back and forth. Plus his barking alone wouldn't keep wild dogs or coyote from getting at the goats, and I needed him to be able to protect them—and to protect Aunt Sue's chickens, which for some reason he never bothered. But then one night he killed another one of the neighbors' chickens. He didn't even eat it or anything, just laid the carcass on the bottom porch step, I guess thinking I'd appreciate the gift.

Dad had shown me how to deal with a chicken killer, though. I found an old protective dog collar in a closet—a giant, hard-plastic cone—and strapped that on Gnarly. He wasn't happy about it, but he couldn't scratch or bite it off. I made sure he could still get to his food and water bowls with it on. Then I tied the chicken's legs together, and its wings tight to its breasts, and tied the whole thing under Gnarly's neck. He went crazy trying to get at it, but couldn't because of the collar—not with his teeth, not with his paws, not scraping against the goat fence, not flinging himself onto the ground and crashing and rolling around.

Finally he gave up and just sat there, looking up at me with his best sad dog eyes.

"Forget it," I said. "You can't kill chickens, Gnarly. You have to take care of the goats when I'm not here. That's your job. No more chickens."

I left the bird there for three days while it turned rancid and rotted—and hoped Animal Control wouldn't show up, which, judging from what I'd seen so far, wasn't likely to happen. The smell nearly made me vomit, and the goats couldn't get far enough away from Gnarly. They ran to the farthest corner of the field every time he climbed under the fence. Gnarly could barely eat for the first two days, and not at all on the third. When I drove out that afternoon to milk the goats, he looked so miserable and pathetic—and stank so bad—that I cut the carcass loose and tossed it away deep in the woods.

It took three Murphy's Oil baths to wash off the smell. But Gnarly didn't kill another chicken.

All of the sneaking around was making me so anxious that I couldn't eat. I felt guilty about lying to the Tutens, and worried about getting caught. Plus I didn't want to hurt their feelings, especially after Mrs. Tuten stood up for me in the meeting with Mr. Trask. I was still getting harassed at school—people defacing my locker, bumping into me in the halls, shouting "Ninety-one!" at me. And someone must have seen me driving the Tundra, because I came out one day to find that it had been keyed down the side.

I couldn't report any of it, though—and couldn't have said anything about the truck even if I'd wanted to, since I wasn't supposed to have it in the first place. I got shakier after every act of vandalism. Once, walking to the truck after school, I suddenly heard footsteps on the sidewalk behind me and turned and shouted "Get away!" But it was just some kid, probably a freshman. He stuttered out an apology, and then practically took off running to get away from me.

The only thing getting me through it all—aside from the goats and Gnarly—were my talks with Mr. DiDio. Mindy had arranged for him to be my counselor—not just my school counselor, but also my mental health counselor. I was supposed to see him once a week during study hall so he could check on how things were going with me. I didn't tell him about the vandalism, or the harassment, and I didn't tell him about sneaking out to take care of the goats. But it was kind of nice meeting with him all the same, sitting on his carpet, having a temporary refuge. So far he hadn't mentioned what happened out at the lake, or anything about Aunt Sue or Book, which I appreciated. I guess he was waiting for me to bring all that up when I was ready.

The day after I yelled at the freshman, I asked Mr. DiDio about confidentiality. "Our talks, or sessions, or whatever," I said. "Are they private, between just the two of us? Like confessing to a priest? That sort of thing?"

Mr. DiDio had made us some herbal tea. I balanced mine on my knee. He got up to add more honey to his. He seemed to like a lot of honey in his tea. Lemon, too. "Yeah," he said. "Pretty much. Unless there's a situation where I'm concerned that you might be in danger. That would include if I thought you might be a danger to yourself."

He offered me the honey bear, but I shook my head.

"Is there a specific reason you're asking?"

I took a deep breath. And then I told him about the goats, and the truck, and sneaking out to Aunt Sue's farm. He listened in silence, mostly looking into his mug of tea, not even nodding or anything. Just listening.

When I finished he didn't say anything for a while. I could tell he was struggling with how to respond.

I held my breath.

Finally he asked if I knew anything about situational ethics.

I shook my head.

"OK," he said. "Here's an example. You're a vegetarian. You think it's unethical—maybe even immoral—to kill an animal and eat its meat."

I nodded.

"But if someone was starving, and only had access to meat. Or if we were talking about nomadic herders in Africa, who only knew the culture they were born into, surviving on their livestock. You wouldn't think eating meat, killing animals, was wrong in those circumstances."

I said no. I wouldn't like it, but no.

"The thing about lying," Mr. DiDio said, "is that it's this corrosive thing. It's bad to the other person, the person you're lying to, but it's just as bad or worse on the person doing it. And it's just flat-out wrong. Usually." He let that sink in for a minute, then he continued.

"But then there's the question of *why* you're telling that lie," he said. "If there's a greater good involved, I guess you might say. And that's where it gets complicated. That's where the situational ethics come into play.

"Do you understand what I'm saying here, Iris?"

"I think so," I said. "Sometimes the end justifies the means. Like if an animal is injured, and suffering, and you know you can't save it. You have to put it down. It's still killing, but you have to do it because you don't want the animal to suffer. I saw that all the time with my dad."

Mr. DiDio warmed his hands on his tea mug. I did the same with mine.

"I want you to ask yourself if there isn't some other way to proceed here, Iris," Mr. DiDio said. "Are you really doing what's right for this situation? There's no easy answer. . . . Maybe meditate on it. And whatever you decide, just promise me you'll be careful."

I could tell he was worried. He shook it off, though, and smiled. Then he lifted his mug of tea and said, "Drink up."

Some of my anxiety dissipated after the talk with Mr. DiDio. I even slept better that night, too. And I caught a break the next day after English class when Shirelle followed me down the hall.

"Hey," she said, grabbing my backpack. "Iris. Stop running away from me. I've been trying to talk to you."

I looked at her expectantly, ready to hear the same thing I'd been hearing from the teachers: *So sorry about what happened. If there's anything I can do, please let me know.*

Instead she said, "I hear you play softball."

"I used to," I said. "In Maine. Who told you that?"

"That white boy Littleberry. The other person you've been ignoring who's been trying to talk to you for the past week. He said he hung out with you before, and that you were a mighty softball player."

"What else did Littleberry tell you?" I asked, thinking about Aunt Sue and her gun.

"That was all," Shirelle said.

She let go of my backpack, and I started walking again. "He saw me take some swings one time," I said. "That's all."

"I don't know," Shirelle said. "He said you nearly killed a boy with a line drive."

I shrugged. "He should have gotten out of the way."

Shirelle stopped again, and this time I stopped with her. "We need you on the team," she said.

"Just like that?"

"Yeah, just like that. We're pretty short on girls right now. Anyway, I'm captain, and it's up to me if you're on the team."

"What about your coach?"

"Coach Davis? What about him?" Shirelle said. "He's also one of the football coaches. What that means is that Coach Davis never comes to any of our practices, and we do everything all on our own. In the spring he'll come out for the games and sign the lineup card, but that's about it. He takes naps in the dugout."

"So why does he do it?"

"Coach?"

"Yeah."

"Money, I guess."

"A lot of money in girls' softball?"

Shirelle laughed. "Oh, yeah. Millions."

I shook my head. "If he's a football coach, don't you think he'll hate me?"

Shirelle looked at me hard for a second. "Look, I won't lie to you, Iris. There's people that are going to blame you for Book

Allen getting in trouble, especially if they lose in the play-offs with him not there. There's always going to be people that are that way, that want to blame the victim or whatever. But you know what I say to them? I say what you ought to say, too."

"Which is what?"

"Which is: Kiss. My. Ass."

I smiled despite myself. "When's practice?"

"Four o'clock. Monday, Wednesday, and Friday."

The bell rang, and Shirelle jogged off to her next class. "Think about it!" she shouted. I ignored the bell and walked slowly, thinking. Joining the team would give me the cover I needed. I could leave the truck at school, drive it out to Aunt Sue's after the bell rang, take care of the goats and Gnarly, and still make it back in time for practice. I wouldn't tell the Tutens that we only practiced three days a week, which meant I'd have longer with the goats on Tuesdays and Thursdays. I'd have to figure something else out for the weekends, but already I felt better than I had in a long time.

I told the Tutens that evening.

Mrs. Tuten was concerned at first. "Are you sure you're ready for something like this, Iris?" she said. "I mean, we're happy for you to take part in extracurricular activities. And we don't mind picking you up from school when you're finished. It's just . . ." She wound her napkin around her hand, first one way and then the other. "It's just, are you *sure* you're ready?"

"I'll still walk the ferrets," I said, not answering directly.

We were at the kitchen table. The Tutens ate pork chops. Mrs. Tuten had made something she called vegetable medley for me, which came out of a frozen food bag and consisted of tiny cubes and balls of carrots, peas, corn, possibly potatoes, possibly green peppers.

Mr. Tuten chewed thoughtfully for a while, his eyebrows practically meeting at the bridge of his nose, and then he finally spoke. "Iris," he said, "I've been thinking this over, and I've decided that you are welcome to use the bike if you would like. To ride it to school. And home from your practices."

Mrs. Tuten started to speak, but he put his hand over hers, and she kept quiet. I noticed the Tutens spent a lot of time like that—not quite saying all the things they wanted to say.

I smiled a genuine smile and promised to take good care of the bike.

Dear Dad,

It's been a while since I wrote. Things are finally starting to look up around here a little. I'm taking care of the goats again, and got invited to join the softball team. I wish my arm was in better shape, but throwing a ball should help. We won't have games until the spring—fall ball is just for practice, like it is back home—but it's already strange to think about playing and not having you in the stands to watch. I'll have to get Mrs. Tuten to cut up orange slices when it's my turn to bring them. I'll have to dig out my glove and limber it up for our first practice.

The rest of the letter was light and upbeat, even kind of chatty. I didn't tell Dad about getting harassed at school, or about my anxiety attacks. I didn't tell him how worried I was about going to court and testifying against Aunt Sue and Book.

I didn't want to think about those things now, not when there were finally good things to focus on. There was time for all that later.

twenty-three

I showed up for softball the next day at the athletic fields behind the school, after racing over to Aunt Sue's to feed and milk the goats. The football team was out in their practice uniforms, running plays on their perfectly manicured practice field while their fifteen coaches looked on, some of them consulting clipboards, some of them barking orders. I scooted away from there as fast as I could, my heart beating double time until I made it past the baseball diamond and the track.

I lifted my old glove to my face. It smelled like grass and clay and neat's-foot oil and Maine. I kept walking until I found the softball team: a dozen girls walking in circles around a weedy, sloping field, heads down, occasionally stooping to pick up rocks, then throwing them into the woods. Some of them had decent arms, but most looked as if they'd have trouble throwing from second base to first.

Shirelle waved. "You're late, girl!" she shouted from across the field.

"Where do we practice?" I yelled back. I hadn't passed a softball diamond yet, though we were at the edge of school property.

She pointed down as I got closer. "Here."

"Here?" While there was some grass, it was mostly dirt and rocks and weeds—even some broken glass. No pitcher's mound, no clay infield, no bases, no backstop, no foul lines or baselines, no batter's box, no bleachers or stands, no warning track, no outfield wall, no scoreboard.

"Yeah," Shirelle said. "Every practice, we try to clean it up a little more first off."

I warmed up my arm lobbing about thirty rocks past the tree line. I also picked up a dozen shards of glass, collecting them in my glove, then jogging over and dumping them in a little pile next to a scraggly pine.

"OK, everybody," Shirelle yelled. "Two laps around, then wind sprints."

I hadn't run wind sprints, hadn't run at all, since leaving Maine. My ankle hurt right away, but I tried to ignore it. My lungs and legs burned just doing the warm-up laps. The wind sprints nearly killed me, but I wasn't the only one. Three girls quit halfway through. Shirelle yelled at them, but they stayed bent over, hands on knees, panting for air.

We partnered off to warm up our arms some more after that. I had a girl named Annie, who told me her shoulder already hurt from throwing all the rocks, so we took it easy, soft tosses and grounders, which was OK with me. Almost as soon as we started, I cut my knee on a piece of glass when I dropped down to stop a grounder, but it wasn't bad—it tore a hole in my jeans, but there wasn't much blood.

"You want to stop?" Annie asked, clearly wanting to call it a day herself. Her glasses slid down, and she pushed them back up to the bridge of the nose with her glove.

"No," I said. "Let's keep going."

Shirelle had basketball practice at four thirty, though, so after an hour she said we'd done enough for our first day. I should have been discouraged. I'd never been on such a sorry field and hadn't been around such sorry players since T-ball. But it felt good to be catching and throwing. Just the feel of the ball smacking into my glove made me smile. Even if I'd amputated my whole leg on one of those shards of glass, I still would have wanted to keep throwing that afternoon.

Shirelle and I walked out to the parking lot together. "Thanks for inviting me to join the team," I told her.

"Oh, sure," she said. "What position you want?"

"Center field."

"You got it."

"Just like that?"

"Yeah," Shirelle said. "Not much of a team, I guess."

I punched my glove. "It'll do."

• • •

The next day, just as I finished milking the goats, a familiar blue-and-white truck pulled into Aunt Sue's yard. It was Animal Control. I froze at the door of the barn, a basket of eggs in one hand, a bucket of goat milk in the other.

The same officer from before, when Book killed Dewey, stepped out of the truck—a short, chubby man with a brown uniform, his long blond hair pulled back in a ponytail. He seemed as surprised to see me there as I was to see him.

He spoke first. "I know you. You're that girl, aren't you?"

"What do you want here?" I asked nervously before he could ask me the same thing.

He pointed at the goats, who crowded around me as if they thought I needed protection. "I come to check on them," he said. "The lady that got arrested, she didn't make any arrangement for the animals. I been coming out every other day."

I knew that wasn't true. I doubted he'd come out more than once or twice since Aunt Sue and Book were arrested. I didn't say that, though. The sun was lower now, shining in my face just over the roof of the house. I shielded my eyes. "I'm taking care of them now," I said. I held up the eggs and milk as proof.

He stepped closer to the fence. "Nobody told me. And the Animal Control Office is gonna have to have something official." He glanced at his clipboard. "From Miss Allen. They got to have some kind of a guarantee from her. You got some kind of a guarantee from her? Because you could be anybody, and they have to have them a guarantee."

I should have lied, gone inside and forged a letter from Aunt Sue, *something,* but I wasn't thinking quickly enough. "What happens if you don't have that?" I asked. "I mean, I can get you something, but what if you don't have anything?"

"Then we got to take them all to the shelter," he said. "This is just temporary — me coming out here. Can't just leave them animals. They usually have to put them down. Somebody might adopt the dog, although from the looks of that one, I kind of doubt it. They don't usually put up farm animals for adoption, though — goats and chickens and such. They just take them to the slaughterhouse."

He said it like it was the most natural thing in the world. I had to fight to stay calm, to not start shouting again, the way I'd done at the boy who walked up behind me at school. I couldn't stop stammering, though, as I assured the Animal Control guy that I would get his guarantee, that he just had to give me a couple of days, that I would bring it to his office, that I would do whatever they needed me to do.

"Just get it by next week is all," he said. "You got to get it signed by Sue Allen. And you got to get it notarized, too. Don't forget about that."

I held it together until after he left, and then it hit me — a full-on panic attack that left me trembling in the barn.

I was going to have to go to the jail. I was going to have to see Aunt Sue.

twenty-four

I drove the Tundra out to the jail the next afternoon before I lost my nerve. I didn't want to say anything to the Tutens in case they tried to talk me out of going—or worse, told me I wasn't allowed to go.

The clerk at the front desk made me leave everything in the waiting room: my belt, my backpack, even a letter I found in my locker at school a week before that somebody had slid inside. I assumed it was from Tiny. On the outside, written in cramped scrawl, it said, "Please give Book Allen this if you see him. From: a friend." I probably would have been creeped out at the thought of Tiny being anywhere near my locker if the note hadn't seemed so pitiful.

When I didn't take off my hat, the clerk pointed and said, "That, too."

My heart sped up when she said it. "I can't," I said. "I need to keep it on."

She popped her gum and didn't smile. "And why's that?"

I didn't want to tell her. I hadn't talked about it with anyone except Mrs. Tuten, and that was only to convince her to call the principal's office and get permission for me to keep my hat on during school.

But I could see I didn't have a choice this time. I leaned on the counter. I had barely slept the night before, worrying so much about today. "It's to cover up one of my injuries. From the assault."

She popped her gum a few more times, then shrugged and said, "Fine."

When my time came, they had me stand in front of a locked door with no window, and when they buzzed and the lock clicked, I had ten seconds to go in. There was a bare table with two chairs, and just enough clearance for my door to open and for another door on the opposite side. There was another buzz and a click at that door, and Aunt Sue came in wearing an orange jumpsuit, followed by a female guard in a brown uniform. Aunt Sue sat in the chair closest to her door, so I sat in the chair closest to mine. The guard stood by the wall.

My hands shook so badly that I pulled them into my lap. Then I sat on them. Then I stuck them in the pockets of my hoodie and clenched them into fists. Sweat spread under my arms, and it pissed me off that I was so terrified, my mind flashing back to what happened at Craven Lake.

Aunt Sue crossed her arms and wedged her hands deep into her armpits. Then she crossed her legs and stared at the ceiling so she could let the whole world know she didn't want anything to do with me. I tapped my foot nervously. I thought about asking the guard to buzz me back out. I didn't think I could go through with this. But then I made myself look at Aunt Sue.

Her face sagged in a way I hadn't seen before. It was as if all her features were melting away. Her eyes were so bloodshot they were practically bleeding. When she uncrossed her arms, I saw that her hands were shaking, too.

"Well?" the guard said. "Y'all here to talk, or we done already?"

"Here to talk," I croaked.

The guard nodded. "Go on, then. Don't mind me."

I put my sweating hands on the cool metal table, palms down to stop myself from shaking. I said, "How are you, Aunt Sue?"

She scratched her nose, looked under her fingernails, then said, "You think I don't know why you're here? Well, it's too late for sorry. Apology not accepted."

I was too stunned to say anything at first. The guard made a noise that sounded like laughing.

"I'm not here to apologize," I said.

Aunt Sue shifted her gaze slowly down from the ceiling until her eyes were level with mine. She didn't say anything else.

"Look, Aunt Sue," I said. "I just need you to sign a thing that says I'll take care of the goats while you're in here. It's for Animal Control. Otherwise they'll take them away."

Aunt Sue laughed this time, but it wasn't a real laugh. She leaned forward. "You think I give a shit about them animals?

You think I give a shit about what you want? How much you love them dumb-ass things?"

The guard shrugged herself away from the wall. "Watch your language there, Sue," she said.

Aunt Sue waved her off. She scratched her nose again, then rubbed it. A thin streak of blood came off on the heel of her palm.

She looked at me. "Book, he already confessed to what happened. Didn't even wait for a lawyer. Just couldn't hardly wait to start talking about it. They played me the video. You seen it? You seen the video?"

I shook my head. No one had told me that Book confessed. I wondered if that meant I wouldn't have to testify in court. My heart started racing; the first thing I was going to do when I left here was call Detective Weymouth to find out.

Aunt Sue leaned forward again, quivering. "You think I still got a job anymore after this? You think you can just take a year off for jail and still keep your job? You ever think about all that before you went and screwed everything up like you did? Little bitch. Little sanctimonious bitch. You know what that word means? *Sanctimonious?* Look it the hell up. You think you're so smart. Better than everybody else. Just like your mother."

The guard put her hand on Aunt Sue's shoulder. "Stop it, Sue," she said. "Just stop. Here." She handed Aunt Sue a tissue. "You got a little blood on you right there. You better press on it to stop the bleeding."

Aunt Sue blotted her nose with the tissue. She nodded at the guard and said, "Thanks, Connie."

I was surprised. "You two know each other?"

The guard nodded and said, "From school." She didn't offer anything else.

I faced Aunt Sue again. "Why did you say that about my mom?"

Aunt Sue inspected the tissue, which had a lot of blood on it, though the bleeding seemed to have mostly stopped.

She laughed again—that same laugh from before. "You want to play with the little goats, be my guest," she said. "I'll be happy to sign a paper for the Animal Control. Only there is just this one little thing. A little problem, you might say, which is that there isn't gonna be a farm anymore, once they cut off the utilities and foreclose on the house, since I can't pay the mortgage, or any other bills. Maybe you can drive them goats yourself over to the slaughterhouse, if they don't repossess the truck first. Wouldn't that be something? And all this for what? For what, *Iris*?" She hissed my name. She glared at me. "I shit on you," she said. "I shit on all of it."

She turned to the guard. "You still party, Connie? You used to be a party girl in school. You think you can get us something in here? I'll give you my checkbook. There ought to be enough for a party. You think you can get us something in here? On me?"

Connie shook her head. "Time to go," she said in a flat voice that she probably used for every visitor. She reached under Aunt Sue's arm and lifted her halfway out of her chair. "Up we go, Sue. You and me go out first, then her."

"Wait," Aunt Sue said. "Wait just a second. Let me make little miss here a proposition, now that she's got me thinking about it." She shrugged away from Connie and sat down again. Then she turned to me.

"You want to take care of them goats, you're welcome to it. But it's gonna cost you. You got to pay the bills for as long as I'm in here. Mortgage. Utility. Truck. Insurance. You do that, you can play with them goats all you want."

I felt ill. "How can I ever do that? I don't have any money."

Aunt Sue leaned toward me. "Farmers' market. You ought to be able to pull in enough from there, now that Reba's giving so much milk. And once Jo Dee kids, there'll be more. I got enough in my checking account for November bills, unless Connie and me spend it all partying. They got my checkbook out there at the desk, locked up somewhere. I'll sign you over that, too. You write the November checks. Then you come back here at Thanksgiving with enough deposits to cover the December bills. You do all that, you can have them goats to do whatever you want with once I get out of here." She leaned back in her chair. "Or else them goats are dead."

Connie shook her head. "That's just mean, Sue. Why you want to put something like that on the girl?"

"None of your business, Connie," Aunt Sue said. "And I'm done talking to her and to you." She stood up. "That's the proposition. Take it or leave it."

I said I would take it.

After they buzzed me out, I got my belt and backpack and Tiny's letter from the clerk, then sat, exhausted and still shaky, on a bench in the waiting room. Fifteen minutes later, Connie brought out Aunt Sue's checkbook and the Animal Control letter. She'd even gotten it notarized.

I held out Tiny's letter. "Any chance you could give this to Book Allen? It's not from me. It's from his friend."

She said she would. I could tell she wanted to say something else, so I waited. "When they first brung Sue here, she told me she didn't know what came over her to have done that out at Craven Lake," Connie said. "She told me she felt really bad about the whole thing."

I stood up. "She didn't sound sorry at all just now," I said.

"It ain't easy for her being in here," Connie said, shaking her head. "It ain't easy for anybody."

The Tutens were out when I got back to their house. I called Detective Weymouth right away, and he confirmed what Aunt Sue had told me.

"Book Allen did admit to the attack," he said. "And once he did, your Aunt Sue kind of had to admit everything, too. It was either that or go into court and convince the judge that her own son is a liar. So it looks like it's all over. Just the sentencing. That won't be until next month."

I had to sit down. I should have felt relieved, but mostly I just felt dizzy.

"Was there a deal?" I asked. "A plea bargain?"

"Yes, ma'am," Detective Weymouth said. "As I understand it. Nine months for Book Allen. One year for Sue Allen. That includes time served. Usually with a sentence that length, they do the time in county jail, where they're at now. It won't be official until next month, when they have their court date and the judge signs off on it. But it's a done deal."

I didn't tell him I'd just been out to the jail, or about Aunt Sue's proposition. I just thanked him for the information, hung up, and sat stone still while it sank in. I was still sitting there at the kitchen table when Mrs. Tuten came home, and I gave her the news. I said Detective Weymouth had called to tell me while she was out. Mrs. Tuten hugged me, and I surprised myself by letting her.

"I know you must have been so worried," she whispered, as if it needed to be kept a secret. "You can get on with your life now. And put all this behind you."

She said some other kind things that made me struggle to keep from crying. It felt good to have someone hold me after all these months, and after everything that had happened. I realized that I was shaking—not much, but enough that Mrs. Tuten must have felt it, because she hugged me tighter.

She was still hugging me a few minutes later when Mr. Tuten walked in the door from work, and he gave me a hug, too, without even asking what had happened.

For a second I thought about telling them everything—about the agreement with Aunt Sue, about going out to the farm, about how I'd lied to them. But I knew I couldn't. They would be angry. Anybody would. They would report me to Mindy and Mr. Trask. They would kick me out.

So I kept quiet, except to thank them for everything they'd done. Then I went to walk the ferrets.

twenty-five

Because I'd continued making goat cheese since coming back out to Aunt Sue's, both refrigerators were already full with containers of finished cheese, not to mention several dozen cartons of eggs, so I had plenty to bring to the farmers' market on Saturday. I had to have an excuse to get away from the Tutens', though, so I told them we were having an early softball practice. Mr. Tuten offered to drive me, but I said I was happy to just ride the bike.

I ate breakfast and walked the ferrets early Saturday morning, then took off on the bike, though I only rode a couple of blocks to where I'd left the Tundra, with everything I needed for the farmers' market stashed in the back.

The Gonzaleses were happy to see me again. They even helped unload the truck and set up the stand. Isabel brought me apple slices, and wanted to play rock, paper, scissors, and dragged over a crate so she could sit next to me and be my assistant. I let her put money in the metal box and help me make change.

I spent a nervous four hours at the farmers' market, constantly looking around for the Tutens' car in case they happened to drive by. I thought I saw them once and ducked under the card table, which must have looked ridiculous, because Isabel was laughing at me when I came out.

"I thought I dropped a dollar," I said lamely—and then felt guilty when she got down on her hands and knees to help me look. I ended up slipping a dollar out of the money box and dropping it on the ground so she could find it.

Somehow, in between hiding and checking out each passing car and pretending to look for stuff on the ground, I managed to sell most of the goat cheese I'd brought—two hundred and fifty dollars' worth. I had opened Aunt Sue's bills and called the bank to double-check the balance in her checkbook. Now I calculated everything I could think of in a little notebook, and figured I would have to make at least that much each Saturday from now until Thanksgiving to cover Aunt Sue's bills. And pray that there was enough hay and grain already in the barn to get us through the winter, that nothing broke down at the farm and needed repairs, and that Aunt Sue would give up her satellite dish. The only way I could figure out to pay for gas for the Tundra was to use the allowance I got from Mrs. Tuten, which meant I'd have to stop eating lunch at school. And I needed Jo Dee to hurry up and kid so I'd have another milker available and could increase cheese production—and sales—that much more.

I felt drained by the time I packed everything up at the farmers' market, but I wasn't through yet. I had to make a quick trip out to the farm to milk the goats, start another round of cheese, feed everybody, and check on Jo Dee. I could barely keep my eyes open when I got back to the Tutens'. I was so tired that I almost forgot to hide the truck and was about to park in front of their house when I remembered. Luckily no one saw me.

"Rough practice?" Mrs. Tuten asked when I finally walked in the door ten minutes later.

I nodded. "Very."

The day should have ended there. A long shower. Dinner with the Tutens. Reading in my room. A letter to Dad.

But then I saw the Saturday paper. The Craven Ravens had lost the night before for the first time all season. They were still in the play-offs, but their perfect season was over. As soon as I read the headline, I knew who was going to get the blame.

It didn't take long.

On Monday, somebody put a three-foot black snake in my locker. It scared me, of course. A small one once bit me on the hand in an old barn back in Maine; my hand swelled up and I had to get a tetanus shot. Another time when I was with Dad on his vet rounds, we saw a six-footer eat a whole chicken.

The girl at the locker next to mine screamed until a bunch of kids crowded around. A janitor went off to find a machete so he could kill it, but I had a sort of calmness, once the surprise wore off. Dad had taught me that the best time to grab a snake was after it tried to strike, so I held up *I Know Why the Caged Bird Sings* to give it a target. As soon as it struck at the book, I grabbed it behind the head. The black snake wrapped itself around my arm, but that just made it easier to carry.

Littleberry, who I hadn't spoken to since that night at the mall before the assault, stuck his head through the crowd of kids. "Whoa, Iris," he said. "Is that a snake?"

"Yeah." I held it out toward him, and he recoiled along with the rest of the kids. The black snake hissed, and they jumped back farther.

I carried it outside and Littleberry came with me, even though I hadn't asked him to. I crossed the athletic fields, planning to let the snake go in the woods. But then when I got to the football field and thought about who had probably put the snake in my locker, and who'd been spitting on my locker, and how panicked I was every time I saw one of them, I changed my mind. I found a big Gatorade cooler in the equipment shed and slid the snake off my arm and into the cooler. Then I carried the cooler out to the fifty-yard line and turned it upside down with the snake still inside.

"Man, Iris," Littleberry said. "I can't believe you just did that. They're going to pee their pants when they lift that bucket up."

I said I hoped they did.

Littleberry followed me to my geography class, peppering

me with snake questions the whole way. I noticed that he didn't have his customary dip.

"Does that kind bite?" he asked.

"If you let it."

"Have you ever been bit by one?"

"Yeah, but only by a little one. It didn't hurt very much."

"They're not poisonous?"

"No."

I said "Bye" once I got to class and turned to go in, but Littleberry grabbed my arm. I recoiled worse than he had when he first saw the snake. His face fell. "I'm sorry," he said. "I didn't mean anything."

I shook my head, embarrassed. "I don't like people to do that," I said. "To grab me."

He apologized again. "The—the thing is," he stammered. "I mean. What I was wondering. The *thing*." He swallowed and tried again. "I just wanted to see if you maybe wanted to maybe go hang out with me again. Like we could go back to the mall. I could, like, buy you a smoothie. Or I know where they have some of those batting cages where you could hit more baseballs and stuff."

When I didn't answer right away, he shifted nervously. "You want to go do something this afternoon? After school? Hang out or something?"

I shook my head. "I can't."

Littleberry pulled his knit cap off and wrung it in front of him. "How come, Iris?" he said. "I've been trying to talk to you, and see if you want to do stuff, but you keep running away and all. I mean, didn't we have fun that one time? I know you've been through a lot. I know it was all terrible and everything, but . . ."

"But what?" I said. "What were you going to say?"

He looked away. "Nothing," he said. "Just that other people have terrible stuff, too, you know. You're not the only one."

"You have terrible stuff, Littleberry?" I said angrily. "Somebody attacked you, too? Somebody beat you up, and did *this* to you?" I grabbed the bill of my dad's cap to pull it off and show him the bald spot on the back of my head, but I stopped.

I remembered the paper he'd written in English class, and what his friends had told me that night at the mall about his dad. But that was his *dad*. It wasn't *him*. It wasn't anything like what I'd been through.

"I'm sorry," Littleberry said, for the third time. "I'm just saying. You know. Some people still want to be your friend or whatever."

I looked at him then—really looked at him, the way I'd done with Aunt Sue: his long hair and his soft cheeks, his peach-fuzz mustache, his dark eyes, the way his clothes hung off him, like hand-me-downs he hadn't quite grown into yet. He probably got what he needed from his dad's closet or the Goodwill store.

He smiled, or tried to, not quite ready to give up, though I couldn't figure out why. "Will you just think about it? And don't be all mad at me, OK?"

The geography teacher, Mr. Nichols, interrupted us. "Miss Wight?" he said. "Are you joining us for class?"

Mr. Nichols walked over to his desk. I started to follow him, but stopped. *Oh, what the hell.*

"Wait, Littleberry," I said. He was already walking away, late for his next class, but in no hurry to get there.

He turned around. "What?"

I said, "Look. OK. Here's the thing."

"Yeah?"

My T-shirt felt damp under my arms. "Tomorrow's Tuesday," I said. "I can maybe hang out tomorrow, but I can't go to the mall, or the batting cages."

He shrugged. "What, then?"

"Have you ever milked a goat?"

twenty-six

Littleberry and I met in the parking lot the next afternoon by Aunt Sue's truck. I brought a bag of Cheetos for the goats, even though I knew I shouldn't be spending the money. But I thought it might help them take to Littleberry if he fed them some. When I told Littleberry what it was for, he ran back to the school to buy more out of the vending machine. While he was gone, I realized someone had broken off the Tundra's antenna, to go along with the key-scrape. I looked around to see who might have done it, but didn't see anyone. I assumed it was one of the football players. I hoped the black snake had bitten one of them at practice.

Littleberry came back with five bags of Cheetos. We shared one on the way out to the farm, though I was so hungry from skipping lunch that I ate way more than my share.

"Will they eat the bags, too?" Littleberry asked.

"Yeah. If you let them. They'll try to get hold of your fingers, too, to lick the Cheetos dust off."

Littleberry looked at the cheesy residue on the ends of his fingers.

"Will they bite?"

"Oh, yeah. You definitely don't want them chewing on you."

Littleberry licked his fingers clean.

"I haven't been around animals much," he said as we pulled into Aunt Sue's. All the goats lined up at the fence to greet us. Huey and Louie were so happy, they started bouncing in the air. Gnarly slobbered all over Littleberry there in the backyard.

"Man," Littleberry said. "I need a shower."

"Just come on inside the fence," I said. "Let the goats have their turn at you." Littleberry pushed Gnarly away and opened the gate. He started to open one of the bags of Cheetos, but Tammy chomped it out of his hand. The other goats crowded in on him to get theirs, and in a panic Littleberry tossed the rest of the bags in the air. Tammy happily chewed on hers—Cheetos, bag, and all—off to one side while the others fought over the rest.

Huey and Louie ended up not getting any, so they turned their attention back to Littleberry—butting his legs and dancing around him. I could tell he liked playing with them. He pushed on their heads. They liked that a lot and pushed against Littleberry harder until he fell into the grass. Then they stood on him.

"Time for milking," I said when the milkers had finished their Cheetos. I helped Littleberry up, and we coaxed them into the barn. Patsy stepped right up onto the milking stand. Littleberry watched closely as I patted and massaged her udder and then squeezed long streams of milk from her teats. Loretta climbed up next.

"Can I do it?" Littleberry asked. I said OK, but it didn't go well.

First he tried to hold her steady by her teats whenever she moved, which Loretta didn't like at all. She *maa*ed and stomped at him on the stand.

"Stop," I said to Littleberry. "That hurts her. You wouldn't pull a woman around by her nipples, would you?" As soon as the words came out, my face reddened with embarrassment. "Anyway, just don't do that."

Littleberry smiled, probably embarrassed, too. "Sorry."

I refilled the grain trough, and that calmed Loretta enough that he could try milking her again. He did a little better, but not much. Mostly he just squirted milk on his pants. Then the guinea hen attacked him, pecking at his pants leg, and that freaked him out.

"Maybe I'll go play with the little goats while you finish up," he said.

I took over with Loretta after he left the barn, Jo Dee pressed to my side the whole time, then it was Tammy's turn. I could hear Littleberry back outside, running around with Huey and Louie. I let Patsy, Loretta, and Tammy out of their stalls while I milked Reba, thinking she would take the longest time, as full as she was.

Littleberry started yelling while I was milking Reba, and I ran outside just in time to see Tammy throwing him off her back. Apparently he had decided to go for a goat ride. I'm not sure how he got on top of her in the first place, but after she threw him off, she butted him hard in his ribs.

Littleberry tried to run, but Tammy chased him and knocked him down. Patsy and the others looked on passively, as if they saw that sort of thing all the time. I couldn't stop laughing as Littleberry got back up and Tammy chased him around and around the field.

"Help me, Iris!" he yelled. "Call off your goat, already!"

But he was laughing, too, and could barely run because he was gasping so hard. But whenever he slowed down, Tammy butted him again from behind.

I finally interceded, grabbing Tammy and holding her just long enough for Littleberry to run to the gate and let himself out. Tammy looked at him for a minute, then dropped her head and started grazing, as if nothing had happened.

I brought the milk buckets with me over to the back steps and sat next to Littleberry.

"Thanks," he said. "I thought she was going to kill me and eat me." Gnarly laid his head in Littleberry's lap. It seemed to be a gesture of sympathy, though he also slobbered on Littleberry some more.

"I doubt she'd eat you," I said. "Probably just your clothes."

Littleberry pulled up his shirt to check for bruises. I couldn't help looking at his smooth chest. He saw me and grinned, and I looked away quickly.

"So," I said. "Think you'd ever want to come out to the farm again?"

He tugged his shirt back down. "Yeah. But it would be good if you could bring the catcher's equipment from your softball team so I could strap it on first for protection."

After we pasteurized the milk and set up the presses, I sat down with Littleberry at the kitchen table and we snacked on crackers and goat cheese, which he said he liked a lot.

Late-afternoon sun angled in through the window, and dust motes danced around the kitchen. I spread more goat cheese on crackers and filled Littleberry's plate again, though I had some qualms about it. I was going to need all the cheese I could make to cover Aunt Sue's bills. And I was going to have to find some way to escape the Tutens' every Saturday morning to set up at the farmers' market. I got tired just thinking about it all: getting out here every day, doing the milking, making the cheese, selling enough every week at the farmers' market, hiding everything from the Tutens.

I poured us two glasses of cold well water and sat down again.

"Thanks, Iris," Littleberry said, and he took a long drink.

"You're welcome, Littleberry," I said.

He set his glass down carefully in front of him, as if he was afraid of breaking it, then scooted his chair over next to mine and held my hand. I tensed up right away, but took a deep breath and told myself to relax. He was just holding my hand. It was no big deal.

Then Littleberry leaned over to kiss me, and I had the same panicky reaction as when he'd grabbed my arm the day before in the hall.

I pulled my hand away and left the kitchen.

Littleberry followed me onto the back porch. "Iris? Are you OK? What's the matter?"

I let the screen door swing shut behind me—between us—and walked quickly back to the barn. I had to lead the goats back in and lock them up for the night.

Littleberry came through the screen door but stopped in the backyard. Gnarly must have sensed something, though, because he started barking hard and backed Littleberry up all the way to the truck, until Littleberry turned around and climbed in.

I finished up in the barn, closed up the house, and petted Gnarly for a while. I hated recoiling from Littleberry like that. I hated that I couldn't just let a boy hold my hand and kiss me.

I finally ran out of chores, or any other diversions, so I joined Littleberry in the truck.

"Sorry I took so long," I said. "And sorry about in the kitchen. I'm just not ready for anything like that, I guess."

"It's OK," he said, gazing out through the windshield. "I mean, you told me before and all. I just thought you might be more comfortable or something out here, you know?"

"Yeah," I said. I didn't know what to say after that. I started up the truck but didn't put it into gear. We just sat there while it idled.

"Hey," Littleberry said. "Remember that night I drove you out here and your aunt was shooting at that car and everything?"

"Yeah," I said. "That was pretty wild. Good thing she didn't shoot us."

"Yeah," he said. "Good thing."

We both lapsed into silence while Littleberry thought up another topic for conversation.

"So," he said after a minute. "Is this what you do with all your goat cheese? You just, like, bring boys out here and let them get beat up by your goats, and then you give it to them to eat?"

"Yeah," I said. "That's pretty much what happens."

"Really?" he said. "Because I was just kidding."

I laughed. "Me, too. I've never brought anyone out here before. You're the first."

I thought about telling him what I was really doing with the goat cheese, but the idea of confiding in him made me nervous. He seemed trustworthy, but how well did I really know him?

But I also knew I was going to need some help if I was going to keep selling the cheese at the farmers' market. I couldn't keep making up stories for Mr. and Mrs. Tuten—not without them getting suspicious about all my Saturday morning "practices," especially when it wasn't even softball season yet.

I was going to have to trust someone, and I realized Littleberry was probably my best option. My *only* option.

I eased the truck into gear and started down the gravel drive away from the farm. I cleared my throat.

"What?" Littleberry looked up expectantly.

I took a deep breath, and then said it. "Would you be interested in a job?"

"What kind of job?"

"A job selling goat cheese." I continued in a rush: "At the farmers' market downtown. Starting Saturday. I could pay you out of whatever we make. I could pay you ten percent." I told him the rest of it, too—what I needed the money for, where I parked the Tundra so he could find it to drive over to the farmers' market, why I had to park the truck there, and why he couldn't let anybody know. I kept driving and talking until the house and the farm disappeared behind us.

I stopped when we got to Cocytus Road—waiting for a car to pass before I pulled onto the asphalt, and waiting for him to answer.

I turned to look at him and he smiled. "Yeah, sure," he said. "I'll do it."

Littleberry sold another two hundred and fifty dollars in cheese and eggs that Saturday. He wouldn't take any money at first. He ended up taking twenty, but then insisted on buying us both some lunch. When I left the house at noon, I had told the Tutens I was bicycling over to the library to study. Craven County was probably the last place in America to still have pay phones, and I used one of them, at a Gulf station near the farmers' market, to call the Tutens and ask if I could go to lunch with a boy from school. Littleberry sat in the truck.

"We're happy to hear you're making new friends," Mrs. Tuten said.

"Thanks, Mrs. Tuten," I said, giving Littleberry the thumbs-up, but feeling guilty about lying to her and Mr. Tuten. But not too guilty. It was what I needed to do to save the goats.

And the part about making new friends—I guessed that wasn't a lie.

twenty-seven

Dialogue Exercise (Note to Mrs. Roosevelt: Do Not Read Aloud to Class)

Hey, Mr. DiDio.

Hi, Iris. Want some tea?

No, thanks. I just had a Snapple.

OK. So what are we talking about today? Anything been going on you'd like to start with?

Well, I had a dream about my mother last night. It woke me up.

I'm guessing it was a bad dream?

Yeah. I had a hard time getting back to sleep.

Do you want to talk about it?

Yeah. Maybe. I had it once before — the same dream. Right after what happened at the lake. The beating. Aunt Sue and Book.

What happened in the dream?

Not a lot. Just my mom calling to me from another room, calling me and calling me, and then hitting me.

You told me you saw your aunt recently. Do you think this might have something to do with seeing her again?

I don't know. Why?

Sometimes a person in your dream can be a substitute for the person you're anxious about in real life.

Oh. I don't know. Maybe. I don't really want to talk about my aunt.

Well, what do you remember about your mom? Let's start with that.

Nothing, really. I was five when she left. Dad said she hit me. I don't remember it, though. I don't remember any of it. Just what Dad told me.

Were you hurt?

I don't think so. Not like I had to go to the hospital or anything. Dad said when he came home that day, I was still telling her I was sorry, but she kept telling me *she* was sorry, and I didn't have to be sorry, that I should never say I was sorry for something I hadn't done.

Why did she hit you?

I dropped the syrup bottle on the kitchen floor. It broke.

Why did she leave?

I guess because she felt guilty. Dad said she was afraid she would do it again. That she had grown up that way, and it scared her—what she might do. But he also said she didn't like Maine. She got restless there. She had a hard time after

I was born and didn't get out of bed much. Even after she got better, she didn't really know what to do with me, so I stayed over at Grandma's and Grandpa's a lot. And Dad started taking me with him on his vet rounds, even when I was really little.

How did your parents meet?

Dad found her in the barn, like a stray animal. He went out to feed the animals one morning, and there was a girl in a sleeping bag curled up in one of the stalls. She was from here, from North Carolina, but I don't know why she was in Maine. Dad offered her breakfast, but after they went inside to the kitchen, he burned the bacon, so she said, "Here. Let me"—like she was an expert cook. Only she burned the bacon, too. She also set fire to the stove. That was one of their stories. Dad gave her a job at his office and let her stay in a spare bedroom. He was older than her, and I guess he was lonely, since he'd never gotten married. So he ended up marrying her. And then they had me.

What did she look like?

Like me, I guess. Only pretty.

Did your father try to stop her from leaving?

I'm sure he tried to stop her. But I don't really know. He never talked much about when she left. And then Grandpa got sick not too long after that, and we had to help Grandma take care of him, and then Grandma got sick after Grandpa died, so we were very busy, and I started school, and I met Beatrice, and we were always together, out doing sports, or at her house, or at my house. There wasn't much time to miss her, I guess.

Do you need a tissue, Iris?

I'm not crying. It's something in my eye.

Do you think about her very often?

Only since the dream started. I guess I did have this idea about her for a while, when I found out how sick Dad was, and then when he died. You know, the Rescue Parent. But I don't know where she is. I used to get letters every once in a while. Just newsy stuff. She traveled to a lot of places with the Rainbow People, camping out in the national parks. And she had a business making dream pillows. They're these hard little pillows that hurt your neck if you sleep on them; they have different herbs sewn inside that are supposed to make you have different types of dreams.

Do you still think of her in that way—as the Rescue Parent?

Not really. People aren't like that in real life. They don't just show up and save you.

Have you seen her since then?

Yeah. It was after she'd been gone for a couple of years. I was seven. I thought she wanted to get back together with my dad and be my mom again. She showed me how to make the pillows and said maybe we could start a mother-daughter business. But she and Dad got into a fight the second night she was there. She was gone when I woke up the next morning. I blamed Dad for a long time, but she probably only showed up because she needed money. I remember she left about twenty of those dream pillows.

What did you do?

I didn't do anything. I made coffee for Dad, and toast with jam. He liked either butter or jam, but never both. And he said he liked me to burn it first, and then scrape the burned parts off. I had been making him toast that way since I was a little kid, and he let me think that everything I did was perfect.

What about the pillows?

We burned them in the old crematorium. I accidentally breathed in a bunch of the smoke, though, and had wild dreams for weeks after that—terrible nightmares. Dad said I used to yell out in my sleep. But every now and then, I would have a nice dream about my mom, too. Every now and then, I still do.

What's a nice dream you have about your mom?

I'm three or four, and Mom lets me curl up in her lap, and it's late in the afternoon and we're sitting by the window with what's left of the sunlight, and she's reading to me, and the little bird in this book keeps asking everybody the same question—"Are you my mother? Are you my mother?" And I'm getting more and more anxious, and the little bird is getting more and more anxious, but then, finally, on the very last page, we finally get the answer we've been looking for.

twenty-eight

The next time we had softball practice, it was so cold I almost couldn't feel my hands. Neither could anybody else. Annie, our pitcher—who threw with too much arc for a fast pitch—whined about it the whole time, which got on my nerves, and Shirelle's, too, but really, who could blame her? Half the girls didn't even show up. Once my shoulder warmed up enough, I hit flies and grounders for them to field, though the freezing aluminum bat turned my fingers purple. Nobody moved much to chase anything, except Shirelle. She and I switched after a while, and then I was the one chasing down everything while the other girls just stood there shivering.

"All right," Shirelle snarled. "Fine. I get it. It's too cold."

"Well it *is*, Shirelle," said Annie. "Can we practice inside? Like in the gym?"

The other girls nodded and said, "Yeah, what about the gym? Why not in the gym?"

"Because they won't let us," Shirelle said. "We are the poor orphan team of Craven High School. Nobody wants us. So we just have to be strong and try harder."

It was meant to be a motivational speech, but Shirelle didn't sound very enthusiastic. And once she said the thing about the "poor orphan team," everybody looked at me. Or, rather, they looked at me and then quickly tried to make it look as if they *weren't* looking at me, just sort of in my direction, over my head, at the ground, whatever.

I wanted to tell them that I didn't care, that it was no big deal—anything to get past the awkward silence. Instead I said, "I have to go, anyway. I have to milk some goats."

"Really?" said Annie. I couldn't tell whether she thought that was interesting or just weird.

"Me, too," said Shirelle. "I have to milk me some goats, too."

We headed back up toward the school. "You're lying, Shirelle," Annie said. "You have basketball."

Shirelle laughed. We all did.

We trudged up the hill from our crummy field, past the football field. The football team and all their coaches were out, running their drills. They had won their first play-off game, even without Book, and had another on Friday. Nobody had spit on my locker in the past week, or left me any more snakes, or vandalized the Tundra again. It seemed strange that nothing had happened. Maybe if they kept winning, everybody would just forget about me—even Drunk Dennis.

Shirelle cupped her hands. "Oh, my God!" she yelled at the football field, as loud as she could. "Is that a snake out there?" A couple of the players stopped their drill and looked over at us, then down at the grass. We couldn't see their faces because of their helmets, but they looked nervous anyway.

We took off running. It felt good to be on a team again.

When I got to the farm that afternoon, I could tell Jo Dee was almost ready to kid. I checked the ligaments on either side of her spine near her tail, which was a trick I'd learned from Dad. They usually felt thin and hard, like two pencils, but they'd become so soft that I could barely feel them. That meant she was close to labor, maybe a day away. Her spine had sunk a little at the end as well, and the tailhead was raised—more signs I'd learned from Dad. Her teats were raw, and she kept twisting her head around and moaning, as if she was trying to talk to her baby. Her udder was shiny and tight and full of milk.

I washed her teats gently with warm, soapy water and rubbed on some Bag Balm that I found in the kitchen with the rest of Aunt Sue's goat medical supplies.

Jo Dee stayed in her stall and pawed more straw into her birthing nest while I milked the other goats and then let them out into the field. She came, too, but drifted off from the others and soon returned to the barn on her own. The next day was Saturday, so I had to load everything into the truck for the farmers' market, but it took forever because I kept going back to Jo Dee, petting her, fussing over her, hugging her, checking and rechecking all the signs. I thought she was going to cry when I had to leave.

I worried about her all night and decided to drive back out to the farm first thing the next morning. I told Mr. and Mrs. Tuten that I had to go to the library again to study and that I had softball practice after that, so I would probably be gone most of the day.

Mrs. Tuten insisted on making a bag lunch for me to take along.

"Goodness," she said. "You have turned into the busiest girl."

I threw everything into my backpack—the lunch, my softball glove, notebooks—and sprinted away on Mr. Tuten's bike. Littleberry had already come for the truck, so I met him at the farmers' market. I was out of breath when I got there. He was in the middle of unpacking.

"I need the truck keys," I said. "Jo Dee is going into labor today, and I have to get out to the farm."

Littleberry grabbed the table and carried it over to our spot next to the Gonzaleses' produce stand. I followed him with one of the heavy coolers.

"You want me to come out when I'm done?" Littleberry asked. "I could ride out on my scooter. If you're tied up with the goat, I could get the truck and come back and pick up everything."

I thanked him and said that would be great. Then I took off.

Jo Dee was nearly crazy by the time I got to the farm. I heard her bleating and carrying on before I even got out of the truck, and when I opened the barn door, she was pacing frantically in her stall. She had a faraway look in her eyes, which were bloodshot. All the others goats seemed worked up, too, except for Patsy, who was her usual calm self.

I hugged Jo Dee and talked to her and sang to her, but that only settled her down a little. I felt for the ligaments again, but they were now so soft that I couldn't find them. Her back was arched and her tailhead fully raised. A string of amber goob hung down between her legs. I'd seen it once before when I helped Dad deliver a calf. He'd said it was the amniotic fluid, and it meant labor had started. I was scared and excited—and hoped I was ready.

It was all I could do to get everybody fed and milked and let them complain in their various ways about how cold it was. I wished the sun would come out—even a cold sun, which it usually was at this time of year whenever we saw one in Maine. The morning stayed gray and overcast, though, threatening rain. I prayed that it wouldn't. The goats hated rain and would do just about anything to get out of it, but I didn't want them all in the barn while I was dealing with Jo Dee.

She started pushing an hour later, and I thought she wouldn't take too long, given how big she was. I held her, paced with her, and slathered K-Y Jelly all over my hands and arms and reached deep inside her to check the position of the kids—or what I had assumed must be the kids. I quickly realized that there was only one, though, and it was a lot bigger than the triplets had been. I couldn't imagine that Jo Dee was ever going to be able to push it out. My excitement vanished and my fear intensified.

I stayed with her in the stall, talking softly, sometimes singing, trying my best to sound calm and reassuring as she shuddered through her contractions. But the kid hardly budged.

She pushed and pushed until her knees buckled. She lay on her side and kept pushing, bleating, and panting—and getting weaker and weaker.

Then, after another hour of contractions, Jo Dee just seemed to give out. Her eyes glazed over, her bleating got fainter, and even the contractions seemed smaller. She still pushed but couldn't make much of an effort.

The other goats started getting noisy outside. Gnarly barked. A couple of the goats—probably Huey and Louie—banged against the stall door.

I pumped more K-Y into my hands and went up inside Jo Dee again. She tried to scoot away. She was so raw and inflamed; everything hurt her. I felt the kid, but not any movement. I probed all around, trying to find evidence of something, anything—a heartbeat, kicking, whatever might be there—but got nothing. The kid wasn't coming out. It had taken too long.

The same despair I'd felt after Dewey's death welled up inside me, but I knew I couldn't give in to it. Jo Dee's breathing grew shallower, and I was afraid that if I didn't do something soon, I might lose her, too.

I checked the kid's legs to make sure they were both facing forward, then I got as strong a grip as I could around the kid's neck and pulled.

Nothing happened.

"Please," I whispered to Jo Dee. "Help me. You have to push a little more. Don't give up."

But Jo Dee closed her eyes. She was done. Desperate now, I found a rope and tied a generous loop on the end, then I spread Jo Dee open as wide as she would go. I slid the loop inside her, but it slipped off when I tried to get it over the kid's legs and neck. It was five minutes more before I was finally able to cinch the rope tight enough so it would hold. I eased out my arms, braced myself again, then pulled on the rope as hard as I could. I kept pulling, and cursing, and sweating, and crying, and wishing I could shut out Jo Dee's screams. She struggled weakly to get away. The goats outside the barn all seemed to be banging against the door now to get in.

Finally the rope gave a little as the kid shifted inside Jo Dee and inched toward me. I strained harder, and the kid inched more until, at last, the legs came out. The head was jammed so tight into Jo Dee's cervix that I thought she would tear. I pulled hard, one more time, and it finally popped free. In short order after that, the cervix gave way for the shoulders, the torso, and the rest.

I let go of the rope and sagged back against the wall. Jo Dee stopped crying. She turned around, and we both just sat and looked at the kid, another billy, as it turned out. It must have died hours ago, judging by how stiff it was. What would Aunt Sue have said? "Saved us the trouble." I waited for the sadness to overtake me, but I was too tired and too numb.

Jo Dee sniffed the kid and nudged it. She seemed confused and kept nudging her baby and licking it. When the placenta came, fifteen minutes later, I wasn't grossed out the way I'd been with Reba. I laid it in the straw, where Jo Dee could eat it if she wanted, and then we were done.

I wrapped the kid in an old towel and placed it in a black garbage bag. I didn't bother removing the rope; I knew I'd never use it again. Jo Dee looked at me, moaned sadly, then looked away. I brought her water and grain. I wiped her off with another rag, cleaned her with warm, soapy water, milked her gently to ease the pressure of her swollen udder, then left her to rest.

The other goats and Gnarly looked surprised when they saw me. I guess it was all the blood on my arms and clothes. I found some rags that were relatively clean and wiped off as much of it as I could, then somehow managed to milk the nannies before dragging myself out of the barn and over to the house.

It was early in the afternoon and still cold, but I stripped off everything before going inside and stuffed all my clothes into the garbage bag with the dead kid.

Blood and viscera had already dried on my boots, and I started to throw them away, too. I'd had them since Maine, though; Dad had bought them for me. I set them on the floor just inside the back door, but shoved my socks and underwear into the bag. Then I went inside the house, got in the shower, and stayed there until the last drop of hot water gave out.

Littleberry came on his scooter while I was in the shower. He drove the truck back into town to pick up the table and chair and sign and boxes, and then drove back out again. He was very sweet to me. While he made coffee, I put on some clothes I'd left at Aunt Sue's, and then he sat with me at the kitchen table while I drank it. I must have been shivering, because he found a blanket and tucked it around me.

We counted the money from the first three weeks' worth of farmers' markets, and it looked as if we might actually make it, or at least be close. All I needed was one more good Saturday. I should have been happy, and I was, but mostly I was just exhausted and numb from delivering Jo Dee's stillborn kid.

Littleberry asked if I wanted more coffee. I shook my head. "No, thanks."

He got up to pour himself some, then sat down again. "I'm sorry about the kid," he said.

"Thanks," I said. "Me, too."

We didn't talk much after that, but I was awfully glad he was there.

twenty-nine

I was melancholy for a couple of days after losing the kid, feeling guilty for not calling a vet, wishing I'd known more and done more. Mrs. Tuten came into my room one night and sat on my bed. She asked if anything was the matter and if there was anything she could do to help. I couldn't tell her, of course, so I just said I got sad like this sometimes but I was sure it would pass. Littleberry continued to be sweet, too. He must have figured out that I wasn't eating lunch, because he brought an extra sandwich to school every day that week, and we ate together under the stairs, where I'd once hidden alone with my Fig Newtons and Snapples. I practiced with the softball team, and played with the goats, and milked them in the afternoons. I babied Jo Dee as much as I could, and all of that kept me from getting too depressed.

One night I called Beatrice. We'd let weeks slip by again without talking, or even e-mailing, which seemed to be our new pattern.

"Iris!" Beatrice exclaimed when she answered her phone. "Perfect timing. I just came in. Well, just came in from fifteen minutes of my mom yelling at me. I was out before that."

"Out where?" I asked.

"With this boy," she said. "We were just hanging out, but Mom got mad about it. These Portland guys are so much better than the ones back home. They're a lot more mature. And a lot more fun."

"Yeah," I said. "I bet." I knew she wanted me to ask about the boy, or all the boys, but I didn't. I wanted to talk about what had happened out on the farm.

She didn't give me the chance, though. "Hold on. Hold on. I have another call. I'll be right back. It's Jeremy. Another boy. I just gave him my number this afternoon."

I waited for a few minutes, but Beatrice didn't come back on, so I finally hung up. I still wanted to talk to Beatrice, just not *this* Beatrice.

A week later, the Craven Ravens lost in the play-offs. It was the Friday before Thanksgiving, an away game at Cartaret High. I heard kids talking about it the following Monday: if they hadn't gotten beat in that one regular-season game, if they'd kept the home-field advantage, if Book Allen had been able to play instead of sitting in jail for some bullshit . . .

I was anxious all day, certain that people were staring at me, whispering things, planning something worse than a black snake in my locker. Nothing happened during school, though—not until that afternoon when I was walking down the sidewalk to my truck in the student parking lot.

Drunk Dennis and his flat-faced friend, Donny, from the field party pulled up alongside me in a black low-rider Chevy.

"You happy now, bitch?" Drunk Dennis yelled out the passenger-side window. Donny was driving.

I kept my head down and kept walking, my cap pulled low, shielding them from my view—and my face from theirs. A few other kids were around, but nobody said anything. Not that I expected them to.

"I asked you a direct question, bitch!" Drunk Dennis yelled. "Are you happy now?"

I still didn't look up, so he kept shouting at me. He said that everybody knew the true story: That I made all that shit up about Book Allen. That I'd been out to get him and his mom from the start. That I was a Yankee whore.

Some boy I'd never seen before said, "Leave her alone already. *God.*"

I wanted to thank him, but I didn't want to stop walking to do it.

Drunk Dennis yelled at his friend. "Stop the car, Donny! Stop the car! I will kick this kid's ass!"

The boy took off running. Drunk Dennis and Donny laughed. They didn't stop their car, just kept cruising next to me, practically up on the curb.

I heard a high engine sound on the sidewalk behind me, like a lawn mower, and I stepped aside to let it pass, but it stopped. It was Littleberry and his Vespa.

Littleberry looked over at the football players. "Hey, guys."

"Yo, Dingleberry," Drunk Dennis said back. "You know her?"

"Yeah, kind of," he said. "I kind of have to talk to her."

Drunk Dennis hesitated. Then he shrugged. "Sure. Whatever. We were done with her, anyway."

Littleberry said, "OK, well, catch you later."

Drunk Dennis and Donny drove off, tires squealing loudly. I waited until they were out of sight before letting out the breath I'd been holding.

"You OK?" Littleberry asked.

I nodded.

He asked if I wanted a ride, and even though the Tundra was just a hundred yards farther, I threw my leg over the seat behind him and climbed on.

A minute later I slid off the back of the Vespa and leaned against the truck, not really sure I could stand up yet. I realized I'd been shaking and that I was worn out from working so hard not to show it.

"You sure you're OK?" Littleberry asked.

"Yeah," I said. "So you know those guys?"

"Unfortunately," he said. "You sort of know everybody in Craven, I guess. We went to kindergarten together. Dennis's family goes to our church."

"You go to church?"

He grinned. "Yeah. I just sort of always went from when I was a little kid."

"What were they going to do?" I asked.

"I don't think they were going to hurt you or anything," Littleberry said. "They're just mad about their football game. People are pretty football crazy around here. I used to be, too. I was the third-string quarterback on the seventh-grade team."

"Whoa," I said. "Impressive." Littleberry was full of surprises.

We hadn't made plans for him to go out to the farm that afternoon, but after what had just happened, I was happy to have the company.

We bundled up when we got to Aunt Sue's so we could take everybody out on a goat walk. None of the other goats would move until Patsy agreed to it, though, and she wasn't interested. I had to bribe her with a handful of grain. Once she started walking, the others followed, bunching up with us and crowding so close to our legs that we had to keep nudging them back so we could move. Huey and Louie danced along on their own. Gnarly, too.

"Do they always bump you like this on your goat walks?" Littleberry asked.

"Yeah," I said. "They just like to be close. Once Patsy

decides to eat, they'll all eat, though. She just needs to find something she likes."

Patsy stopped a few minutes later—almost as if on cue—and pulled a long strip of pine bark off a skinny tree that had fallen onto the trail. It flapped out of her mouth like a giant piece of taffy while she chewed. Loretta, who did everything her mother did, went second, as usual, and the rest had some, too, except Tammy. She nibbled on leaves.

Littleberry and I shivered in our coats, cold once we stopped moving.

"They're like people," he said after a while.

"You mean the way people are always eating pine bark?"

Littleberry laughed. "Yeah. There's that. But you know what I mean. Like Patsy there is the leader and everybody else is the follower, only there's the one over there, Tammy—she's like the rebel. She wants to do her own thing and not be like everybody else. The black sheep of the herd."

"Black *goat*," I corrected him. "So which one would you be? If you were a goat."

He grinned. "A Tammy. Definitely a Tammy."

"And what about me?" I asked.

Littleberry took a step away and crossed his arms. He looked at me, then nodded a serious nod. "You'd be a Patsy. I'm pretty sure."

I liked hearing that but couldn't imagine what he'd seen in me to make him say it.

Patsy got tired of the pine bark after a while, and so we

went farther down the trail until we came to a giant honeysuckle bush, which everybody attacked, even Tammy.

I looked around to make sure there wasn't any laurel or rhododendron, which were poisonous to goats, then sat on a log next to Littleberry.

"So this is what you do besides milk them and let them butt you?" he said. "Just hang out with them in the woods?"

"What's wrong with that?" I asked. "They're a lot better than most of the people I know."

"You mean like me?"

I smiled. "I'll let you know. I'm still figuring you out."

"Nothing much to figure out," Littleberry said. "I'm a professional goat-cheese merchant."

"And I'm your boss."

The goats had practically flattened the honeysuckle in their feeding frenzy. When the girls jerked hard on one side, Huey and Louie pulled back as hard as they could on the other.

I elbowed Littleberry. "So there is one thing I wanted to ask you about."

"Oh, yeah?"

"Yeah. That essay you wrote. About the head wounds."

He shifted uncomfortably. "What about it?"

"I don't know," I said. "I was just curious about why you wrote it."

He shook his head, as if he was trying to get something out. "It was just something. Nothing. I had to come up with a topic. That's all."

"But wasn't it about your dad?" I asked. "That's what your friends told me."

"It wasn't exactly about my dad," he said softly, looking down. "Just his head wound. And anyway, I don't like talking about it."

"Why not?"

"Why do you think? Because his brain is messed up from what happened. Because it won't heal up. Because he thinks my sister is my mom, and my mom is my sister. Because my mom has to tie his shoes to get him dressed. Or sometimes I have to do it. Because he just sits there and watches TV all day. Or else he spends half the time down at the VA hospital watching TV there. But you probably already heard all about that from my so-called friends."

He spat on the ground, but at least it wasn't tobacco juice. In fact, I couldn't remember the last time I'd seen him chew tobacco.

"So why *did* you write about it?"

"I don't know," Littleberry said. "Why did you write about your dad and the pet crematorium?"

My feet were cold. I stood up and stamped the ground some more and wrapped my arms around myself. "Because I miss him."

Littleberry stood up next to me and shrugged his backpack over his shoulder. "Well, I guess that's it," he said. "We both miss our dads."

Neither of us knew what to say after that, so we stood

there, quiet in the fading afternoon and the deepening cold, waiting for the goats to finish up with the honeysuckle.

We finally had to pull them away from what was left of the bush and coax them down the trail back toward Aunt Sue's farm.

Halfway to the farm, I felt the back of Littleberry's hand brush against mine. Then his fingers found my fingers, and the next thing I knew, we were holding hands for the second time.

I almost asked him what he thought he was doing, but since I wasn't sure what I was doing—letting him, holding his hand, too—I kept quiet. I liked the feel of his hand. I liked his warm touch. I liked walking with him there in the woods.

The goats followed along dutifully, tired from the walk and full of honeysuckle, ready for milking and the warmth of the barn.

Gnarly ran ahead of us, and a minute later I heard him barking wildly. Something wasn't right.

I saw it as soon as we got close enough to see the farm. There was a black low-rider Chevy parked next to my truck, and familiar voices coming from inside the barn.

It was Drunk Dennis and Donny. They had wooden kitchen matches and were taking turns flicking them off the side of the box, trying to start a fire.

thirty

"Well, hello," Drunk Dennis said when he saw me and Littleberry and the goats, standing together in the barn door. "Check this out."

He flicked a match and sent it sailing into one of the stalls. I ran past him and stomped out the fire. It was the stall where Jo Dee had delivered her stillborn kid.

"What the hell are you doing?" My heart was racing.

Drunk Dennis turned to Donny. "We must have been aiming at the wrong hay before. That other stuff wouldn't catch." Donny took the matches and flicked one right at me. I swatted it down and stomped it out, too.

"That's enough," I said. "Just quit it."

Littleberry stepped toward Drunk Dennis. The goats inched forward with him. "Y'all knock it off," he said. "This isn't cool at all."

Drunk Dennis took the matches back from Donny and flicked one at me, too. "Shut it, Dingleberry," he said. "We got business with this one, not you."

Donny grabbed a pitchfork and aimed it at Littleberry, poking lightly at his chest and backing him up against the milking stand. Donny pressed the pitchfork a little harder so the tips cut into Littleberry's jacket.

Littleberry cursed. "Damn, Donny. Fucking stop it, man."

I closed the stall door between them and me. "What do you want?"

Drunk Dennis stuck the wooden end of a match in his mouth and chewed on it. He seemed genuinely perplexed by the question. He turned to Donny.

"What *do* we want?" he said. "I forgot."

Donny shrugged, still pressing the pitchfork into Littleberry's jacket. "Burn it down, maybe?"

"I don't know," Drunk Dennis said. He plucked the match out of his mouth, struck it on the side of the box, and threw it at me. It burned out before it landed. "There's probably a law against burning down a barn or something. And you know this little bitch would tell on us."

Littleberry tried to reach for the pitchfork handle, but Donny jabbed him. Littleberry was leaning so far back, I was afraid he would fall over the milking stand.

"Leave him alone!" I yelled. "You're going to hurt him. Leave him alone."

They ignored me. "What do we want?" Drunk Dennis said again, rubbing his chin and looking up at the rafters. "What do we want?"

He looked back at me.

"I think we'll just take a goat," he said. "Maybe the one that came to school that day. We'll have a cookout with the little dude. A barbecue. They got barbecues up North?" He tossed another lit match at me. I swatted it away, but it caught dry hay and I had to stomp it out, too.

Drunk Dennis hooked his thumb at Donny. "Me and him, we're members of PETA. I bet you didn't know that. You know what it stands for—PETA?"

"Yes."

"No, you don't," Drunk Dennis said. "It stands for People Eating Tasty Animals." He laughed at his own joke. Donny did, too.

"We'll even pay you for it. We're honest gentlemen. How much you want?" he asked me. "How about a dollar? One dollar for a goat. I know you love them goats. God knows what you do with them all the way out here, all by yourself. That's why I'm offering so much money. One whole entire dollar. Come on out here and get it."

I didn't move or speak. I had to think of something, fast.

"What's it gonna be?" Drunk Dennis said. "You selling us a goat, or are we just *taking* us a goat?"

Littleberry cursed at him and struggled to stand up again, but Donny pressed the pitchfork harder, shoving him farther into the milking stand. I was afraid Littleberry was going to get hurt.

"Fine," I said finally, opening the stall door and stepping out. "You can have one."

Drunk Dennis seemed surprised at first, but then laughed and pulled out a wrinkled dollar bill. He lifted his hand toward me.

"Leave her alone, Dennis!" Littleberry yelled, but Dennis ignored him.

He tucked the dollar into my jeans, sliding his hand in my pocket and keeping it there. He pulled me toward him while feeling my leg at the same time.

I stepped back out of his reach, and seized on the only idea I could come up with.

"I'll need a knife," I said.

Drunk Dennis snorted. "Yeah. Right. Like I'm going to let you have a knife."

"How are you going to get the goat home?" I said. "Put him in the trunk of your car?"

"No way," said Donny. "I just got that car. No way."

"You want him for your barbecue, fine," I said, struggling to look as calm as I sounded. "Let me get a knife from the house and I'll slaughter the goat. I'll butcher him and bag up the meat. But then you have to leave us alone."

"I thought you loved him," Drunk Dennis said.

"I do," I said back. "Which is why there's no way I'm letting you be the one to kill him."

Drunk Dennis looked back and forth between Donny and me. I suspected that this had gone further than he had intended it to. He probably hadn't had any idea what he wanted to do when he showed up here, except to scare me.

"Keep Dingleberry out here, Donny," Drunk Dennis said. "I'll go in the house with this one to get the butcher knife."

"Get two," Donny said. "You keep one. In case she tries something."

"Yeah," Drunk Dennis said. "Right. Good idea."

Patsy and the other goats were still crowded together just inside the barn door and wouldn't let us go past. Drunk Dennis kicked at Patsy, but she lowered her head and he backed off.

"It's OK," I said. I rubbed Patsy's head and scratched under her chin. "You guys go graze. Go play. I'll do the milking in a little while. I just have to take care of this first." I didn't look at Huey.

They let us through, but then it was Gnarly's turn. He stood guard on the back steps to the house and started barking wildly and trembling, until I shushed him and told him to go. He bared his teeth at Drunk Dennis but then went to the corner of the house and stood watching as we went inside.

Drunk Dennis told me to sit at the kitchen table while he went through the drawers for some knives.

I didn't sit. "I have to go to the bathroom," I said.

"Bullshit," Drunk Dennis said. "You're going to try to call somebody."

"The only phone is right there," I said, pointing to the wall.

"You got a cell phone?" he said.

"No," I said. I turned my coat pockets inside out to show him.

He looked me over, to see if I might have any other place to hide a cell phone, and decided I didn't. "All right, go. But I'll be standing right here in case you're up to something."

"I just have to pee," I said.

"Yeah," he said. "Whatever."

I walked down the hall, but instead of going into the bathroom, I opened the closet and pulled out the .22. It wasn't loaded, but Drunk Dennis didn't know that.

I held my breath as I turned back toward the kitchen and nervously approached Drunk Dennis. It took him a second to realize what was going on. I stopped five feet away and pointed the .22 straight at his chest. His eyes widened so much they practically took over the rest of his face. His mouth moved, but he couldn't seem to say anything. I took a step toward him, and he turned and raced out of the kitchen and through the back door.

Gnarly took off after him, snapping at his heels. Drunk Dennis vaulted over the fence into the goat pen, and Patsy and the others attacked him immediately. Gnarly squeezed through the fence and joined the goats chasing Drunk Dennis into the barn.

I heard Dennis screaming at Donny—"Haul ass! She's got a gun!"—and then they both ran out of the barn. The goats and Gnarly chased them twice around the field, then through the gate. Donny stopped to open it, but Dennis just vaulted over the fence again. The chase continued over to Donny's car, where Gnarly tore off one of Donny's tennis shoes and the goats slammed their heads into Donny and Drunk Dennis as they jerked open the doors and wrestled their way inside. Huey and Louie kept butting the doors even after Dennis and Donny locked themselves in.

I stood on the back steps with the gun, trembling hard from adrenaline, or fear, or both. I had to sit down.

Littleberry stood in the doorway of the barn, shaking his head. He looked dazed.

Drunk Dennis and Donny drove off, spitting gravel out from under their tires, nearly losing the road at the first curve in the long driveway before the car righted itself and they disappeared into the trees.

The pitchfork had torn holes in Littleberry's jacket and shirt, and raked a two-inch cut across his chest. I had to coax him into the house to let me clean it. He didn't say anything the whole time, except "OK" and "Thanks." I felt vulnerable—and angry that Drunk Dennis and Donny had made me feel that way. Neither of us could talk about it just yet.

I loaded the .22 and brought it with me to the barn. I gave it to Littleberry, and he held it while I milked the goats and fed Gnarly and the chickens. Then we went back over to the house, where I hid it under the porch steps.

We were both silent on the drive back into town, except when Littleberry gave me directions to his house. He'd left his scooter at school, but he said he'd get a ride the next day with his mom. So much had happened that afternoon, I thought it should be midnight by now, but dusk was just settling in. I worried about leaving the goats and Gnarly out at the farm, but didn't know what else to do. I couldn't stay there with them — not overnight, anyway.

I pulled into Littleberry's driveway. I saw the shapes of people in the living room. There was a warm orange glow to the house. It had a red door, blue shutters, and a white fence around the small front yard.

I grabbed Littleberry's arm before he could climb out of the truck.

"You OK?" I asked.

He nodded. "*You* OK?"

I nodded, too.

He looked at me then for the first time since the barn. His eyes were watery. He swallowed and blinked. I put my hand on his cheek and kept it there.

thirty-one

Mr. Tuten wasn't back from work yet when I got home. Mrs. Tuten was cooking dinner. I walked into the kitchen and gave her a hug—my arm over her shoulder.

She smiled. The only other time we'd hugged was the day I found out Book and Aunt Sue had confessed and I wouldn't have to go to court.

"Well, *Iris,*" she said. And that was all. But she was still smiling after I pulled my arm away.

"Anything I can do to help?" I asked.

She waggled a spoon toward the laundry room. "We're a little past due cleaning the litter box and putting down some fresh litter. And Hob and Jill need their walk."

Mrs. Tuten followed me into the laundry room. I scooped up some ferret pellets so she could do her inspection. She sniffed them, sifted through them with a toothpick, stabbed the toothpick through a pellet as if it were a cocktail wiener, examined it through her glasses, and then nodded her approval.

Hob kept trying to chase cats during the walk, but Jill didn't want any part of that business, so they pulled hard in opposite directions. I needed some time away to think, though, so we did a couple of laps around the block. I couldn't tell the Tutens about what had happened with Drunk Dennis and Donny. I couldn't tell anyone, not even Mr. DiDio, who didn't know I'd gotten permission to take care of the goats. But how was I going to protect the goats and Gnarly? And how long could I keep up this secret life, anyway? The Tutens were nice people; they would be so hurt to find out I'd been deceiving them—no matter what my reasons, no matter how desperately I needed to save the animals. I had almost enough money to give to Aunt Sue on Thanksgiving to cover the December bills, but what about after that? It was getting colder. Fewer people would be going to the farmers' market. One bad weekend, one rainy Saturday, one snowstorm, one power outage on the farm—a thousand things could go wrong.

Littleberry found Drunk Dennis the next day at school and hit him in the face. Drunk Dennis was a lot bigger. Littleberry got a black eye and a bruised jaw. People who saw it said that Littleberry would have kept fighting if a couple of teachers hadn't broken it up.

I heard all about it during fourth period and rushed to find him as soon as the bell rang for lunch. He was waiting for me under the stairs.

"Are you all right?" I touched his bruised face, and he flinched.

"Yeah," he said. "I'm fine. They're probably going to suspend me, though. They called my mom. She's coming once she gets off work. I'm supposed to be going to the bathroom right now, but I wanted to see you before I go back to the office."

I sat down next to him on the dirty floor and leaned against the wall. "I wish you hadn't done it."

Littleberry rubbed the back of his right hand. "I had to do *some*thing."

"Well, you didn't help things much," I said. "You just got yourself beat up."

"I hit him a couple of times."

"Great. And now people are going to ask questions. They're going to want to know why you got into a fight with him."

We didn't say anything else for a while. Littleberry wiped his palms on his jeans, then inspected them. Then he leaned against my shoulder.

"Sorry, Iris."

I kicked at an old empty milk carton. "I guess it's OK," I said. "I appreciate you standing up for me. Just don't do anything dumb like that again."

Littleberry tried to grin, but I could tell it hurt his face.

• • •

Shirelle caught up with me after English and wanted to know about the fight.

"Dennis is telling people you pointed a gun at him, out at your farm," she said. "What's up with that? Is that why they got in the fight? And what the hell are you doing with a gun?"

I said I didn't want to talk about it, but Shirelle was persistent. "We're teammates, Iris. So tell me. If you're in some kind of trouble, maybe I can help."

"I can handle it," I said. "But thanks."

"Maybe you can and maybe you can't. But sometimes you got to let your friends help you, and they can't help you if they don't know what's going on."

She picked up my backpack and slung it over her shoulder, then we walked down the hall together. She handed it back when we got to my locker, though she didn't let go right away.

"Sometimes you just got to trust people, Iris," she said. "At least a little."

So I told her—about the deal with Aunt Sue, about hiding what I was doing from the Tutens, about Drunk Dennis and the field party and the vandalism—and about what had happened at the farm.

Shirelle was so mad, she was ready to fight Drunk Dennis and Donny herself.

"I never could stand those boys from the second I ever met them," she said. "They're not even first string. Donny, he's like the water boy or something. Dennis plays on special teams, and that's about all."

She said she'd talk to her cousin, whose name was Tyreek. She said he played tight end on offense and linebacker on defense.

"Tyreek will definitely straighten out those boys."

"But you just said he's on the football team."

"So?" Shirelle said. "They don't all think the same way about everything, you know."

"They don't?"

Shirelle shook her head. "Not Tyreek. He's no knucklehead. He went to Boys' State last year, and you have to have the grades for that." She rubbed her hands together. "Oh, yeah," she said. "I'll make sure Tyreek has a word with Dennis the benchwarmer and Donny the water boy."

Littleberry was waiting for me again that afternoon, sitting on the hood of my truck.

"So?" I asked.

He threw gravel at a spare tire mounted on the back of somebody's Jeep. "So I'm suspended for three days."

"What did you tell them?" I asked. "About why you got in a fight."

Littleberry blushed. "I just told them it was about a girl."

That made me smile, even though I was still worried. "And Drunk Dennis—what did he say?"

"Same thing. I said it first, and he did his snorting thing, but then he said it, too. I guess he didn't want them finding out he was trying to commit arson."

I didn't ask why Littleberry wasn't home or how much trouble he was in with his mom. It couldn't have been too bad if he was here waiting for me. He got into the truck before I could ask if he wanted to, and we drove out to the farm.

I did the milking and gathered the eggs and started new cheeses, then I pitchforked up old goat turds out of the barn to inspect them—the same way Mrs. Tuten examined Hob's and Jill's. They were all nice, round pellets, which meant everybody was OK. I'd been reading one of Aunt Sue's goat books, and it recommended checking the goats' eyes, too—something I remembered Dad always doing—to make sure the tissue under their eyelids was red. If it was white, that could mean the goats had parasites that were stealing nutrients out of the food they were digesting, not leaving the goats with enough for their red-blood-cell supply, making them weak and sick.

They all looked good. We wheelbarrowed the turds over to the manure pile next to the barn.

The work usually had a hypnotic effect on me, but today I stayed anxious, flinching at noises and scanning the driveway. I kept the .22 next to me while we worked and carried it along when we took the goats for another walk. Patsy and the others had been so great the day before, chasing off Dennis and Donny, that I decided to reward them by letting them forage through the woods for as long as they wanted.

We eventually made it all the way to the Devil's Stomping Ground, and I felt relieved once we got there, sure that we were safe, that no one would find us. I hadn't been there since the day I buried Dewey. I leaned the gun against a tree and sat next to the stones I had piled over Dewey's grave so no animals would dig him up and so I could find him easily whenever I came back.

Littleberry sat with me at first, but after a while he got up and started hopping with Huey and Louie. They liked it when Littleberry fell down, and butted him when he tried to get up. I draped my arm around Patsy. She let me lean on her while the boys played, and we girls all watched.

Snow started falling while we were there—light flakes, not enough to bother the goats at first. I caught some on my tongue, opened my arms, and turned my face to the sky. But the peacefulness didn't last long. The snow picked up, soon falling heavily, and the goats hated that. They huddled close to one another and *maa*ed nervously. Gnarly whimpered and whined. So we headed back home in the darkening afternoon.

As we walked down the fading trail, I thought about a winter day last year in Maine—a day I went out with Dad in snowshoes, down by a frozen creek not far from our house. We did that every week or so to look for traps people set there illegally. If we found one, we'd take long sticks and poke the center plate to make them spring shut. We had been walking for half an hour that day when we came across a bloody patch in the snow. A trail of blood led away from the creek, and we followed it. Something struggled up ahead in the snow, and we approached slowly. It was a white fox. One of his hind legs was caught inside the jagged teeth and iron jaws of the trap, which he had dragged with him for fifty yards before he collapsed.

We couldn't free him. Every time we got close, he snarled and lunged and tried to bite us. He couldn't move otherwise, couldn't crawl any farther. Blood pumped out of his leg every time his heart beat.

Dad always carried his rifle when we went out on these walks. He lifted it off his shoulder and pulled several bullets from his coat pocket and slid them into the magazine. "You should walk away now, Iris," he said. "Let me take care of this."

But I wouldn't go. I stayed next to him as he aimed and fired—twice, to be sure. We freed the body together, carried the trap back home to throw in the trash, and kept the fox with our other frozen animals until later in the winter, when we built the new crematorium.

After we got back home, Dad stared out a back window, not saying much. I remembered him coughing then, and I wondered now if that was the first time I had heard the cough, or if it had been there for a while and I just hadn't noticed before. I put my arm around his shoulder and stood there with him for a long time. I loved my dad so much right then that it made my heart ache. And now, walking home from the Devil's Stomping Ground, I loved him so much that I almost wished my heart would stop so I wouldn't have to feel that deep ache of love, and the bottomless ache of loss.

"You OK?" Littleberry asked after we shut the goats up in the barn and fed Gnarly and hid the gun back under the steps. We seemed to be asking each other that a lot lately.

"Yeah," I said, because how could I even begin to explain?

He didn't believe me, I guess, because he put his arms around me, and we did an awkward sort of hug. We stayed like that for a couple of minutes, with the snow falling harder around us, and the early winter wind picking up, until I melted, and let my head rest on his shoulder, and closed my eyes to the beautiful, terrible world.

thirty-two

Littleberry came out with me to the farm again the next day and insisted that I let him milk all the goats. It took him forever, but he was proud of himself, so I tried to be patient. The truth was I wanted the goats all to myself, but I guessed Littleberry had earned the right. That didn't stop me from standing right next to him the whole time, though, and giving him plenty of advice.

"Don't pull on Patsy's teat the way you did last time. And lock the kids in the stall or they'll go straight for the milk. And be sure to put plenty of grain in the trough for Tammy."

We had just finished and stepped outside the barn when a familiar truck pulled into the backyard. It was Tiny's. I squinted through the glare on the windshield and saw Shirelle and a black guy I didn't know squeezed together with Tiny in the cab.

There was another car behind them—a black low-rider Chevy. Inside that were Drunk Dennis and Donny.

Littleberry reached for the .22. The goats crowded the fence close by. Gnarly's fur stood up, and he planted himself in front of us as Tiny, Shirelle, and the guy—who I assumed was her cousin Tyreek—climbed out of the truck.

Shirelle waved, and she and Tyreek came right over. Tyreek was the same height as Shirelle—about five eight—but twice as broad. He had a hard look on his face, but that must have just been from squinting to see us through the afternoon sun, because it softened when he smiled.

"You Iris, right?" he asked, pulling a knit cap over his shaved head.

I nodded warily, wondering what they were doing here.

"Nice to meet you," Tyreek said.

Then he turned to Littleberry. "I've seen you around school. Your name Doogleberry? Something like that?"

"Littleberry," he said, shaking Tyreek's hand.

Tyreek asked what the gun was for.

I pointed at the black Chevy, and Littleberry swung the barrel over that way, too. Dennis and Donny still hadn't gotten out. Tiny stood next to his truck, wearing his short-sleeved football jersey, but no jacket or hat. He gave me a shy wave.

"Why is *he* here?" I asked Shirelle.

She shrugged. "Muscle?"

"Yeah," said Tyreek. "Them boys—I call them Thing One and Thing Two—they needed a little persuasion to come out here and make things right. So I got Big Man in on the job to help me."

"Tiny?" I said.

"Big Man. Tiny. Same-same," Tyreek said. He waved Tiny over. "You can put down that rifle," he said to Littleberry. "He's all right."

Tiny lumbered toward us as far as Gnarly but stopped there. Gnarly growled. "Hey, Iris," he said. "We brung out Dennis and Donny. They come to apologize. There ain't going to be no more trouble."

I didn't know what to say. Tiny studied his shoes. Then, not looking at me, he said, "That was me left them letters in your locker for Book. I don't know if you knew that or not. I got a letter back from him in the jail, but they won't let me visit. I guess I could of just mailed him my letters instead of leaving them for you at your locker, but I didn't think to ask. Thanks for bringing them in. I know what he done to you was wrong, and he sure is sorry for it."

He glanced up under his hooded eyebrows to see how I was taking what he said, then went back to memorizing the details of his shoes.

"All right, then," Tyreek said. "We got that out of the way. Time to party."

He pointed to Donny's car and wiggled his finger. "Things!" he shouted. "Yo!"

Drunk Dennis and Donny crawled out of their car.

Tyreek turned back to me. "You got anything to put down over their car seats, and maybe the trunk? That would be great if you did. And if you got a couple of shovels, too, the Things would appreciate it."

"I have a roll of Visqueen in the barn," I said. "And shovels. Why?"

"Oh, just a little something we got planned."

I went for the plastic and the shovels, the goats buzzing around me the whole time. When I came back out of the barn, Donny had backed his car over to the manure pile.

Littleberry stood off to the side with Tiny and Shirelle, all of them grinning huge grins.

Tyreek was laughing. "Thing One and Thing Two—they volunteered to take some of your goat poo off your hands."

Tiny giggled. "You don't mind, do you? It's for my mom's garden. I didn't want to get it all over my truck, so they said why not load it in their little car to bring over to my house." He giggled again.

"Yeah," said Tyreek. "Kind of like how you volunteer for community service instead of going to jail, or having your ass beat and your coach told about what you did—shoving around a girl, trying to burn down a barn—so you get kicked off a football team next year."

I smiled—still a little wary—and said they were welcome to take as much as they wanted. The turds were mostly dry, pinkie-size pellets. They didn't smell especially good—kind of musty and grainy—but they didn't exactly stink, either.

"If you're going to fill up your car with manure, you could

do a lot worse than goat," I said. "You can probably just vacuum afterward."

It took them fifteen minutes to fill up the trunk and the backseat. There was still plenty left.

"What about the front seat?" Tiny said. "They could sit on some of it. Hold it in their laps."

Tyreek seemed to be considering the idea. Dennis and Donny both looked like they were ready to cry.

"That's OK," I said. "That's probably good enough. Just make them promise not to ever come out here again."

Tyreek looked over at Dennis and Donny. "Well? What about it, y'all?"

"Yeah," said Tiny. "Y'all learned you a lesson or what?"

Dennis and Donny nodded. Neither had spoken a word since driving up to the farm.

"All right, then," Tyreek said. "Y'all can take your dookie and go. I just got to get a picture first. Y'all stand right over next to the car. Leave the trunk open."

They all pulled out their cell phones—Tyreek, Shirelle, and Tiny—and snapped pictures of Dennis and Donny and the car.

"You want one, Iris?" Shirelle asked.

I shook my head. "Just one more thing, though," I said. I walked over to Drunk Dennis and tucked a dollar into his shirt pocket.

"You can have this back," I said. "I'm keeping the goats."

thirty-three

The following Thursday was Thanksgiving, and the Tutens surprised me with a tofu turkey—a Tofurky. Everything else was the same as a usual Thanksgiving dinner, except the no-meat gravy. Another surprise, or sort of a surprise, was Aunt Nonny, Mr. Tuten's great-aunt, a tiny woman who was ninety-four. She lived in a retirement home called Cravenwood. She kept calling me Alice. I tried correcting her, but she had her mind made up.

"What year are you in school now, Alice?" she asked at one point. I was keeping her company in the living room, waiting for dinner to be ready.

"I'm Iris," I reminded her.

Aunt Nonny looked at my face, her eyes blinking behind her thick glasses.

"You're Alice," she said firmly.

Mrs. Tuten walked in, and I looked at her. "No, Aunt Nonny," Mrs. Tuten said. "She's Iris. Remember?"

Aunt Nonny turned to Mrs. Tuten. "Well, don't ask me."

"Don't ask you what, Aunt Nonny?" Mrs. Tuten said.

Aunt Nonny shook her head. "Never you mind."

Mrs. Tuten turned to me and whispered, "She gets a little confused sometimes."

Aunt Nonny wasn't having any of it, though. "It's not polite to whisper!" she barked.

Mr. Tuten intervened. "Time to sit down, Aunt Nonny," he said. "Time to come and eat."

Aunt Nonny eyed him suspiciously. "What are you serving?"

"It's Thanksgiving dinner," he said. For some reason Mr. Tuten was wearing Mrs.Tuten's apron, the one that said, *What part of IT'S MY KITCHEN don't you understand?*

Hob and Jill raced into the room and careened off all of our legs, including Aunt Nonny's.

"Rats!" she yelled. "Rats in the house!"

Mr. Tuten took her arm and practically dragged her into the dining room. "They're ferrets," he said. "Not rats."

Aunt Nonny didn't miss a beat. "Lock 'em up!" she said. "Before they eat the rats! Lock 'em up tight!"

Mrs. Tuten filled Aunt Nonny's plate with potatoes and creamed onions and green-bean casserole. Then she added a wedge of Tofurky with no-meat gravy.

Aunt Nonny clutched my forearm with her thin, veiny

hand. "What is this we're having tonight?" she asked, looking down at the Tofurky. "Is this some kind of a pâté? A liver pâté?"

"It's still daytime, Aunt Nonny," Mr. Tuten said. "And that's called a tofu turkey."

Aunt Nonny ignored him. "Watch out for the boys," she said to me. "Boys will try to get you. That's all they want to do is to get you. How fast do you run? I mean today? How fast do you run? You have to run fast when it's time."

Mrs. Tuten tucked a napkin in Aunt Nonny's lap.

Mr. Tuten nudged the Tofurky, maybe to see what it would do. It didn't do anything.

Aunt Nonny fished up some potatoes and a creamed onion. "That's quite a lump," she said. "I don't care for lumps." Mrs. Tuten scraped the creamed onions off Aunt Nonny's plate but left the potatoes.

"Much better," she said. "Now, Harry? Harry? When is your mother coming over?"

Harry was Mr. Tuten. I'd never heard his first name before. Mrs. Tuten always called him Mr. Tuten. He finished chewing whatever he had in his mouth, swallowed, then said, "Mother said to tell you she's sorry she can't make it, Aunt Nonny. She's not going to be able to come today."

Then, under his breath, he added, "Since she's *dead*."

I laughed so hard that I choked on my Tofurky. Mrs. Tuten raced into the kitchen to get me a glass of water, and Mr. Tuten jumped out of his chair and pounded me on the back. Hob and

Jill, who'd been hiding under the table, came out to look and started dooking like crazy. Aunt Nonny held out her plate to no one in particular and said, "More lumps."

Once she finished eating, and talking about dead people who she thought were still alive, Aunt Nonny wanted to watch football. She said she liked the Dallas Cowboys, and if they weren't on, somebody was sure going to hear about it from her. She was all ready to make some serious trouble for the networks, but we found a channel with the Dallas game, so everything turned out OK. She fell asleep after about a minute. Mrs. Tuten found three creamed onions in one of the pockets of Aunt Nonny's dress.

After we had Aunt Nonny cleaned up, I asked if I could borrow one of the Tutens' cars. They had let me take it a couple of times before, for quick trips to the grocery store. I was hoping they wouldn't mind.

"I thought I would go to the jail," I said. "Since it's Thanksgiving. To see my aunt."

Mrs. Tuten's mouth dropped open in surprise. "Are you sure, Iris?" she asked.

I told her I was. I said that Aunt Sue was the only family I had left, and I thought I should at least try to visit her. I couldn't tell Mrs. Tuten that I had to show Aunt Sue the check register for all the bills I'd paid in November, and the farmers' market deposits to prove I'd earned enough for the December bills.

"Just be careful, Iris," Mrs. Tuten said as I loaded a couple of Thanksgiving dinner plates into the car.

Mr. Tuten put his hand on my shoulder and handed me his cell phone. "You can call us if you need to."

Dad and I never had the traditional Thanksgivings like other people did—not after Grandma and Grandpa died. I thought about that as I drove to the jail. Instead we went out for Chinese. The first few years we had to drive all the way down to Portland, but once they opened the Panda Palace, out next to the L.L. Bean outlet, we stayed in town. We ordered three meals: one for him, one for me, and one for my mom. Dad and I got the same thing every year: Peking duck for him, *moo shu* vegetables for me. I don't remember when I started ordering for Mom. For months after she left, I set a place for her at Grandma's and Grandpa's until Dad told me it was making everybody uncomfortable and I had to stop.

He didn't say anything about the Chinese, though, even though neither of us ever ate it and it just went to waste. I don't know why I did it, exactly. I think I had it in my head when I was little that Thanksgiving was the time of the year when people might come home after being gone, even if they'd been gone for years. After a while it just became a habit, a part of our ritual, even after I stopped expecting Mom to show up.

Last Thanksgiving I didn't order for Mom at first. Dad ordered his Peking duck, and I ordered my *moo shu* vegetables, and then I didn't say anything else. Dad kept looking at me, and the waitress just stood there, pencil hovering over her order pad.

"Are you sure you don't want anything else, Iris?" Dad asked.

"Yes, yes," the waitress said. Her name was Sally—her American name, anyway—and she knew us. "You want other order, too?"

I finally said OK, how about just some eggrolls this time. Sally wrote that down.

Dad and I kept them in the refrigerator for three weeks before one or the other of us got around to throwing them away.

It wasn't a regular visiting day at the jail, but I was hoping they'd relax the rules because it was a holiday. I got lucky: Connie, the same guard from last time, was on duty and convinced her supervisor to let me in. They let me bring in the plate of food for Aunt Sue, too, after they inspected it. They said they'd take the other plate to Book.

"What'd you say that was again?" the supervisor asked.

"Tofu turkey. Tofurky."

I knew they remembered what it was called; they just thought it was funny and wanted to hear me say it again.

The Aunt Sue who walked into the visiting room was smaller than the one I'd lived with out at the farm. She was smaller than the Aunt Sue I'd visited several weeks earlier.

Connie had her hand on Aunt Sue's back as they walked in, and I almost had the sense that Connie was carrying her. I breathed easier at first, seeing her looking so weak and vulnerable. But the old Aunt Sue reemerged as soon as she sat down and I offered her the Thanksgiving dinner.

"They already fed us ours," she snapped. "Don't expect a thank-you, because I didn't ask for it, either."

Connie pointed. "It's Tofurky, Sue. You ought to try you some. I bet you never had any of that."

Aunt Sue twisted up her mouth; I thought she might spit, but she didn't. She untwisted her mouth and looked at me with dull eyes. She wore the same orange jumpsuit, or one just like it, with the words *Property of Craven County Jail* stenciled on the front.

"What do you want?" she said.

I wiped my sweaty palms on my jeans. "I have the deposit slips. For December. For the bills. And what I paid out in November."

Connie had let me bring the checkbook into the visiting room. I laid it on the table between us. "Here it is."

Aunt Sue picked it up and examined every entry. Then she went through the register a second time. Then she looked up at me.

"Now I guess you got to go to work on the January money."

She stood up and gestured to Connie that she was ready to leave. "You want to keep them goats, I expect to see the same thing all over again by Christmas."

I was already tired just thinking about it, but underneath all of that I was happy—joyful even.

I'd saved the goats for another month.

On the way out of the jail, I asked if I could see Book. I hadn't planned to. I was still afraid of him, but I also remembered him crying out at the lake and begging Aunt Sue to let him stop.

He wouldn't look at me when he came into the visiting room—a different one from the one I'd been in with Aunt Sue; Book's was on the men's side. He crossed his arms and tipped back in his chair and stared at the ceiling. His face was puffy, and he'd put on weight. He didn't say a word at first. I felt nauseated just seeing him, and suddenly wished I hadn't come. I reached into my pocket and pulled out a letter from Tiny, who still left them in my locker, probably out of habit. The guard, whose badge said *Smith,* stepped forward and grabbed the letter before I could pass it on. He opened it, read it, stuffed it back in the envelope, and then handed it to Book.

"I guess he can have this," Smith said.

Book chewed on his bottom lip. He cupped the letter between his hands. Then he started crying, although he didn't make any noise—just tears slipping down his cheeks and falling on the table. He looked back up at the ceiling.

Then, in a faint voice, so faint I almost didn't hear it, he said he was sorry.

I stared at him, though he still didn't look at me.

I thought about him being in jail for the next several months. I thought again about him crying out at Craven Lake and begging Aunt Sue. I started to feel sorry for him, just for a second. And then I thought about him not stopping until she finally said he could.

"OK, Book," I said. "I've gotta go."

I wished Littleberry was around, but he'd gone to Raleigh with his family to visit his grandparents, so I made a quick trip out to the farm, then went back home to the Tutens'.

Mr. and Mrs. Tuten were watching an old movie, *To Kill a Mockingbird*. I'd seen it before with Dad. It was one of his favorites. Aunt Nonny was back at the nursing home.

Mrs. Tuten scooted over to make room for me on the couch. "Would you like to watch with us, Iris?"

I surprised myself by saying yes. It was the first time I'd done anything like that with them. I was tense at first. It didn't help that Mr. and Mrs. Tuten both had ferrets in their laps. But I must have relaxed after a while, because I fell asleep around the time Scout put on her ham costume for the school play. When I woke up, hours later, the lights were off and I was stretched out on the couch under a warm blanket. Someone had tucked a pillow under my head. Someone had even taken off my shoes.

thirty-four

I'd seen plenty of diarrhea before, on vet rounds with Dad, but nothing like Huey's. I noticed it as soon as I got to the farm the next afternoon. I had told Mr. and Mrs. Tuten that I was going to a movie with Littleberry; they didn't know he was still out of town. My hands shook badly as I tried to hose Huey off, but the diarrhea just kept running down his legs. The nannies huddled away from him at first; Louie danced around as if it was some sort of game.

Then Huey started staggering. He weaved his way into the field, but then veered back. It was clear that he didn't know where he was going. He stumbled into the side of the barn.

"Huey!" I shouted. "What's the matter, boy? What's the matter?"

He walked in a circle next, his head turned back toward his left flank, as if he couldn't move it anywhere else. He kept circling in that direction, around and around, head turned, diarrhea running out behind him almost constantly.

I chased after him, frantic with worry, and tried to hold him still. I reached my hand under his chin to lift his face and check out his eyes. He felt hot; his eyes were dull and cloudy. He looked right at me, but I could tell he didn't see me.

"I'm here, Huey," I said, hoping he could still hear my voice.

He dropped to the ground and started convulsing.

"Huey!"

I dropped down beside him and held him until the convulsions subsided. The ground was cold and damp, and soaked through my jeans. Huey's neck was rigid, with his head still turned back. I tried to straighten it but couldn't. He moaned.

"What's the matter, Huey?" I kept saying. "What's wrong?" Gnarly and Patsy and the rest of the goats crowded around us in a protective circle, including Louie, who had stopped playing.

"Huey!" I yelled his name one more time, but he still didn't respond. The diarrhea continued, even as he lay there. He seemed paralyzed.

The November sky darkened. There hadn't been sun all day, and the late afternoon threatened to turn into night much too soon.

Huey was shivering now. I ran into the barn for a blanket and brought it back outside. I wrapped him in it, scooped him up, and carried him into the barn. I laid him in clean straw. Patsy and the others followed us.

"Just wait here," I said to Huey. I turned to Patsy. "You watch out for him, OK? I'll be right back."

I ran over to the house, wishing someone was there to tell me what was wrong, to tell me what to do. But who was I going to call? My dad? Aunt Sue? The Tutens? Littleberry? I fumbled through Aunt Sue's goat-care guide, the one I'd been reading, but couldn't find anything that helped. I stared at the phone, as if I expected it to tell me what to do, struck by how completely alone I was. I tapped myself on the forehead with the receiver. I had to think of something. I *had to*. I'd lost Dewey, and Jo Dee's kid. I'd lost Dad. I'd lost Beatrice. I couldn't lose anyone else.

I kept tapping, harder, until my head finally cleared and I did the obvious thing—I grabbed the phone book. It was several years old, but probably still good for most numbers. The first two vets didn't answer, but I jotted down their emergency numbers in case I couldn't reach anyone now. The third number just rang and rang and rang.

"Come on! Come on!" My fingers shook as I dialed.

An old man answered at the fourth number I called.

"This is the Herriot residence."

I sagged against the counter in relief.

"I have an emergency," I said. "Can I speak to the vet?"

"I'm the veterinarian," he said. "But I'm retired." I strained to understand him through his thick southern drawl.

"Please," I said, "can you help me anyway? My goat is sick, and none of the other vets are answering. It's an emergency."

"Well," he said, "all right. What's the problem you have?"

I described all of Huey's symptoms.

"How old is your goat?" he asked.

"A couple of months."

"Uh-huh, I see."

"So can you come out here?" I said. "Please? I'll pay you." Though I had no idea how I would do that.

"How old are you, young lady?" he asked.

"Sixteen."

"And is there someone else there?"

"It's my aunt's farm, but she's not here."

"Is she coming back soon?"

"No," I said. "She's not here. She can't be here. Nobody's coming."

He said, "Well, OK, then. We'll just have to handle this ourselves. From the sounds of it, it's one of two things, and probably it's goat polio."

I sat down on the kitchen floor, deflated. *Polio . . .*

"That's the better diagnosis, actually," Dr. Herriot said. "If you get to it in time, you can treat goat polio. If it's the other thing—listerosis, which is a bacterial infection and needs antibiotics—we've got a tougher situation."

I leaned back against a cabinet, the handle digging into my side. "So what do I do?"

"Goat polio is a thiamine deficiency. Does your aunt have any thiamine? If you're raising goats, you likely have some in the house. Go look wherever you have to look. I'll wait on the phone."

I slammed open the doors to Aunt Sue's goat paraphernalia cabinet, riffling through it all—bottles of stuff, books and pamphlets, cheese-making equipment—until I found what I was looking for. A large bottle with a dropper. I raced back to the phone.

"Got it!"

"All right," he said. "Good. Good. Now, here's what we do. Write this down. You have a pencil? Write this down."

He gave me the dosage for Huey's weight—which I estimated, but it was the best I could do. He said I had to give it to him every six hours over the next twenty-four.

"If you're going to lose him, it'll be a day to three days after the onset," he said. "If he's going to improve, you might see it in just a couple of hours, but you might not. You just have to stick with him, give him his doses when they're scheduled."

"He looks so bad," I said, twisting the phone cord. "I don't think he can even see me anymore."

"That's blindness. That's a symptom, too," Dr. Herriot said. "But even that can clear up. You just have to wait and see."

"But what caused it?" I asked, worried that the other goats might get sick, too.

"Moldy feed. Moldy hay. Too much grain," he said. "Your goat needs plenty of free-choice roughage, which is where he gets his thiamine. Too much grain, not enough of the other, that's your recipe for goat polio."

I knew I should get back to Huey, but I was afraid of getting off the phone—afraid of being alone.

"Is there any way you could come out?" I asked again. "Please?"

"I'm truly sorry, but it takes me too long to get anywhere these days," Dr. Herriot said. He sounded tired just from our phone conversation. "You just call me when you see improvement."

"I understand," I said. "Thank you. I'll call back." And I hung up.

Huey lay on his side, twitching, but not convulsing the way he had been before. Drool puddled under his face. I had to turn his body up so I could work the dropper into his mouth and squeeze the thiamine down his throat without him drooling it right back out. He managed to swallow it, and I yelped with excitement. Patsy went back outside to be with the others, but Louie kept running in and out of the goat door.

I held Huey's head in my lap and told myself again that I couldn't panic just because something was wrong. That didn't help anything. And stuff was going to happen. It was a farm. They were goats. They ate stuff they weren't supposed to, or ate too much of something. I'd given them too much grain because I was so happy to see them, and happy to be with them, but that was stupid. I should have known better. And there wasn't much roughage left in the field. The goats had stripped most of the saplings, pulled up most of the grass and weeds, stood as tall as they could with their front legs against the fence, or against any tree, to get at every branch and leaf they could reach. I should have been taking them on more goat walks. Winter was coming. I had to figure things out.

There were a hundred things to figure out. And the feed and the roughage were just two of them. The most pressing, though — the one I'd been trying not to think about — was that I was going to have to confess everything to the Tutens. I had to stay with Huey, see him through this, keep giving him the thiamine, reassure the other goats and Gnarly. I couldn't leave. But the Tutens were expecting me home any minute.

Huey seemed calmer now — asleep or unconscious or in a trance. I hugged him, kissed him on his long, sloping nose, then slid out from under him. His breathing had softened. I just needed to get through the next six hours, hope he'd hang on, and give him his next dose. And then the six hours after that. And the six hours after that.

I coaxed the nannies into the barn one by one for milking: Patsy, then Loretta, then Jo Dee, then Reba, then Tammy. I thought about Littleberry trying to climb on her for a ride the first time I brought him to the farm. I wished he was here now.

I finished the milking and gathered half a dozen eggs from the roosts out of habit. It had gotten dark out, well into night. Gnarly and I shepherded the goats into their stalls and chased the chickens inside as well. I fed everybody, checked on Huey, who was still breathing in the same soft way, then went in the house to call the Tutens.

thirty-five

Mrs. Tuten listened on the phone while I explained the situation, including the agreement with Aunt Sue. I expected her to be furious, but she wasn't. She just said, "I see." I tried to apologize but she cut me off: "No time for that right now."

They drove out to Aunt Sue's right away. Gnarly went crazy barking and snarling when he heard them on the long gravel driveway, and I had hold of his collar and was shushing him by the time they pulled up to the house. Huey's condition hadn't changed from the first dose of thiamine; he still lay on his side, unresponsive. Louie hadn't been able to settle down yet in the barn and just wanted to stay near me, so I'd let him follow me out to collar Gnarly and greet the Tutens.

Mrs. Tuten got out of the car and knelt down by Louie. She ignored Gnarly; I wondered if she didn't like dogs, since they tended to lunge at her ferrets during their walks.

"Is this him?" she said. "Is he all better?"

"No," I said. "This is his brother, Louie. Huey's in the barn. He's still sick."

Mr. Tuten lifted a wicker basket and a small cooler out of the backseat of their car.

"We brought dinner," Mrs. Tuten said. "It's only leftovers, but it will have to do. Mr. Tuten, would you be kind enough to take everything inside the house?"

Louie rubbed against Mrs. Tuten's thigh, and she patted his head, which he likely didn't even feel. I was pretty sure she'd never touched a goat before. Mr. Tuten headed for the back door with the basket and the cooler. Mrs. Tuten stood up, though she kept her hand on Louie's head.

"Now," she said. "Let's go see this sick goat of yours."

I had my sleeping bag, but Mrs. Tuten made Mr. Tuten drive back into town to get his summer hammock for me to use in the barn. I argued with them—or actually with her. I'd slept in the barn before; I didn't mind; I just had to stay close to Huey. But Mrs. Tuten insisted.

"There are mice in that barn," she said. "I heard them. And I can only imagine what other sorts of vermin."

"You just heard the chickens," I said, but Mrs. Tuten wouldn't listen. Mr. Tuten drove off while we washed the dishes from dinner, which had been vegetable medley and pork chops again.

When we finished, Mrs. Tuten put her hands on her hips and looked around, as if she'd been too busy to fully inspect

Aunt Sue's house until now. "It could certainly use a good cleaning."

Mrs. Tuten said she thought it best if she and Mr. Tuten spent the night, since I was going to be out in the barn with Huey. And they *were* the foster parents. I knew there was no use arguing with her about it, or about much of anything. I was still waiting for her to be angry. She probably was, but she seemed to be one of those people who turned helpful in a crisis. As long as the crisis lasted, I figured her anger would stay in check.

Mr. Tuten helped me tie the hammock up in the barn. It had gotten colder, and a late-autumn wind whistled through cracks in the walls. I pulled on my hoodie and down jacket and a pair of insulated jeans I hadn't worn since the winter before in Maine. Dad had had a pair just like them. Louie finally settled down and went to sleep with the other goats. Patsy lifted her head at any noise we made, just checking on things.

Mr. Tuten had to get up early for work in the morning, so around eleven he went upstairs to sleep in my old room. Mrs. Tuten stayed up to help me give Huey his second dose of thiamine. She shivered the whole time—she only had a thin jacket on—so I promised her I would crawl into my sleeping bag in the hammock if she would go back inside the house and go to sleep on the sofa, which she did.

I sat up with Huey for a long time after that, though. I turned off the overhead bulb so it wouldn't disturb the animals, but I had a battery-powered lantern of Aunt Sue's that I kept on so I could still see. I sang some songs to Huey that my dad used to sing to me. Not lullabies this time, but old songs like "Me and Bobby McGee," and "Teach Your Children," and this strange one by Neil Young called "After the Gold Rush," part of which was about getting on silver spaceships and leaving Earth.

Huey shifted in my lap—not much, more like stretching out, then relaxing. His neck wasn't so stiff anymore, and his head wasn't turned so hard and rigid toward his flank. Maybe it was a sign that the medicine was working. "Huey?" I whispered. "Can you hear me? Hey, little guy. Are you there?" He seemed to relax a little more in his sleep, or coma, or whatever it was, and I finally crawled into my sleeping bag in the hammock and fell asleep.

Mrs. Tuten came back out to the barn what must have been hours later. The squeaky barn door woke me, but it took a few minutes to remember where I was—bound up in the hammock, with my sleeping bag so twisted around me that I thought I'd never be able to pull myself out. I'd left the lantern hanging on a nail, on a post next to Huey's stall, and could see Mrs. Tuten in the dull light of it—wrapped in one of Aunt Sue's blankets, sitting in the straw.

"Mrs. Tuten?" I said, still trying to get free of my bag.

"Oh, don't get up, Iris," she said, her voice low and husky, from either deep sleep or lack of sleep. I had a feeling that she might have insomnia a lot of nights, though I'd never actually seen her up late before. It was just the way she always seemed to be tired, sometimes staring off at nothing when she didn't know anyone was around.

She said, "I came out to check on things. Are you all right? I'm sorry to wake you up."

"It's OK," I said. "You didn't wake me up. It's time to give Huey his next dose." I squinted to look at Mr. Tuten's watch, which he'd let me borrow. "In about an hour."

I finally made it out of my sleeping bag and tumbled onto the barn floor. Then I crawled over to Huey's stall with Mrs. Tuten and sat in the straw next to Huey, who seemed to be snoring. I'd never heard a goat snore. It was kind of a muttering, spitting, whistling sound.

"You really should go back to sleep, Iris," Mrs. Tuten said. "You could go inside the house, where it's warmer. I can wake you up when it's time for the medicine."

"That's all right, Mrs. Tuten," I said. "I'd be too worried about him, anyway. I was hoping he'd be better by now."

"He will be soon," Mrs. Tuten said. "I'm sure he will."

I didn't say anything. I'd learned the hard way that things didn't get better just because I wanted them to.

I thought Mrs. Tuten had nodded off to sleep, wrapped in her blanket in Huey's stall. But then she started talking.

"My mother," she said, "would have died to know I was sitting here in a barn like this."

"How come?"

"Oh, she was very, very proper," said Mrs. Tuten. "And she liked a neat house. I had to wear skirts or dresses at all times in public, and anytime I sat down on the floor, I was expected to fold my legs back to the side, like I'm doing now." She stroked Huey's neck. "And we did not have pets. We weren't really around animals at all that I can remember."

"None?"

"We did go to a petting zoo once. And there was a picture of me when I was three, sitting on a pony at a birthday party." She stopped talking, but I could tell she wasn't through.

She unfolded her legs and pulled her knees up in front of her. She hugged them and clasped her hands together to hold on. "Mr. Tuten and I were determined that when we had our daughter, she would have lots of animals," she said. "Dogs and cats and fish and hamsters. Whatever she wanted. We fenced in the backyard, but we never did have the animals. Except Hob and Jill, of course. But they came much later."

"Your daughter didn't want pets?" I asked tentatively, a bad feeling in the bottom of my stomach. They had never mentioned any children. There were no pictures of a daughter in their house, or none that I'd seen.

"Alice," Mrs. Tuten said. "I always thought that was the prettiest name. I think it confused Aunt Nonny at Thanksgiving, seeing you there. She thought you were Alice, all grown up. I'm sorry about that."

"It's OK," I said. "Alice *is* a pretty name."

Mrs. Tuten nodded. "I know it's an old-fashioned name — it was even then — but I did always like it."

"My mom and dad felt the same way about my name," I said.

Mrs. Tuten smiled. "I like your name. Very much," she said. "Iris is my favorite flower."

"My dad said he liked it because Iris was the messenger of the gods," I said. "She traveled between heaven and earth on a rainbow." I wasn't sure why I was telling her that. I stroked Huey's neck the way Mrs. Tuten had been doing, first down, toward his shoulder, going with the direction of his hair, then back up so I felt the bristly ends. It reminded me of running my hand over the carpet in Mr. DiDio's office.

"We just liked the sound of *Alice,*" Mrs. Tuten said.

"Where is she now?" I finally asked.

Mrs. Tuten had that look I saw on her when she thought she was alone. "We only had her for a few days," she said. "She was so tiny and so frail. She was in such a hurry to meet us that she came out too soon. They tried everything to stop her, to stop the early contractions. And then they tried everything to keep her alive. We got to hold her only once while she was alive, with gloves, in the incubator. She was as small as a kitten. As small and as light. She never made a sound. She was such a good baby."

"I'm so sorry, Mrs. Tuten," I said. She seemed far away, though we were just a few feet from each other in the stall, sitting on either side of Huey in the dry straw.

"It's all right, Iris," she said. "It was a long time ago."

The lantern flickered, making shadows dance around the cold barn walls. The wind had died during the night, but I could still see my frosty breath, and Mrs. Tuten's, and shallow puffs from Huey's nostrils that came out in little chugging sounds, like a far-off train. Then Huey lifted his head. Just a little. He looked at me, or at least he opened his eyes in my direction. Then he settled back down.

I checked Mr. Tuten's watch again, even though only a few minutes had passed. Mrs. Tuten was shivering again. I wondered if it was from the cold or from thinking about Alice. I suggested we go ahead with the next dose, since we were close enough to the six-hour mark, so she held Huey while I got the dropper and the medicine.

Huey opened his eyes again after I gave him his dose, and this time he kept them open. He sort of shrugged, and then he stood up. He wobbled, but he stayed standing for a couple of minutes. Mrs. Tuten was beaming. I thought she might even start clapping. I hugged Huey gently—laid my cheek against his side and my arm softly over his back. I was so happy, I couldn't speak.

He pulled away from me after a few minutes and took a few steps around the stall, but before long he settled back down and nodded off to sleep again.

After I laid the blanket over him, I realized Mrs. Tuten was silently crying. "It's all right, Mrs. Tuten. I think he's going to be all right. It probably just tired him out getting up for a little bit."

"I know, Iris," Mrs. Tuten said, wiping away her tears. "It's just the happiest thing."

Louie woke up and came over to Huey's stall, about as casually and sleepily as if he'd just gotten up to go to the bathroom, then he lay down next to his brother. I stood and stretched and peeked out the barn door. Gnarly poked his head out from under the porch steps, where he'd been sleeping lately—I guess it was warmer there. Stars still lit the sky, but a faint light crept over the tree line, too, east of the farm. Mrs. Tuten stepped outside with me, and we looked at things together for a while. Gnarly crossed the backyard and leaned against my leg, still half asleep. One of the goats *maa*ed in the barn. I couldn't tell for sure which one, but it kind of sounded like Huey.

"I'm sorry I lied to you and Mr. Tuten about coming out here," I said. "But I don't know what I would do if I didn't have the goats. And I don't know what they would do if they didn't have me."

"I know, Iris," Mrs. Tuten said. "I can see that."

Patsy came out of the barn and stood between me and Mrs. Tuten, pressing her shoulders against our legs to let us know she was there, too. She studied the sky with us for a while, then shook her head, as if she didn't quite get the point.

Mrs. Tuten reached down to pet her.

"Tell me this one's name again?" she said.

"Patsy. She's the herd queen."

After a few more minutes, Mrs. Tuten spoke again. "There are some things I need to say to you, Iris, and I need you to hear them." She let out a breath as if she'd been holding it for a long time. "The first thing is that you should not have gone behind our backs to come out here to the farm, and drive your aunt's truck. You should have told us about the agreement with your aunt. You have apologized, but the one thing we cannot have, if you are to continue living with us, is any more lying. That has to be understood."

"Yes," I said, hope filling my chest at the words "continue living with us." Still, her tone was serious, and I worried that she was going to order me to stay away from the farm. But I couldn't agree to that. Ever. "I do understand," I started. "But the goats—"

"Let me finish," Mrs. Tuten said.

So I waited.

"The second thing," she said, "is that we're going to have to clear this arrangement with Mindy and Mr. Trask. We'll need their permission for you to continue coming out to your aunt's farm, to take care of the goats. It's probably a formality, but we need to do this right."

She knelt down to scratch Patsy under her chin. I couldn't believe what she'd just said. I wanted her to repeat it, to make sure I'd heard her right, that I wasn't imagining things.

Mrs. Tuten looked up. "And finally, you have to let us help."

thirty-six

Mrs. Tuten and I had an appointment with Mindy and Mr. Trask two days later. Huey had almost completely recovered, but Littleberry was staying with him out at the farm anyway, just to make sure he was OK. Reba and Louie stayed close by, too.

Mrs. Tuten stopped me when she parked the car downtown and said she didn't think we needed to mention that I'd already been driving the truck and going out to the farm to take care of the goats and Gnarly.

"It might be best to just make a fresh start," she said. "Let the past be the past."

The receptionist escorted us right away down the hall to Mr. Trask's dark-paneled office. Mindy was already there, and we sat with her in a row of spindly chairs. Mr. Trask blinked at us from behind his desk, which was bare except for a single yellow number-two pencil. I wished he'd turn on more lights.

He looked at his watch and pressed a button on the side—probably the stopwatch function. "You asked to see me?"

I took a deep breath, thanked him and Mindy for meeting with us, then nervously explained as well as I could about how much the goats meant to me, about the situation with Animal Control, about my visit to the jail, about the agreement with Aunt Sue. I showed them a copy of Aunt Sue's letter giving me permission to take care of the animals. I showed them my report card from school and told them I'd joined the softball team, which I hoped demonstrated what Mr. DiDio called "a healthy balance of activities." Then I explained my proposed schedule for visiting the farm, handling the cheese production, and working at the farmers' market—all things Mrs. Tuten had suggested I do.

"I recently accompanied Iris to the farm," Mrs. Tuten interjected, "and was able to see for myself how well she can manage things. One of the goats fell ill, and I was very impressed with how Iris dealt with the situation."

Mindy scribbled notes as we talked, and seemed to be nodding, which was always a good sign. Mrs. Tuten had spoken with her on the phone the day before—they had talked for more than an hour—but she still asked a couple of questions, which Mrs. Tuten and I took turns answering.

Mr. Trask looked at his watch again and started drumming on his desk with the eraser end of his pencil.

Mindy stopped writing. "Do you have any questions you would like to ask, Mr. Trask?"

He said he didn't. We waited to see if he would say anything else.

He didn't.

"Well," Mindy said finally, "I can't say I think it's at all fair for Iris's aunt to put this financial burden on her, just so Iris can see the goats. I've actually never heard of anything like it. But I do see how important this is to Iris. I've spoken with Mrs. Tuten at length about it, and I'm convinced that Iris is capable of handling the arrangement—or at least should have the opportunity to give it a try." She nodded earnestly again. "As long as Mr. and Mrs. Tuten are comfortable with it," she added. "And Iris continues to do well in school."

I was ready to celebrate, a huge grin on my face, but faltered when I looked at Mr. Trask again. His mouth was twisted into some strange species of frown that made his lips disappear. He picked up Aunt Sue's letter, glanced at it, then laid it down in front of him.

"I have to disagree," he said, sliding the letter back across his desk toward me with his pencil. "Miss Wight has shown poor judgment in the past. There were repeated incidents of vandalism to Mrs. Allen's property earlier this year—including vandalism to the new truck. I do not see sufficient evidence that Miss Wight is mature enough to take over the care of the animals, or to take on these financial responsibilities."

"I already told you why I did all of that!" I said, gripping the chair arms so hard I thought they might break off. I hoped they would. "But you wouldn't listen to me!"

Mr. Trask leaned back so far away from me that his chair threatened to tip over. I started to say more, my anger boiling over, but Mrs. Tuten stopped me.

"Iris," she said, laying her hand on my arm.

She had a determined look on her face. I'd seen it before—the last time we were in Mr. Trask's office, and two nights ago when she and Mr. Tuten showed up at the farm to help with Huey.

"Could I get the two of you to step outside?" Mrs. Tuten said to Mindy and me, smiling a thin smile. "Just for a few minutes. I think it would be a good idea if Mr. Trask and I had an opportunity to speak. Alone."

Mr. Trask's strange frown deepened further, practically on the verge of turning his face inside out. He checked his watch yet again and shook it, as though he thought it might have stopped working.

Mindy and I stepped into the hall. "I'm sure everything will be OK," Mindy kept saying, though I doubted she was certain of that herself. "Mrs. Tuten can be very convincing—a very forceful advocate."

I kept my hands clenched into fists, not sure what I would do if Mr. Trask didn't change his mind.

Finally, after fifteen long minutes, Mrs. Tuten opened the door and invited us back in. She was still smiling, but it was a different, fuller smile this time.

"Mr. Trask has reconsidered," she said once we sat down. "Iris may visit the farm and take care of the animals and use her aunt's truck. And Mr. Trask has also agreed to let Iris have access to some of the funds from her father's estate during those months when she may not be able to earn enough at the farmers' market, though of course we hope that won't be necessary."

Mr. Trask didn't say anything. He'd taken off his watch and it was lying facedown next to the yellow pencil.

I stood up again, but I wasn't sure why. Mrs. Tuten was still smiling, and we just looked at each other, and she nodded. Everything seemed frozen in that moment. I didn't know what to say to thank her. There weren't enough words.

I thought about how hard it must have been for Mrs. Tuten to lose her baby, and I thought about her sitting up all night in the barn with me and Huey. I thought about all the things she and Mr. Tuten had done for me. And now this. After losing Mom, and losing Dad, and losing Beatrice, and losing Maine, I couldn't have imagined there could ever be this much good left in the world.

Mindy was the first to move. She stood up and hugged me, and Mrs. Tuten came over and hugged me, too. I was so happy that I started crying and couldn't stop. I heard Mr. Trask's chair scrape the floor, and I heard him walk out, but I kept crying, and Mrs. Tuten and Mindy kept hugging me, and I didn't mind that at all.

I begged Mrs. Tuten the whole way home to tell me what she'd said to Mr. Trask to make him change his mind, but she refused. She must have told Mr. Tuten later that night—I actually heard him laughing—but I could never get him to tell me anything, either.

Littleberry and I drove out to the farm early the next morning before school with a giant bag of Cheetos—with the Tutens' permission. The goats were especially glad to see us. I was ready to get back to milking them twice a day, every day, to increase cheese production.

They were ready for a party.

thirty-seven

Mr. and Mrs. Tuten gave me an iPod for Christmas and added me to their cell-phone plan. Shirelle gave me a softball team T-shirt and a copy of the picture she took of Drunk Dennis and Donny and the goat manure in Donny's car.

And Littleberry wrote me a poem—actually a limerick. He gave it to me on Christmas Day, when the Tutens invited him over for dinner.

There once was a girl from Maine who
Raised goats and she had quite a few.
When I saw how she loved them,
And cared for and hugged them,
I wished that I was a goat, too.

It was my favorite present.

Later, when I walked Littleberry out to his Vespa, he asked if he could kiss me.

"Well, *yeah,*" I said, my heart thumping. *Finally.*

"I'm a really good kisser," he added, as if I still needed him to talk me into it.

So that was my second-favorite present.

Hob and Jill watched us from the Tutens' front window, and I'm pretty sure they were dooking the whole time.

I wandered back inside after Littleberry left, kind of in a daze. Mr. and Mrs. Tuten were watching football with Aunt Nonny, but I still had to drive to the jail to give Aunt Sue the January money. I was meeting up with Littleberry again after that, to go out to the farm.

"You be careful," Mrs. Tuten said. "And call if you need us."

Aunt Nonny told me to watch out for snakes.

I brought a pack of crackers and some goat cheese for Connie, the guard. She ate it standing up in the interview room while Aunt Sue and I sat at the table.

I told Aunt Sue she looked good, which was true. They must have had her doing stuff outdoors. She just sniffed. "I been working out. So what?"

Connie waved a cracker at her. "It was a compliment, Sue. Have some manners."

Aunt Sue sniffed again.

I showed her the check register, or tried to. She wouldn't

look at it at first, so I laid it on the table between us, just as I'd done when I visited on Thanksgiving.

She flicked at it with her index finger.

"They had us in court last week," she said. "For the sentencing. Book nine months, me a year."

"I know," I said. Detective Weymouth had called to tell me a couple of days earlier.

"Why didn't you come?" Aunt Sue asked. "I'd of thought you'd enjoy the show."

I shook my head. "No, I wouldn't have. And you wouldn't have wanted me there."

The conversation hung suspended on that note for a minute. I didn't know what to say. I wasn't glad that she was going to have to spend a year in jail, but I wasn't sorry about it, either.

I'd never told Aunt Sue about the polio, or about the stillborn kid, so I talked about those things for a little while. She seemed interested but didn't respond. Then I started talking about milk production. I said it was still strong overall—especially from Reba and Jo Dee—but had slipped some in December from Patsy and Loretta and Tammy. That seemed to get Aunt Sue going. She said it was probably getting to be about time to call over to Black Marsh Farms for their Rent-a-Buck.

"Maybe give the milkers another month or so. They won't taper off too fast. It'll be gradual. And they might not ever stop altogether. But you'll know when it's time. Then take a couple of the nannies offline, get them knocked up, let them have their kids, then they'll be right back producing. You might ought to do the three of them at once—Patsy and Loretta and Tammy. Cheaper that way with the Rent-a-Buck. You just have to hire him the one time."

Things went quiet again after that, except for Connie in the corner still eating her goat cheese and crackers.

"There's something else," I said.

Aunt Sue rolled her eyes. "What now?"

I steeled myself, knowing how she'd react to what I was about to say, then blurted it out: "When you get out of jail, the end of September, I want you to let me have all the goats. Not just the wethers."

Aunt Sue's head snapped back. "You want *what*?"

"I'm saving your farm," I said, as evenly as I could. "I'm giving you this money every month—and I want the goats in return."

Aunt Sue laughed. "That supposed to be your idea of a joke?"

"It's not a joke," I said. "I want them to live with me."

"Live with you where? Last I heard, you were moved into town with Peg and Harry Tuten. Peg and Harry let goats live at their house? Got them a spare bedroom?"

I'd never considered the possibility that Aunt Sue might know Mr. and Mrs. Tuten. It surprised me to hear her say their names.

"I'll find someplace for them," I said. "I've got time to line up something."

Aunt Sue glared at me. "Let me spell it out as plain as I can," she said. "You ain't getting a single solitary one of them milkers. Not in September. Not ever."

I just looked at her. I crossed my arms and sat back in my chair and just looked at her. I don't know if I thought it would unsettle her, or make her nervous, or make her crack, but that's what I did.

Connie sighed. "What the hell, Sue. You say you're sorry for what you did to the girl. So prove it, why don't you? Let her have the goats. Looks to me like she earned them."

Aunt Sue didn't respond. She just looked down at her hands, still raw and calloused from all those years working in the warehouse at Walmart, and from keeping up the farm, and from whatever chores they had her doing now at the jail. She sat that way for a couple of minutes—the longest minutes of my life.

"Fine," she said finally. "Whatever. You can have them. I'm tired of them damn goats, anyway."

She looked up at me. "But not until September. Not until I get out." The meanness was gone from her face; it was almost as if she was asking my permission.

I don't know what came over me. I reached across the table and cupped my hand over one of hers. She let me, though only for about a second.

Neither one of us said anything else after that. I was ecstatic, though I tried not to show it. I was thinking about the goats, and thinking about where I might keep them. Maybe the Gonzaleses had room on their vegetable farm. Maybe I could call Dr. Herriot and see if he had any ideas. Maybe the Tutens knew someone with a field and a barn.

I didn't have a clue about what was going on in Aunt Sue's head.

"I guess that's it, then," I said, standing up to leave. I only got as far as the door before she called after me.

"Iris."

I turned around. "What?"

She had that same old hard face on again, though—the one I first saw back in August the day she picked me up at the Raleigh airport.

"You still owe me another four hundred dollars for those truck tires you jammed holes in with the ice pick," she said. "Don't think I forgot about that for one single minute."

Connie laughed. "Good godamighty, Sue," she said. "You just don't ever quit, do you?"

I hesitated when I left the visiting room. I thought about seeing Book. Not that I wanted to. The visit with Aunt Sue had worn me out, but I had another one of Tiny's letters with me.

I waited for Connie to come back out to the front desk and passed it on to her. She stuck it in her pocket.

"You sure bring it out in your aunt Sue," she said.

"Yeah," I said. "I guess I do."

Connie handed me the empty goat-cheese container. "You're going to be all right, Iris," she said. "I can see it in you. Every time you come for these visits."

"I sure hope so," I said.

Connie smiled. "No hoping to it," she said. "It's just what is."

I had one more Christmas present—from Mr. DiDio. He'd given it to me at our last counseling session, the day school let out. It was an old poem by a Sufi poet named Rumi, called "The Guest House," and I liked it almost as much as Littleberry's limerick, though I still didn't know what a Sufi was.

"This has helped me through a lot," Mr. DiDio had said. "I thought you might want to have it."

I pulled the poem out of my pocket while I waited for the truck to warm up. I'd been carrying it around with me all week, and every time I read it I thought about my dad. It was the kind of poem I bet he would have written if he hadn't been so busy all his life taking care of everybody's animals, and taking care of me. I planned to copy it down for Dad the next time I wrote him a letter.

This being human is a guest house.
Every morning a new arrival.

A joy, a depression, a meanness,
some momentary awareness comes
as an unexpected visitor.

Welcome and entertain them all!
Even if they're a crowd of sorrows,

who violently sweep your house
empty of its furniture,
still, treat each guest honorably.
He may be clearing you out
for some new delight.

The dark thought, the shame, the malice,
meet them at the door laughing,
and invite them in.

Be grateful for whoever comes,
because each has been sent
as a guide from beyond.

thirty-eight

I drove over to Littleberry's house from the jail, and we loaded his parents' grill into the back of the Tundra for smoking some hard goat cheeses so we'd have something new to sell at the farmers' market.

I couldn't stop thinking about that kiss from earlier, and halfway to the farm I pulled off to the side of the road for a few minutes so we could do it again.

Mrs. Tuten had given me a bundle of apple wood from Roxbury Mills, a nursery just outside Craven, and I'd had it soaking in a tub of water for a couple of days. Once we got out to the farm, we set up the grill next to the back porch, lit the charcoal, then went into the barn to milk the goats while the coals burned down just right. When the embers were ready, we spread on the waterlogged apple wood, double-wrapped a couple of hard chèvre blocks in cheesecloth, and closed them up on the grill.

We were just finishing up when I heard the phone ringing inside the house, which startled me. I hadn't heard it ring in months, since Aunt Sue and Book went to jail.

It was Beatrice.

"Hey, Iris," she said. "Merry Christmas."

"Hey, B. Merry Christmas." It had been weeks since we'd last spoken, and we'd barely said three words to each other then.

"I called the other number," Beatrice said, "and the lady said you were out at the farm."

"Yeah."

"So how are you?" she asked.

"I'm OK," I said, not really sure I wanted to talk to her. It had been such a good day; I didn't want anything to ruin it. But I didn't want to be mean or rude to Beatrice, either. "What about you?"

"I'm OK, too. That lady—Mrs. Tuten—she said you were with your boyfriend."

I laughed. "He's not my boyfriend. He's just a friend." I looked out the kitchen window at Littleberry, who was throwing sticks for Gnarly to fetch. "Well, I guess he might be sort of my boyfriend."

"That's great," Beatrice said, and she sounded sincere. "I'd love to meet him sometime."

I wasn't sure if she was going to continue talking, or if she was waiting for me to respond—and what, invite her down to

Craven County? I tried to imagine Beatrice here but couldn't. The silence stretched on.

Beatrice finally broke it. "I just haven't talked to you for a while," she said. "So I thought I would call." She paused again. "And I wanted to tell you that we moved back home—me and Mom and Sean. Mom and Dad have been talking about things, and they're seeing a counselor. So I'm in my old bedroom again. I'm here right now. It's pretty weird."

I had to sit down at the news. "Wow, B. That's huge. When did this happen?"

"Just a week and a half ago," she said. "I already went back to school, and rejoined the team. Just before Christmas break. Coach had us doing conditioning drills in the gym. He just about started crying when I showed up. He didn't have another pitcher. Everybody says to tell you hi. Coach says to tell you we could sure use you back in center field."

I stood up again by the window. Littleberry was still playing with Gnarly, pretending to throw the stick in one direction, then flinging it somewhere else. Gnarly fell for it every time, tearing off in the wrong direction, happy as he could be.

I tried to imagine a life in Maine after all I'd been through here—tried to imagine myself back playing center field again for my old high school. Littleberry looked over, saw me at the kitchen window, and waved.

"I wanted to tell you something else," Beatrice said in a shakier voice. "I wanted to tell you how sorry I am. For everything.

For being such a bad friend. For letting you down. For my whole family letting you down. We just got caught up in our own stuff, you know? We should have been there for you—I should have been. But everything got all twisted up."

"I know," I said, and I realized that for the first time in a long time I wasn't mad at her. "Life and all that."

"Yeah. Life and all that."

I had all but given up on our friendship, but suddenly I wasn't so sure. This sounded more like the Beatrice I had known all my life, and talking to her now, hearing a different voice, I thought maybe I *would* see her again. Maybe I would go back to Maine. At least for a visit. Someday.

Tammy came over to the fence then, probably to see where I'd gone off to. She crammed her head through and of course got stuck. She *maa*ed in her usual desperate way, and the other goats crowded around, too, as if they hadn't seen it all a dozen times before. Littleberry stopped playing with Gnarly and ran over to help her. I was starting to wonder if Tammy didn't do it on purpose, like a little kid who just wants attention.

I told Beatrice I had to go. She sounded genuinely disappointed until I promised I'd call her back, that we would talk again soon and I'd tell her everything that had been going on with me. I said there was something I had to take care of right at the moment, though.

I said it was a goat thing.

ACKNOWLEDGMENTS

I could not have written this book without the help of my friend Lee Criscuolo, who generously shared her stories, time, expertise, cheese, and goat poo samples—and who didn't lecture me too much about my bumbling attempts at milking. Thanks also to Mehitabel, who was the unrivaled star of our goat party, and to the late Rosie, Lee's no-nonsense herd queen. Both were kind and patient despite my clumsiness and showed great restraint in not hooking me with their horns or butting me out of their barn. I'm just sorry that Rosie didn't live long enough to see this book in print and to have the opportunity to eat it.

Thanks to Marie Rizza for her beautiful, operatic rendition of the goatherd song, and to the Padovan-Hickman family, who taught the viewers of *Wife Swap* all they needed to know about contra dancing and living off the grid in King George County, and who also taught me a thing or two about goats. Thanks to my many friends at the Unitarian Universalist Fellowship of Fredericksburg, who cheered this book along, and thanks to my friend Jill Payne and the staff and volunteers at CASA (Court Appointed Special Advocates) who believe that every child matters and who show it every day through their amazing work and dedication.

Thanks to my agent, Kelly Sonnack, who wasn't able to make it to the grave-digging party for Rosie, but who has been there for everything else — and for me — throughout the writing of this book. Thanks to my wife, Janet, who read countless drafts of *What Comes After* and helped shape the manuscript in countless ways. Thanks of course to my own goat girls — Maggie and Eva and Claire and Lili — who remind me every day how blessed I am. Thanks to Maryellen Hanley for all her brilliant work on the haunting, resonant cover and design, and to all the good people at Candlewick Press for believing in this book and in so many wonderful books by other writers that might never have been published without their faith and vision.

Thanks especially to my editor, Kaylan Adair, who could not possibly have done more for a story and its author. I am forever grateful for her kindness and support — and for her fierce and loving pen.

Finally, thanks to a girl whose name I don't know but who inspired this book, and who has had to go through a lot more in life than anyone ever should. I pray that she has found her own goat family, her Mr. and Mrs. Tuten, her Mr. DiDio, her Littleberry and Dr. Herriot and Shirelle, and that her story turns out to be as hopeful, and full of promise, as Iris Wight's.